Seeing Dell

Seeing Dell

by Carol Guess

CLEIS
PRESS

To my parents

Published in the United States by Cleis Press Inc., P.O. Box 8933, Pitts-burgh, Pennsylvania 15221, and P.O. Box 14684, San Francisco, California 94114.

Book design and production: Pete Ivey
Cover photo: Phyllis Christopher
Cleis logo art: Juana Alicia

First Edition.
Printed in the United States.
10 9 8 7 6 5 4 3 2 1

Library of Congress Cataloging-in-Publication Data:
Guess, Carol, 1968–
    Seeing Dell / by Carol Guess. - - 1st ed.
        p. cm.
    ISBN 1-57344-024-8 (cloth). - - ISBN 1-57344-023-X (paper)
    I. Title.
PS3557.U3438S44   1996
813' .54--dc20   95-43309
                                                                 CIP

CONTENTS

ACKNOWLEDGMENTS

I am indebted to Eva Cherniavsky and Tonia Matthew for their faith in my writing, and to Marcus Elmore, Esther Eppele, Alison Guess, Mary T. Lane, Letta Neely, and Lori K. Sudderth for affection and encouragement.

Special thanks to Lizanne Minerva, Julie Thompson, and Nichola Torbett for love, guidance, and keen good humor.

I am particularly grateful to Felice Newman, Frédérique Delacoste, and Leasa Burton at Cleis Press for their patience, persistence, and belief in my work.

"What you risk reveals what you value."

Jeanette Winterson
The Passion

CHAPTER 1

Copeland

THE night I came home drunk was the night I woke up sweating, four in the morning, unable to remember Dell's face. At first I thought she was gone for good, but after I smoked a few cigarettes and drank some coffee, she came back to me. Heavy-lidded eyes. High cheekbones, very prominent. Thin, bright lips. Solid chin, with just enough flesh underneath it. Dell was an athlete in high school, and it showed, not just in her face, but in the way she moved. She walked as if her shoes were new, and she wanted to show them off. And if you were the sensitive type, you could practically write a poem about the way she sat: back straight but not stiff, her legs slightly apart, not prissy and ladylike, but not like a man, either.

That was Dell for you all around: not girly, not at all like the women I'd dated before. "Honey," one of them would say, before I'd even had a chance to get both trouser legs on, "Honey, how do I look?" Then would come a show. Prancing around, fixing things that didn't need fixing. Dell was different. She didn't prance, and she didn't mince words, either. What she said was always just exactly what was on her mind. She liked to tell stories, but when she did you knew what they were; she didn't mix fact with fiction. I'd never heard anyone talk like Dell, and haven't since. We'd sit, drink coffee for hours, and Dell would say everything she was thinking. After she'd talked herself tired, she'd hold her mug up to her lips, ready to drink, but then before she did she'd look me in the eye, very direct, very Dell, and say, "What about you? What do you think of so-and-so or such-and-such?" The first time she asked me, I was floored. What do you say when someone asks you a real question? But I wanted to please her: that happened right off the bat. So I tried. I tried to tell her things. I tried to locate the words inside my head, offer them up in ways someone else could understand.

Dell was a driver, like me. Funny thing is, though, that's not how we met. Oh, I'd seen her before, in and around the office, but she kept her distance from the rest of us. She was the only lady cabbie, and that seemed to make her feel like an outsider. Or maybe being an outsider was simply what Dell did best. "You gave me inside," she said once; it took a while to figure that one out. But back then we didn't speak, not ever even a "hello," and that's something I regret. First time we talked was in Wilson's Shop Mart. I don't like grocery stores (not many public places I do like), so I do my shopping Sunday morning, when most of Carlstown is on its knees. There I was, picking at the oranges, trying to find a few that weren't wilty looking, when up beside me comes Dell, pushing a cart full of Cheerios and TV dinners. She was tearing off one of those plastic baggies, trying to follow the perforations, so she didn't see me, and I figured I'd push my cart over into the pasta aisle so we wouldn't get stuck making small talk, which is another thing I hate. So I pushed, but Dell gave her cart a shove at the same time, and the carts skidded, locked wheels, made a grinding noise that set my teeth on edge. "Goddamn!" she said loudly, glaring at me like I'd done it on purpose.

"Hey, lady, don't look at me." Then she must've recognized me, because she did something weird: leaned her head back, and guffawed to bring the roof down.

"Copeland." She put a hand on my shoulder, surprising me with knowing my name and all. "Copeland, don't go calling me a lady. I'm a cabbie, same as you."

"Yeah?" I was still mad. "Well, you sure don't know much about driving a grocery cart." She just laughed louder and longer, as if everything I was saying was sitcom material. I didn't get it. But her laughter was sort of infectious, it was so thick and raucous; pretty soon I was laughing too. I let the orange I was holding drop from my hands; it rolled down along the aisle 'til it stopped against a display of soup cans rising in a shaky tower towards the ceiling. That just made us both laugh harder; the guy standing by the fruit scale shook his head, as if we'd embarrassed him.

After that, she said "Hey, Cope" when she saw me in the office; one day I got up the nerve to join her on the stoop for a smoke. It felt like just friends at first, nothing heavy. But then it changed, slowly, like water when you turn the tap from cold to hot, one finger underneath to test the temperature. One night when we were sitting outside waiting for the next call, she turned her face away, like it was nothing special she was asking. "How'd you like to come by my place later tonight, Cope, and watch some dumbass TV?"

I snorted into my coffee, liking the way she swore. "Sounds good." I kept my eyes fixed on a Honda parked across the street. "Sounds good to me."

" 'Bout ten?" She tapped her cigarette against the stoop; the ashes twisted and fell.

"Be there." I got up, went inside. Picked up a newspaper I was too nervous to read.

That night was about her voice, curling like smoke, and her hands, rough like a man's, unyielding. For Dell, stories were sex; when I didn't want to leave the next morning, I kept her talking in bed 'til it was time for us both to head for work. I showered at her place, borrowed a sweatshirt, rubbed my teeth with a washcloth, let the stubble stay. But I thought she might want to keep things low key at the office for a while, so I suggested we drive in separately, arrive five or ten minutes apart.

Dell looked at me like I'd suggested we walk the twenty miles. "Why would we want to do something stupid like that?" Wrinkling her face up. "Do you think I care what anyone has to say about my private life?" Then she put her hands on my hips. "Besides, Copeland, folks are gonna know about me and you eventually."

Sometimes around Dell, I found myself doing the opposite of the thing I'd been thinking I should do. That first morning-after was one of those times. We drove together to work in her car with the windows down, singing to a beat-up Clapton tape I found stuffed in the glove compartment. When she pulled into the lot, James was leaning out the back door, emptying the ashtrays. "Whoah, now," he said, letting the ashes fall more on the steps than the grass. "Whoah, now," again as he leaned inside the door and motioned with his hands. Said something neither Dell nor I could hear; next thing we knew, Dennis and Pit were hanging out the doorframe, whistling and carrying-on.

"I knew it was coming," Dennis' voice was gruff. Dell just smiled without showing her teeth. "Got one question for you, girl," he called after her as she brushed past him and into the office. "How come you picked him, huh? I could show you a better time." Even from ten feet away, I could see Dell's back muscles stiffen; my mouth tasted sour, and I caught myself calculating where his body would fall if I punched him this way or that. Would his head clear the table? I felt my fingers curl into a fist, but I took Dell's lead and held the violence in, like a breath. I didn't need to care what a trouble-maker like Dennis thought. I was happy. Happy in a real way. So I ignored him, found my clipboard, signed in, took the next call out.

No one but Dennis ever said a thing about me, at least not to my face. But then, most of the guys I count for friends. Me and James go fishing once or twice a month; Brad and I make bets on the NFL every year. Chas and I went to the same high school, had a couple classes together. And Pit dates a cousin of mine, short blonde named Maggie. They were all there at Dell's funeral; Pit cried almost as hard as I did. Only Dennis was missing; I heard from someone a while ago that he'd joined the army. Not sure what I think of that, if I'd want him defending me against foreign invaders or not.

For Dell, things got bad after a while. Dennis seemed to have it stuck in his head that since Dell was seeing one of the guys, it was open season for all of them. For a time it was just Dennis being stupid and cruel; Dell stood it, and asked me to keep my mouth shut. She wanted us both to ride it out, to wait for Dennis' jealousy to find another target. But nothing changed; some months later, James picked up the teasing, and then Chas too. Brad even got his feet wet; only Pit stayed out of it entirely. Oh, they never said anything while I was around, but Dell would come home, move too slowly, and I'd know. To be fair, I don't think any of the guys but Dennis realized just what they were doing to her. They thought it was a game; when she didn't respond, they pushed harder. They didn't want to break her, just share a joke at her expense. I think they thought she brushed it off; maybe they even thought she liked it. But I saw her at home, and knew they'd struck a nerve.

I turned into a knight in my own mind. Asked her to let me talk to them, even take them on. But she said no, no, no—didn't want me even to mention her name when I was around the guys. Thought things might get worse. Instead, about a year and a half after things took off between us, she decided to leave Carlstown Yellow and take a job driving for Parker's, a service that does shuttles back and forth to the airport. I didn't like the thought of smoking on the stoop without her, and I knew it would make planning time together more difficult. As it was, we had things pretty simple. But the cost was too high. She needed to be clear of Dennis and spiteful gossip, needed to be a woman alone someplace where she could start over, keep her distance from the men around her. And secretly? Secretly I was relieved. I didn't like the jealousy in Dennis' eyes, or the way he watched her when she talked on the telephone. Once I caught him in the locker room holding onto the sleeve of her jacket. Just holding onto it, almost as if it was an arm. It made me shiver, so when Dell handed in her resignation I wasn't all doom and gloom. She signed on with Parker's the next day; that was how, two years and three months later, she came to be driving west on the highway at two fifty-three in the afternoon, through thick snow that was rapidly turning to freezing rain.

I don't love lightly. When we took each other, we did it for our whole life long. Problem is, there's no "our" anymore: my life's still chugging away, but hers ended some time back. Highway, ice, semi—don't ask me to describe it. The way it happened, the police had routed things to a single lane, no more than a crawl, so I had lots of time to verify that the car that'd been cut in half was Dell's. If I hadn't had passengers in the back, I would've driven my cab under the wheels of that semi to join hers. But even in wild grief, I couldn't take what wasn't mine to begin with, so instead I pulled over, got out and tore for the car, or what was left of it. When this policeman with a big barrel stomach grabbed hold of me, wouldn't let me near her, I swung at him; I remember watching my own arm go up, come down like it was a slow motion replay. He just caught it. "Calm down, bud," he said. "Nothing I can do about it."

"That's Dell's car." I remember I pulled out my license, as if my name might somehow prove my words. "That's Dell's car," about a thousand times. Kept saying it: "My Dell's in there. My Dell's in that car," even after it was clear to me that, really, she wasn't.

They told me she died instantly, and I'd like to think that's true. But I've never believed anyone in this life except Dell, and she was the one person couldn't verify her own experience. As I watched the tow truck haul away the pieces of the wreckage, I let my hands go limp by my sides. These hands knew Dell's body like my feet know this trailer I've lived in going on twelve years now. In the dark, eyes closed, I knew where to find her. Without any place for my hands to rest, what use were they? They needed to learn their uselessness. I picked up a piece of glass smeared with oil, wiped it across the back of one hand until the blood started. Then I got in my cab like a zombie, started her up, drove my passengers to their destination: front door service, no charge, sorry for the inconvenience. The woman tipped me anyway. I still remember her face.

"Always will," I'd said once. I don't say such things easily. "Forever," I'd said once. Why say it twice? What would it mean the second time? For some people, there's only one other person who can make it worth all the godawful trouble of not being alone. For some people, only one other person's breathing isn't static, and only one other person's hands don't feel like weapons. That was Dell for me. She was just right. No use trying to replace something that fit the first go around.

The fellows helped some after the funeral. Mostly what I wanted that first year was to be left alone; after they figured that out, they gave me what I needed. But time kept on, and they got restless. Started asking me when I was going to get over it. Hadn't I grieved long enough, Chas asked one morning. Didn't I miss bed company, James wanted to know. They started to push me to get out, to see people, to "live again." It was no use explaining that living wasn't an option anymore, that the only reason for staying alive was the picture of Dell's face that I'd discovered painted on the insides of my lids when I closed my eyes. I've always had a keen memory; photographic, you might say. I'm Carlstown's best cabbie because I can glance at a map once and remember it, for always, down to the very trees. It was so with Dell's face; when I realized this, I began spending time with her: saving my evenings to sit in our old brown chair, my eyes closed, exploring every pore of her skin, talking to her, in case somewhere she might be listening. That was living, for me. But the guys wanted something else, something showy and brash. James was the worst. He kept trying to fix me up with this Patty or that Marlene, 'til finally I'd had enough of it, and said yes just to get him to shut up. His face went all relieved then; I think he'd begun worrying that I was a faggot. "OK, James," I said, "bring 'er on." He grinned away like I'd told him he'd won the lottery. Not his fault he didn't understand: he wasn't exactly faithful to his old lady himself. Chas had stories; he'd run into James more than once talking up the same girl, half-pretty, and definitely not his wife. I suppose my grief just didn't register on his scale.

The woman James wanted me to meet was named Kathy. "You'll like her," he said. "She's got long hair, very shiny. Great legs."

"What kind of stuff does she like to talk about?"

"Oh, whatever you want. She's lively. Whatever you want to talk about, Kathy can handle." James scratched his elbow. "You can always ask her about her job. She delivers mail."

So I told him all right, I'll call her, we'll go out to dinner. I'll have dinner with Kathy. I won't like it, but I'll take her out to dinner.

"Copeland." James ground his cigarette in the ashtray. "Dell's been gone more than three years now."

"I know, James. I know it. I said I'll take Kathy to dinner, OK? Just don't talk about it more. Just don't ask me how it goes."

I worried a lot the week before my date with Kathy, mostly about what kinds of questions to ask, how to keep the conversation going. I wasn't concerned with impressing her, or even liking her, since there wasn't going to be a second date. But I wanted her to feel comfortable, and to know that I'd listened well. So I thought about it, and finally decided I'd start off with questions about envelopes, then move on to stamps. For example, their stickiness. How did it happen? Who drew the pictures, and how did they pick which famous people to feature? Maybe I'd ask her which celebrities were coming next. Was there going to be a Madonna stamp? Had anyone ever tried a do-it-yourself sort of dealie, with space above the number for you to color in your own design? Too, I thought I might share with her my personal feelings about the mail. Something about the thought of handling other people's letters has always appealed to me. When I was little, I used to pretend that I had ESP and could see right through the envelopes. I'd touch them lightly, run my fingers across the stamps, scrunch my eyes up, imagining I knew what they were waiting inside to say.

But as soon as I mentioned her job, she shook her head so that her curly hair jiggled like sprung wires. "Oh, Copeland, let's not talk about boring stuff! I'm ready for fun tonight." We were in the car, on our way to Red Lobster. "So, what movies have you seen lately?" She didn't wait for a reply, but described the plot of a flick she'd seen the week before, about a man who's hired by the CIA to kill a spy who turns out to be a woman he'd dated years earlier. "And they fall in love all over again. And it's so hard for him, cuz he has to shoot her." She pulled out a tiny compact, and began re-applying peach-colored eyeshadow. "That's how he makes his living. Talk about bum jobs." Laughing. "So James tells me you like fishing. Are you a sportsman?" She snapped the compact shut. "You look like you might be a sportsman, Copeland. I always find men who work with fish and animals very attractive."

Red Lobster wasn't too crowded, so we got a booth. While the waitress filled our glasses with water, Kathy scanned the menu. "Oh my. So much fried food. I'm trying to reduce." She closed the menu, stuck her hand down her shirt sleeve and adjusted her bra strap. "I was on the Oprah diet for a while. I think I'll just have a dinner salad. Maybe I'll also have a bite of yours, Copeland?" Smiling across the table. "Men don't have to worry about their figures like ladies do. It's hard work, you know. Some men never appreciate those kinds of things." I looked down at the list of side orders. I wanted hush puppies, and I wanted fried shrimp. Those were two things I knew for sure.

When I arrived back at Kathy's apartment complex later that evening, she sat very still in the car, without even reaching for the door handle. It took me a minute to realize that she wanted me to get out and open the car door for her. As I walked her to her apartment, I said, "Goodnight," and "Thank you for your time."

She paused, keys in hand. Beneath the glare of the bug light, I could see the thin orangey line of her foundation make-up where it ended along her chin. There were tiny creases in her eye shadow; for a moment, beneath the dense, spontaneous spot-light, Kathy looked like a human puzzle, made up of hundreds of tiny painted squares. I wondered what color her skin really was. "Copeland," turning away from me towards the door, "would you like to come in for a while? I bought a bottle of wine yesterday; I'll never finish it all by myself." The keys in her hand clicked against each other; a car pulled up three apartments down. "I have cookies too, the Pepperidge kind, with mint in the center?"

Kathy's door was mud-colored; as it shut behind her, I let out a deep breath that whitened and vanished slowly in the cool evening air. Inside my car, I cranked up the radio, cranked up the heat, and sweated home, singing loudly, erasing the evening with lyrics that were little more than pronouns and improbable innuendos strung together. Back in the trailer, I headed straight for the brown chair and pulled up the empty microwave box I used for a footrest. Then I closed my eyes, found Dell, and began to narrate.

James kept his word, never did ask me how the date with Kathy went. I thought he might let up after that, but he came at me periodically with phone numbers, snippets of dialogue, vital statistics. Mostly I let them go, but gradually adopted the practice of going out once a month or so with some woman he'd suggested. I was afraid of being called a queer; too, I was afraid of losing the camaraderie I felt at the office. The ribbing we gave each other when we got lost or took a passenger to the wrong stop. Sharing smokes. Listening to the oldies station. Weekend fishing trips. The invitations, every so often, to family things: Pit's birthday, Brad and Katie's wedding. And to be fair, some of James' women were nice enough, though never nice enough to call back twice. The only exception was a secretary named Maureen. We hit it off OK; midway through our first dinner together, she came right out and explained that she wasn't in the game for herself. What she wanted was a father for her thirteen-year-old son. Someone who could take him out weekends, toss a ball around.

Of all the offers, pleas, and bargains each date implicitly contained, Maureen's was the only one that even remotely interested me, mostly because it was upfront. She wasn't trying to pull something, wasn't hiding anything from me. She knew what she wanted, and she was going to find it, if not with me, then with the next fellow, or on down the line. But too, it had to do with Joey, her kid. He was lively, a tall-for-his-age redhead. Smart, her son was. Real smart, and real creative. He liked acting, and took advanced English and history at school. On our third date, she showed me some of his schoolwork; talking about Joey, I could feel myself moving towards her, and I could feel myself allowing Maureen to move closer to me. So we went out several times, and I got to liking her in a quiet sort of way. One night I sat in the brown chair and talked to myself, the way I sometimes do, trying to come to some sort of decision. Because Maureen was starting to count on me, and I needed to decide whether I could handle that, whether I wanted it. So I sat down and—I swear, it felt like a sign—just at that moment the phone rang; when I answered it, the voice on the other end said, calm as could be, "May I speak to Dell?"

After I'd explained the whole long story to Jody Phelps, a friend of Dell's from high school who was calling to dig up info for the alumni newsletter, I sat back in my chair, tried to pick up thinking where I'd left off. But instead of Maureen, instead of Joey, all I could think was Dell, Dell. The accident came back again. I tasted fear on my lips, felt the sting of glass and then blood on my hand. This may sound mean, but after that I never called Maureen back. She might've tried a couple times—I don't have a machine anymore so I don't know. But that was the end of dreaming about fatherhood for me. I couldn't be a husband if I was married in my head to someone else. For a while after that I gave up going out altogether. Then the holidays rolled around. Then New Year's. Then Nora came along, and things shifted: not for the better, either.

With Nora, things were different right away. Not different like with Dell, but different from Vera, Heather, Marsha, all the other faceless women I'd driven round-trip to cheap restaurants. Nora was stubborn, not clingy but determined. She liked me right off, and when I showed the littlest bit of interest (she wasn't pretty, Nora, but she knew how to make pretty happen), she jumped the train and hung on for dear life. She had a mean streak, and that showed right away too; soon as I saw it, I thought to leave. But seeing Nora was like galloping a horse for the first time: no matter how much you want to think you're in control, you can't help but notice that you're not. At first, I wasn't sure how to get out without destroying her; pretty soon, I was more worried about being destroyed myself.

On New Year's Eve, Carlstown Yellow runs the usual save-a-life special: call a cabbie if you're too drunk to drive, and we'll cart you home for free. I do the holidays because most of the other fellows are family men; a day's a day to me. So I was on when the call came through from the barkeep at the Metropolis. Said he had some gal threatening to make trouble if she didn't find a quick ride home. "Get someone out here fast," he said, so I flew, and that's how I met Nora.

When I pulled up, she was standing just inside the doorway, and

staggered out to meet the cab. "You called Yellow?" I said, not expecting an answer.

"Yeah," she climbed in easily, even though she'd been weaving,
"but I prefer red."

Passengers tell you right off what kind of a ride they want from
you. They draw lines, or they want you to cross them. They let you
know, too, where they want you to take them. Sometimes it's where
they say they're headed; sometimes it's someplace else. Nora wanted
a good time, but she also wanted intimacy. I knew the first would
make her act foolish, but the second? The second would make her
clever. So I grew curious in spite of myself, wondering how her clev-
erness would show. I watched her face in the mirror, and that
intrigued me also: I couldn't tell what she was thinking. Usually I
can, with almost all my passengers I can, but Nora was unreadable
then, and in fact, the whole time that I knew her.

I didn't reply, just wrote down the time on my clipboard. I turned
up the radio, hummed a little, wondering if she'd want to start a
conversation. But everything in the back was quiet; pretty soon, I
started wandering: thinking some about Dell, some about the chores
I had waiting for me back home. When I reached her house, though,
everything stopped and started all over again. She put her face close
to the glass and I wondered what she was gonna do, glad that the
divider was bullet-proof. I didn't trust her. She looked like the kind
of lady who might carry a pearl-handled gun in her pocketbook.
Besides, she was dead drunk, ready for nonsense. My shoulders stiffened, but I was still curious, even if I wanted to know what she was
up to more than I wanted her to do it.

She didn't disappoint me. She pulled out a little cylinder, dark
green, and scrawled her phone number in red lipstick across the
glass. Backwards, so I could read it. Pretty sharp thinking for a
drunk, and she knew it, because she laughed as she opened the door
and said, "I'm more coordinated than you think."

I didn't call her, of course. She called me. The phone jangled
almost off the hook one evening a few days later; I tried ignoring it
(I was thinking about Dell), but it grew harsh and insistent. When I
picked up, it was Nora, her voice calmer but still opaque. "Copeland?
You drive, right? Remember me? New Year's Eve?" There was a
pause; I shook my head, then remembered that she couldn't see me.

"Yeah, I remember."

"When can I come over?"

We wound up in bed almost immediately. I picked her up at her place; she had to run back inside for her checkbook, invited me in, and we just stayed. I try not to remember now what happened in her room, because some of it scares me. It wasn't good sex, but it wasn't bad sex, either. It was just different. She was hell-bent on being in charge. I remember that she hit me, that I grabbed her hand as it came down a second time, and told her to stop, told her I wasn't like that.

"Like what?" She smiled, and it was creepy but sexy too and I felt confused and didn't answer. When I got home the next morning, I washed my hands before I even climbed into the shower. Letting the water run over my wrists, I noticed the scars: that happened after Dell died, almost immediately. I don't know if I'm sorry now or not.

She pursued me, Nora. And even though I was afraid of her, I found myself liking the feeling of falling—not falling in love, but falling into trouble. Trouble was what my life was lacking; trouble, not love, might distract me from Dell. So Nora and I started hanging around; pretty soon, though, her meanness expanded, seeping out in public places, at inappropriate times. It felt simple at first, like something I could isolate about her, and ignore if I chose. I didn't find out 'til later that it was poison: something that spread fast through her blood, branching out 'til it fueled every part of her, down to her painted toes. Like one night when we were at a party, and James came up to find out who it was I had hanging on my arm. "Good to see you with a lady, Copeland," he said, and the thing was, he meant it. They all did—Chas, Brad, Pit, all the rest. They wanted to see me happy. "Good to see you with a pretty lady handling your arm." He made a little bow to Nora. "Maybe you and your lady friend can come by our place sometime, have yourselves some dinner with me and the wife." Now, invites don't come easily from the boss, let me tell you. Maybe Nora didn't understand, or maybe she thought the whole thing was a joke. But she tilted her head, looked him up and down.

"Yeah," squeezing my elbow, "maybe on a leash."

I found out later that she was insulted. "He was talking like I'm your property," she said, and I understood why that would hurt an independent type like Nora. But James meant well, and she missed that—the meaning-well part. It was the part she always missed. She'd take my words, or someone else's, and twist them, making them something ugly or cold or angry, when they weren't, when they weren't at all. It was that, but it was some other things, too. It was hard to be with Nora. It felt like work. I'd come home exhausted, tired of watching what words I used, tired of reassuring her that she was beautiful, that I liked sleeping with her. Tired of thinking up new ways to respond to "I love you" without using the same words myself.

My fault for staying with her. My fault for not telling her the truth sooner, for using her to distract me from Dell. After four months, I couldn't take it anymore. But I didn't want to just stop calling like I did with Maureen. I felt I owed her something, if only for her time. So I thought we'd go out to the bar, like she'd been begging me to do. She could drink while I nuzzled club soda and tried not to remember the feel of my lips against a whiskey glass. I'd tell her gently that I couldn't see her anymore; if she cried, no one would notice. That's what dark and smokey bars are for. But I didn't think she'd cry; I figured she'd pout, try to talk me otherwise, then sulk while I drove her home.

So there we were, come full circle to the Metropolis. She had two White Russians; I had a club soda with lime. We danced when the mood hit her, sat down when her feet hurt. I felt like I'd already done the deed, had to keep pinching myself to remember that the evening wasn't over yet. As she trotted off to the ladies' room, I dug my nails into my palms: do it, Copeland, I told myself. Get it over with. Tell her what you've been thinking. Tell the lady what's on your mind.

"Nora," I said as she sat down in her chair, arranging her skirt around her legs, "Nora, there's something I've been meaning all night to tell you."

"Uh-huh?" She was looking over the little plastic card that advertised fancy drinks. "The Pink Flamingo," one side said; there was a picture of a reddish-looking drink with bubbles at the top, and a little plastic flamingo stuck in the glass.

"I want to tell you about it now."

"Well, honey, go right ahead!" She wasn't drunk, but she was starting to feel pretty good about the evening. She stretched her arm around my shoulders. "Tell Nora all about the thoughts running around that big old brain of yours. Copeland, you just tell Nora all about it."

"Nora, it's this." I glanced down at my fingers, which looked wet in the dim light. "I don't think we should see each other anymore."

Nothing but quiet, though I felt her push back her chair.

"Nora, I'm sorry. I'm sorry it didn't work out."

She stayed quiet; I was afraid of her eyes. When I finally glanced up, she was looking away, at the neon clock over the cash register. "Nora," I tried to take her hand, but she shook it away from me. "Nora, I'm sorry. Can you talk to me? I mean, tell me how you're feeling."

"How I'm feeling?" She stood up and flicked her skirt at me, making it look like an accident, but letting me see the inside of her thigh. Then she bent over the table, put her hands on my shoulders, her face right up in mine. "If I were a man," her lips touched my ear as she spoke, so that I felt her words as much as heard them, "if I were, Copeland, I'd rape you." She shoved me backwards, walked out, leaving me to whistle into my club soda, to amble up to the bar and casually pay the tab. The worst of it was, I wasn't even drunk, so I had no excuse to offer the faces peering in on me, no dizzy rejoinder to toss back when the comments came. I took care of it quick, though: as I stood there watching the barkeep make change, it occurred to me that one sip of whiskey would change every aspect of how I was feeling. So I ordered whiskey, and then more, and more, and then so on. You know the funny thing? It didn't even feel like giving in. It felt natural, almost like a good thing. Like this was what I had to do to survive. Like being a drunk was better than going home, shooting myself, or (don't think it didn't occur to me) shooting Nora.

That was what Nora brought out in me: violence. I suppose I brought it out in her, too, though I'm inclined to think that in Nora it was already vine-ready and growing. By the time I staggered home, it was nearing midnight; the only thing I remember is that the dark seemed to follow me in. I fell right asleep, without even taking the time to wish Dell goodnight. Maybe that was the problem. Not speaking to Dell, I mean. Because four hours later I woke, sat straight up, sweat tickling my back and chest. Somehow even in sleep I knew I'd lost her: I couldn't remember Dell's face. Tried and tried, but she was gone, leaving nothing even to replace her. Just darkness with some white fuzzy stuff when I closed my eyes. No Dell.

I lit like a fuse. I yelped, cried, carried on as if I were on fire. Without seeing Dell, I knew I couldn't go on living. So I tore into my boxes of photographs, thinking pictures on paper might make the picture in my head come clear again. They didn't help, though, and I paced around the trailer, choking on tears, stumbling, until I stepped on a pop can I'd left lying by the TV set and cut the edge of my foot. That's when I sat myself down, tried to talk some sense into my own damn fool head. I took deep breaths, swallowed a couple aspirin to ward off the hangover I could almost already see. Then I brewed coffee and sat out on the doorstep, drinking it black, chain-smoking, willing myself to stay quiet, sick at heart for having hit the bottle again, wondering what to do to keep the taste down in my throat. I was more than afraid I'd end with my face in a whiskey glass. So I put my head in my hands, the way they do on TV or in the movies when someone's grieving. And you know what? It worked. Because I saw her face again, very suddenly: eyes that strange almond color, lips just naturally lipstick-bright. I was seeing Dell again. I breathed deeply, filling my lungs with relief. She hadn't left me. I reached a hand up, even said "thank you" aloud to who-ever might have been responsible. Then I went inside, called in sick to work, slept all afternoon, into evening.

When I finally woke up, it was maybe half-past six, and I flipped on the TV to see if I could find the news. I usually don't bother with it—got enough grief in my own life—but that night I wanted to see what had happened to the world while I'd been snoring off my hang-over. I had this odd feeling, as if something important might have taken place without my knowledge, simply because I'd turned my own night and day upside down. What if there was a war on, I remember thinking. What if I needed to go register for the draft? I must've been groggy still, because my logic was watery. So when I heard the knock at the door, I ignored it, thinking it was my imag-ination playing tricks. "There's no war on," I told myself; probably even said the words aloud. "There's no war on, and no one's coming after you to register, Cope, so just stay put." I leaned back, turned up the sound 'til I couldn't hear much of anything except the lady announcer's nasal accent.

Why was I surprised when the door opened? Maybe I'd been concentrating so hard on recovering Dell that I'd completely forgotten about Nora, or maybe I thought she had too much pride to come tagging after me. But there she was, make-up streaked under her eyes, hands on her hips, still wearing the same skirt and leotard top she'd had on the night before. She looked like she hadn't slept, and perhaps that was so. "Copeland," she walked on in while I cursed myself for leaving the door unlocked, "how come you don't answer when a body knocks? You think you're too good to open the door for a lady visitor?"

I stood up, pushed back my chair, started to lower the sound, then thought the better of it and just snapped the set off. "I wasn't expecting visitors."

"Copeland." She glanced at the chair, then back at me, and I nodded. When she sat down she slouched forward; I hadn't realized how tired a woman could look 'til that day. Her eyes were all smeared with mascara lines; her lipstick was bitten off, so her lips looked orange and raggedy. I almost touched her, not out of love or greeting but in pity. Then I stopped myself. Dell used to say, "Pity's no present," and I believed her, the way she said it. I didn't want to give Nora something I didn't believe in.

"Copeland." She said my name again. I stayed standing, even though there was a chair within arm's reach. "I came by...do you know why I came by?"

"To apologize?" Just thought I'd try it out.

"Because I love you." She reached out a hand, touched the sleeve of my t-shirt. "Copeland, I love you. I want us to be together."

I couldn't make words form into any kind of reply.

"I want you to let me into your life. You haven't given me a chance. I just want a chance. I want what Dell had."

"What Dell had?" I didn't want to be hearing her correctly.

"Copeland, Dell wasn't unique. She might've seemed special to you at the time—no, I know she did, and she was special, in that you loved her, and she loved you back. But the love you had for her—it's not a once-in-a-lifetime deal. People love more than once in their lives. It's the way human hearts are made." She took her handbag off her shoulder, let it drop to the floor, and then stood up. Moved towards me, 'til the tips of her pointy-toed boots almost touched my toes. "Cope, if you could love Dell, you can love another woman. And if you find the right one," she took a lock of her hair and twisted it around her finger, "she'll love you back properly, and it'll be better than it was with Dell. Not so childish. I know how it was with her, Copeland; I've talked to James. I know how you two were together. Like best buddies, like two boys out on the town. It won't be like that with me. I can do better than Dell, Copeland; I'm different. I can show you how you make me feel."

I've never hit a woman in my life. I've never had cause to. I didn't then, but all the while Nora was talking, my fingers were digging into my palms, needing something to do, something to keep my hands from going at her. But Dell wouldn't have wanted me to defend her with violence. She hated the way some men cultivated cruelty as a defense, and she made me see it and hate it too. So I walked real slowly into the kitchen. I took the dish towel from the refrigerator, twisted that towel 'til it looked like a cigarette.

"Dell was my life." I could feel my blood travelling to feed my heart. "You can't be her. You're nothing compared to her, just a speck of dust, something I want to sweep away from me."

"Copeland."

"Dell was my life."

"Copeland, listen to yourself! She's dead, Copeland! She'd been dead more than four years now. You're walling yourself in, burying yourself. You have to stop mourning, Copeland. You have to give up the ghost."

I snapped the towel against the TV set. I snapped it against the chair, then picked up the grey pillow I use for my back, threw it past Nora, towards the clock on the wall by the bathroom. I missed, but Nora snatched up her handbag. She was scared, I could see it, and I felt sorry: angry as I was, I hated letting my violence escape. But it was so bottled up, so tight. I didn't know what to do with it except throw things. I couldn't imagine ever feeling calm enough to eat, read, sleep again.

"Get out," I said to her. Then something changed, something dropped across her face like a shadow. It was as if she realized, only then, that she hadn't lost me; she'd never had me. It was a rigged game from the start. Her lips began to move slightly, as if she were grinding her teeth, or rehearsing words silently to herself. She took a step backwards, then another. Put her hand on the door. Took a deep breath. I just watched, as if I were watching a movie: it didn't seem real anymore. She was just some half-pretty distraction I'd dreamed up to keep from thinking about Dell.

"Copeland," calmly, "Copeland, you bastard." Then her voice began deepening, filling the space she'd only just recognized between us, expanding into something angry and fierce, into what it had been waiting to become, the way a river wants all along to be feeding the ocean. "Goddamn, Copeland, she's not dead for you, is she?" Nora turned the handle on the door, moved out onto the doorstep. "You're still seeing her. You still live with her, you bastard!" She walked quickly to her car, holding her skirt up and her head high, without once looking back. I just shut the door, slammed it shut; no need to fill my ears with Nora's kind of music.

I thought about her last little speech, though: not just that night, but the next night, and the next. On Thursday, I came home from work, fixed dinner around six the way I usually do. But this time, I made enough for two people. I took out two plates, laid one on either end of the table. Put out two forks and knives, two napkins, two glasses.

I had to see if it was true.

CHAPTER 2

Nora

HOW was I to know that he was married to a ghost?

People should have the history of their desires tattooed across their bodies. Too many men have made love to me, only to have the palms and backs of their hands tell me they weren't in love.

James was different. He came right out and explained his situation, down to the last detail, more than I even needed or wanted to know. He opened his life's history to me, let me page through the story of his wanting. Was that why, finally, he became uninteresting? All plot and no style, a cheap paperback with broken binding.

I met James at the Metropolis. That night I was there with Susan, a buddy of mine from high school. We were both cheerleaders, and pretty, back then; not anymore, though we can still pass for pretty when we have the time. Her hair's still mostly blond, and my figure hasn't changed much. We're both divorced: senior year marriages that flopped fast; no children, thank God. Susan and I take the Metropolis Saturday nights when we don't have dates. I should mention that that's not often. We're both—how should I say it?—in demand. Pass-for-pretty single ladies aren't too ready a commodity, these days. But every once in a while, Susan and I make it to the Metropolis. We buy good beer or fancy drinks and watch young couples dance, the girls burying their earrings in the boys' necks, the boys bewildered by the girls' breasts. If someone buys one of us a drink, we send it back. It's not about finding someone, it's about being alone with another person in a private public place.

That night we were watching MTV on the set above the bar. Some comedy special; I remember because Susan laughed, and snorted beer out her nose, and that got the barkeep chuckling at both of us. Then a man came in, someone whose name I didn't know but who I'd seen around, not at the Metropolis, but at Casey's Steakhouse, and a couple other family-type spots uptown. He always had a wifey-looking tag-along on his arm: very, very pretty, and very,

very placid. Tonight he was sporting single; you could tell he was out to make trouble. He didn't know it yet himself, but anyone watching him could just predict. Men who are about to commit adultery all walk the same way; it's in the hips, and the swing of their arms.

Leave it to me to become someone's trouble. Leave it to me to be some sweet-faced wife's nightmare. I didn't start things, though; Susan nudged me, but I shook my head no. I wasn't interested in anything just then. Flirting is a hobby of mine, but like all hobbies, you have to be in the right mood to enjoy it. I wasn't in the mood. I just wanted to talk to Susan, drink some beer, chat up the barkeep. When James walked up to us—right up to us, without even casting an eye or sending a drink over first—I was mostly annoyed. He wasn't what I was looking for. I needed a man without a ring.

So it's a mystery to me how we got to talking, but we did, and the talk went on and on, an argument about basketball that heated up until Susan dropped out (mostly for lack of material; she's not a fan), and we were both half-drunk. I did something lousy then, the first of a long series of lousies that came out of my involvement with James. I let Susan go off without me. She was playing with her compact, her lipstick—stuff she does when she's bored. Sort of an unspoken signal between us, I guess. But I didn't want to drop the talk with James. I was trying to persuade him that Dean Smith was God, and he wasn't having any of it. It was fun: I knew the game, he knew the game, I was moving pretzels around on the bar, mapping plays, citing stats, and he was coming back at me with the same thing in a louder, deeper voice, and clumsier diagrams, sketched with his longish thumbnail on paper napkins. So we were engrossed, but Susan was tired, bored, and approaching lonely. Finally she tapped me on the shoulder. I was exploiting the James Worthy connection for all it was worth; she shrugged, I shrugged her off. I barely noticed when she left. She'd driven; I knew it didn't matter. I was going home with James.

I went home with James.

Turned out his wife was away visiting her mother with their two kids. Turned out he'd never done this sort of thing before. Oh, I know: that's what they all say. But in his case, I believe it was true. He hadn't; I was the first. What made it so weird, and what took some getting used to, was his conviction that I was somehow inevitable. He has this theory, James. Thinks—oh, hell, it's hard to explain without sounding crazy—thinks he's pre-destined to love more than one person at once. First time he tried to explain it to me, I thought he was drunk. And he was, of course, but he still had the theory, whole and complete, the next morning. It's the only one he has; he clings to it like a religion. Thinks it explains his whole life; maybe it does. Maybe I just need a theory, too, to explain why my life's been such a roller-coaster. "I prefer red," I told Cope the night I met him, and it's true. Red's the signal for full stop, but also for go: romance, passion, anger, blood. Maybe red should explain all of my stories; certainly red was how it was with James.

His house was just what I'd expected: a suburban spread, one room for each of the kids, a flowery master bedroom with its own full bath, a living room with white carpeting, a breakfast nook with window seats and an imitation Tiffany lamp to shed light on each morning's Wheaties. It made me want to puke, both because that's something I've never wanted, and because it's something I'll never have. I grew up in a trailer that was practically a tent; I have a house now, a tiny number, almost a shack, that I rent at half-price because I've agreed to patch it, bring it up to livable again. I like fixing things, so that's not bad. But sometimes when I was with James in the Grand Hotel (as I took to calling it), I felt the first sproutings of something I'd have to call jealousy. Here was so much, and he didn't even know he had it. His kids would grow up taking carpeting for granted, thinking everyone ate breakfast in sunlight, on patterned window-seat cushions, thinking everyone watched television on huge color sets. They were born with remote controls in their little paws, and I couldn't help resenting them for it.

If the house was what I'd imagined it would be, James himself was not. The Laura Ashley draperies in the bedroom? Sashes like scarves, light and soft; perfect for tying a lady's wrists to the bed-posts. That was how he put it: "a lady's wrists." As if he wanted me to be a lady! No, he liked me because I wasn't. And he did like me, I saw that right away; it didn't seem to be only about sex. Told me later it was my ardor for basketball that did it: "Not many ladies can talk sports and flirt at the same time." I didn't have it in me to tell him that he must've been hanging out with the wrong kinds of ladies.

That first night, we did the drapery thing for a while, until I got bored, wanted to eat something. We had Ben and Jerry's, slept a little, got up, played some more. It was good but I've had better. He hadn't, and I could see by the look in his eyes that he was falling faster and harder than I was. It was like that the whole way down, with James. I sometimes wonder what his eyes look like to other people, without that open wound in the center that showed when he spoke to me. By then, it was almost into Sunday evening. His wife was supposed to come back early Monday, but I wasn't taking any chances. He let me out the back ("the neighbors, you understand"). I gave him my number, took his. Set sail the pieces through the window of a city bus.

I didn't call him, of course. He called me.

After that first night, I didn't think I'd go back. Like I said, I needed a man without a ring, someone who'd have me over to stay, not just for the weekend's entertainment. But when he called the second time, maybe two weeks later, I was having an off night: boss scarred his throat screaming me up at work, PMS, Susan was dissing me. I felt unbefriended, tired of falling asleep with the set on. Truth to tell, I was beginning to worry that my luck with men was running out. So I said, OK, I'll come over, just for a little while. That night changed things. Made a one-night stand into an "almost maybe." I nearly married James, and it was because of that second night. What happened was simple: we talked. What's harder to explain is why that mattered. When I say "talked," I mean really talked. Not about sports, and not "a little harder, honey," either. No, James opened up to me, and he did it suddenly, less like a flower unfolding than a gunshot in a parking lot. We were sitting on his sofa, the clock ticking away (wife, kids at some concert), when he took my hand, looked me straight in the eye, and asked, primly and properly, "May I tell you my story?"

If you could make a living reciting your history to strangers, James would be a millionaire. He started off with his childhood, ran me through twenty-two years of snow fights and swimsuits and proms and frat parties, hit his wedding (she was a virgin; "still is," he said, and I had to look down at my wine glass), birth of kid number one, buying Carlstown Yellow, birth of kid number two, building up the business, buying out Checker Cab of Carlstown, money, money,

money. He ended with the house in suburbia like it was a punctuation mark—an exclamation point or a question mark, I'm still not sure which one. Then he swerved, and things got interesting.

He wanted to talk about emotions. Go right ahead, I told him, thinking this was his prelude to foreplay, or a euphemism for talking dirty. And maybe it was, for James. He started in. "Do you ever feel," he began, and I waited for the kicker, for something horrible or simply stupid—some piece of my body eulogized, some torrid fantasy he'd fail to execute. "Do you ever feel like you're completely alone in the world?" He turned his head away from me, gazed out at the manicured lawn. "Do you ever wonder if anyone can really understand you? Do you ever think that your thoughts might be crazy, but no one will tell you?" His voice got lower; the music in the background framed each question like a picture, and for a moment I felt close to him, close the way I'd only ever felt maybe to Susan, or my best friend Lizanne in seventh grade. The stem of my glass seemed to disappear in the dim light as I set it down on the table. Why is it people never talk to each other anymore? Why is it that the big questions seem like preludes to fantasy, something vaguely obscene, something you tell your mistress but hide from your wife and kids?

I did something uncharacteristically corny: took his hand and kissed his knuckles. "Tell me." If he read desire in my eyes, he was reading me right. "Tell me more—why?"

We never slept together again, James and I; that wasn't what he was after. James wanted someone to talk to, someone to ask questions, someone to listen to his probing answers. Above all, he wanted someone whose mind worked similarly to his—similarly enough to comprehend his wildest mental flights, yet differently enough to push him off course, keep him from coasting. I did that for him, and got the same thing back in return. Eventually it wasn't enough. But initially it felt like everything, if only because it was so completely new.

What amazed me was the degree to which our conversations felt adulterous. We had nothing to hide, and so appeared frequently in public, our philosophical musings unwhispered, carried on underneath the noses of friends, townsfolk, colleagues. We never touched after that first night, not even to hug good-bye, or to tap one another's shoulders in enthusiasm, warning, empathy. The space between us was as precisely bounded as if we'd marked it off in ink; yet there was no question that we each believed we were having an affair. Certainly it was a very loud love affair. Lasted two years, right out in the open.

James' theory about his heart divided convinced me early on that I would always be a mistress, never a wife; I also had no real desire to split up a Happy Suburban Family. I missed sex, but after it became apparent that James wanted words and not caresses, I began taking care of that myself, carrying on a second affair with a youngish man named Troy who worked in a drugstore. Troy was good in bed, but above all he was quiet, and that was what I was looking for. Talking to James wore me out. Besides, I liked the neatness of the arrangement: talking to one person, fucking another. No lines crossed. Everything in its place.

As our second December approached, James began talking about leaving town for Christmas. I didn't think much of it—he'd gone to his wife's parents the year before; it seemed to be a tradition. Soon, however, he began musing about how much he'd miss me. What's to miss, I wondered. The trip would take a week, maybe a little longer; one week off wouldn't kill us. But James was melancholy, more pensive than usual. Long pauses punctuated our once-lively conversations; I began to feel wary, to wonder what would happen when he returned.

He arrived back in Carlstown on December thirtieth, and called me up that evening. "Nora, I have wonderful news for you. Margaret and the kids are staying up in Adair for New Year's. I told her I had to get back to town to organize cabbies for the New Year's special. Nora, we can celebrate New Year's together. I'll meet you at the Metropolis, and we'll take it from there."

It seemed like a good idea at the time; I'd planned to spend the evening at the Metropolis by my lonesome anyway. Having company on New Year's is no small thing, so when I hung up I felt grateful. I even called Susan and told her about it, though she was reluctant to view the news as good fortune. Susan didn't like James; I couldn't tell whether it was because I'd left her alone too long the night I met him, or because something about the man struck her as odd, the way it did many people, most people, myself included sometimes.

I got dolled up the night of the thirty-first. Sheer black stockings, the kind I never wear because they snag too easily, and snags cost money. Black pumps. A red dress, velvet, no sleeves, cut straight across the neck, no cleavage, but a back so low you could almost see my stocking band. The skirt hit just above the knee; it was an expensive get-up, and I have to admit I was hoping James would notice, take the hint, maybe unreel the curtain sashes again for me. I was talked-out, didn't feel like celebrating the beginning of another year with a dictionary in one hand and a thesaurus in the other.

I waited, nursing a mint-flavored drink that Alex, the barkeep, had whipped up for me. I like sweet drinks, the frothy kind, the kind with lots of sugar in them. I've never liked candy, cake, any of that stuff, but sweet drinks give me a trembly buzz I especially enjoy. I was sitting in almost the same place as I had the night James and I got started; when he came in, it was big time deja-vu. We joked about it, but his eyes weren't joking, and he wasn't chatty like usual. So we just sat, not saying much of anything, and watched the place fill up, all kinds of people. From our spot at the bar, we could see the dance floor: visible heat, red, blue, and yellow lights flashing. The TV sets above the mirrors showed muscular men in striped boxers gyrating to the beat of a rap song, though not the song that was playing. A tall man began swirling his hips and waving his arms perfectly in sync, becoming a column of smokey motion. Beside him: a chubby redhead, her hands on a dark-skinned woman's hips, their legs pressed tightly together, merged bodies an S, moving almost faster than the solo man beside them. The redhead's eyes were closed; the dark-skinned woman's throat was tilted back. As I watched, their dance became something more supple, an embrace, or a wave good-bye.

The Metropolis is going gay, gradually but still going. We talked some about that, about why and what we thought of it. "Everyone deserves a place," I said, but James shrugged, two short shrugs, the way he does when he's about to pose a question.

"Did God make Adam and Eve, or Adam and Steve?" That annoyed me, because it wasn't a real question, not something you could actually answer "yes" or "no" to, but a rhetorical question. A question that's not one, only pretending to be.

It got towards midnight, and the only deep thing James had said was the Adam and Eve bit, and to my mind that didn't even count. Mostly I felt relieved; I was tired of talking, hoping maybe tonight to see a little romance, what with Margaret gone, and the New Year and all. When it was close to the count-down, I got up, tapped my toe against the leg of his chair.

"You gonna dance with me or not, fella?" When I put my hand on his knee, he smiled as if he'd been waiting for me to ask him. As he stood up, he slipped something from his jacket into the pocket of his slacks. I noticed, but didn't ask; figured it was a key, money, something he didn't want to leave for whoever might steal his jacket. The dance floor was crazy-crowded; they had the big video screen cued up to Times Square, and the microphones were on over the dance floor. I used my elbows to make space, and James used his big clumsy feet. We danced underneath the strobe, slow, to a very fast song.

I like public things, public celebrations; I get very happy and loud. When the ten-second countdown started, I jumped, little jumps because of my heels and tight skirt. "TEN!" I yelled, so loud the guy next to me pretended to put his hands over his ears, but in a nice way, and he winked at me, and I winked back. "NINE!" I shouted. "EIGHT!" Everybody was shouting but James. "SEVEN!" "SIX!" I grabbed his shoulders and shook him a little, I was so hyper. "FIVE!" James' hand went into his back pocket, found something, grabbed my hand, put it in my palm. "ONE!" I kissed him, dropped it, and he scrambled to the floor, looking for whatever it was. "Darling, I'm sorry," I said. For a second, it looked like he was going to be trampled. A tall, skinny man in a dress with a trailing boa tripped over his back, sort of yelped, and I thought, goddamn, we'll both be killed by a drag queen on the dance floor of the Metropolis. But James stood up and dusted himself off; steering me by the elbow, he walked hard and fast over to the pool tables in the back.

The music started back up again; an old disco single, something I wanted to dance to. "Please, James, let's dance at least one more." James didn't answer, but put his hands on my waist, lifted me right up off the floor. Set me down on the pool table, and then—in front of at least seven or eight people, with Donna Summer panting in the background, whirlpools of smoke and neon pulsing, and the clock pushing six minutes after twelve—got down on his knees. Lord, if I didn't get faint then. I know what it's supposed to mean when a man goes down on his knees before a lady in public. It's never happened to me before, but I know what it's supposed to mean. And he did the deed: took out a small velvet box, battered but not cracked, opened the top, and held out a gold ring, clunky with an oval-shaped diamond and two tiny rubies.

What do you say to a married man when he proposes?

You say, "James, what about Margaret?"

You say, "James, this isn't legally possible."

You think, "This isn't what I want," and it wasn't. I wasn't in love with James. I didn't want to be somebody's sounding board, though I liked the places our conversations sometimes took us. But James was a diversion for me, a stop I'd made because I was too tired and scared to keep going. It shook me up, the ring and all. I hadn't realized he was in that deep; I couldn't help wondering how real it was. After all, the only thing I did for him was listen.

So I took the box, closed the lid, handed it back to him. Hopped off the pool table, put my arm around his shoulders. "James, you're drunk. You're married. You need to go home, get some sleep, take this back to Sears first thing Monday morning."

"Nora, I'm serious." He closed his hand over the hand I'd put on his shoulder. "I want you to marry me. I'm going to divorce Margaret; I've been thinking about it for months. As soon as the papers are finalized, we'll make it legal." He held the box out. "Take it; it's yours. I bought it for you. I want everyone to know how I feel about you." Several onlookers clapped; a small, dark-haired woman in a hat gave a wolf whistle.

"James, you're a married man. How will Margaret feel? What will the kids think?"

"Leave that to me. That's my worry. You deserve this; you're my wife more than she is. Please." He pushed the box forward, but I pulled my arm away from him, stepped back. I started wobbling, the way I always do in heels when I'm nervous. A man in jeans took his girlfriend by the arm, walked her away from the scene.

"Take it, Nora, please. You know I love you."

I clenched my hands into fists. "No, James."

"Nora."

From behind me, I heard someone echo both our names in the high, tremulous tones of mimicry. Laughter. Who were these people?

"Absolutely not."

"Nora!"

"I don't love you, James. I don't want your ring."

James held the box in his hands. My legs were shaking; I leaned against the pool table, ran my fingers through my hair. For a moment, I thought he was going to speak, but he stayed quiet. Then he opened the velvet cover, and put the ring in his palm. In the dark shadowy spaces around the pool tables, the diamond stood out like a beacon. James raised his palm above his head, then clamped his fingers down quickly around its light. "Wear it."

"James." I didn't like the rough edge to his voice. "James, stop it." The disco music had ended, replaced by a slow duet.

James reached over, pulled at my neckline, and dropped the ring down the front of my red velvet dress. I put one hand to my chest and bent forward; I could feel the diamond shifting against my skin, scratchy and cold. The crowd of seven or eight had expanded. We'd become more fun than Times Square on the big screen. The ring tumbled. I tried reaching my hand down, but the neckline was too tight.

I straightened up. I looked James in the eye.

"Wear it," he said.

I knew what to do to make the ring fall.

I shimmied. I rolled my shoulders and swirled my hips, like a belly dancer in a B-movie. I waved my arms, twitched my toes, thrust my thighs, did the Hulu, the Pump, the Charleston, the Bus Stop. I don't need a dance floor, you fool, I thought; I don't need a strobe, or a microphone. All I need is an audience. The ring fell free, several people clapped, someone whistled; James bent down, picked it up, and walked out of the bar.

I watched him go through the window of a half-empty glass.

Then yes. I said, "But I prefer red." Red for passion. Red for dead stop. Why is it that one color means both?

No more married men. I looked at Copeland's hand for a ring: no ring. How was I to know it was invisible? All I wanted from my driver was to clear the words *wear it* from my head. To rub James' touch off my shoulders. To erase the pattern the ring had traced in invisible ink as it danced across my chest and belly.

How was I to know he was married to a ghost?

Sometimes I think everybody is married to someone in their

36

head. That we live by attaching ourselves to a memory, and don't dislodge ourselves from it until we find another. Maybe Copeland wasn't different, but there was an intensity to his love for Dell that made it hard to understand. It took time for me to realize that she was less a memory than a ghost. I figured it out before he did; I say that because when I broke the news to him the night we said our angry good-byes, he looked shocked, rather than angry. Shock followed by revelation; his last expression was one of recognition.

He hadn't mentioned Dell's name to me until some time into our relationship; it was even longer still before I understood what she meant to him. That first night, I took Copeland for a sweet-faced single boy stuck working New Year's Eve. I was drunk, humiliated, and stupid enough to think that a one-night stand would ease the pain of watching James walk out of my life for good. I figured he wouldn't be back; I thought I knew James well enough to know that it was all or nothing with him. He was looking to cure his heart of its addiction to the number two; he wanted someone to be everything for him, so he could concentrate on the number one, so he could ease the split that burdened him. I'd refused, and now he'd eventually look elsewhere. I wished him luck but figured he'd run through life feeling discontented. James' mistake was thinking it was possible to be anything but split in two. No one can be everything for another person; it's not a mistake to want that, but it's a mistake to think you can find it.

I was putting off mourning the loss of someone, putting off thoughts about how I'd fill my time now that I had no one to talk to, no one to meet for lunch, dinner, odd hours for coffee. I wasn't expecting anything from my driver, but the kindness etched in Copeland's face surprised me. So I pushed him, hoping he'd sway easily. I wanted sex, and a long sleep in someone else's bed. What I got was heartache; there might be a lesson in that, but I'd prefer not to think it through.

I tried the lipstick trick. When he didn't call, I took matters into my own hands. I wasn't drunk by then, of course, just curious. What would he look like through sober, daylight eyes? I half-expected a horror, but he was so beautiful. Copeland has hair the color of mahogany; it's long, just past his shoulders, and he wears it in a ponytail, always held back with a blue elastic band. Not the same one; he has several. I know because I asked, and he pulled open a drawer: socks, cigarettes, blue elastic hair bands. His eyes are dark brown, and his skin is olive. His features are economical, very evenly spaced, nothing stands out in particular. But the combination is handsome. He picked me up in the yellow cab ("It's mine, and it's paid off," he said, right away); I climbed in the front seat, then realized I'd forgotten my checkbook.

I really had forgotten my checkbook. I'd remembered it a few minutes before he came by, but somehow managed to forget it again. Yeah, OK, I wanted to sleep with him. But not because I wanted sex so badly; what I wanted was a mark on him. I wanted to make sure he wouldn't forget my name; sex seemed the quickest way to do it. "House tour," I said, and he fell for it. There's only a living room, kitchen, bathroom, and tiny bedroom: house tour, yeah, right. It didn't take long. In the bedroom, I shut the door so I could show him the poster on the back: Matisse, big blue ladies holding hands in a circle. Don't know why I like it, but I do. It cheers me. He scrunched up his face when he looked at it, tugged on his chin. Then grinned.

"Looks like the definition of fun."

I laughed, grabbed his hands, kissed him. That part was easy.

Passion was harder. He and I didn't have the same ideas about some things; sex was one of them. I don't understand soft sex the way I don't understand bland food. Cream of Wheat? Why? Kisses are fine, kisses are lovely, but they need to travel, and they need to travel fast. I've had boyfriends who held me down, and I liked that; I had a girlfriend once, too, and that was another way I liked it. But with Copeland, everything was soft, slow, so gentle I almost forgot he was there. It didn't take long for me to realize that he wasn't; what I couldn't be sure of was why. I never did figure out whether he really liked things so careful and light, or whether he just wasn't all that into it with me. I've come to settle that it must've been some of both: Cope is cautious by nature, a little boring, but Dell's memory had a whole lot more to do with it.

After that first time, we started seeing each other every so often, then regular, then steady on. But with Cope, it was never what I expected. Usually with a lover, things move forward or stop dead; there's not a lot of lag time. It's on or off. With Copeland there was no momentum; pretty soon, it got to feeling stagnant. Came a time when I knew I needed things to move forward. But for that to happen, I had to know what he was holding back.

Copeland kept me just slightly at a distance, always some part of him I couldn't reach. We'd be talking together in bed, after sex or before, and I'd look him in the eyes, trying to lose myself, when somehow he'd stop me. It wasn't that he'd turn away or close his eyes, nothing so obvious. Just a feeling I'd get that told me to stop, to lower the intensity. Not to put my emotions into words. It felt like I was drowning; I had that feeling with Copeland a lot. My throat would go tight, and I'd turn my face towards the bluish curtains, breathing deeply. He stopped me from being myself just when it mattered most; I thought then that I couldn't ever forgive him for that. But, I have, because I learned why later. Dell. The dead girl. Dell.

It took some time for me to figure out that old Cope had a secret beyond a lover's usual secrets: the *Playboy* stash on top of the refrigerator, the canceled engagement, the six-year-old in Idaho, the disease that might or might not recur. I figured it was some permutation of the above, or maybe whiskey; turned out I was wrong on the first count, right on the second. One night I asked him to take me to the Metropolis; he got antsy, coughed, did the little avoidance dance alkies do 'til he came right out and said it: "I don't like bars much, now that I'm not drinking." OK fella, I thought, no biggie. I've got your number. But I didn't; whiskey wasn't much of a secret. Dell came later.

We'd been together maybe a month, we were in Cope's kitchen, and we were cooking tacos, my specialty. Copeland was chopping tomatoes and lettuce, I was frying meat, heating sauce in a pan. Something about the evening—the smell of the shells baking, the sounds coming in off the highway—something reminded me of cooking for my ex-husband, and I said so to Cope. "You know," I told him, "I wanted that divorce from Ray so badly I could taste it. I've never doubted for a minute that it was the right thing to do. If I'd stayed, I'd have six kids by now, and I'd still be in that kitchen, frying chicken wings and cubed potatoes. Sure wouldn't be cooperative cooking like what we're got here."

Copeland shook his head, the way he did when he agreed. He had the head signals for "yes" and "no" mixed up, and always shook his head for "yes," nodded for "no."

"You're right there, Nora." He liked it when I noticed the way he helped with cooking and cleaning things. I did notice, too, and I didn't take it for granted.

"But you know, Cope," I turned down the heat under the sauce, "even though I was crazy-happy about the divorce, after Ray was out of my life, I felt his absence like a presence." Ordinarily, Copeland and I tiptoed around the subject of relationships, past ones and our present one, as well. We'd share all kinds of intimate details about our lives, but leave obvious gaping holes, and never call each other on it. But something about the evening was making me pensive, less cautious than usual about sharing details of my life with Ray. I remember thinking that it felt new, but not risky. "I'd wake up, turn to him, and then my hands would shake when I realized I was in bed alone. Do you ever think," I rummaged around for spices in the cabinet, then remembered that Cope kept them in the refrigerator, "that our bodies have memories, just like our minds? I think my shoulders and hands sometimes remember Ray, all on their own." Copeland was quiet; I shook pepper into the sauce.

"Does this need more of something, and if so, what?" I held out the wooden spoon. But he'd moved to the door, his back towards me; his head was bent a little to one side, his shoulders forward. While I watched, he put one hand in his pocket, the other on the doorframe. We both stayed still for I don't know how long. When he finally turned around, took the spoon, tasted the sauce, I could see from the set of his brows that he'd been holding sadness in. So I called him on it. I stuck the spoon down on top of the counter, marched over to turn off the stove.

"We're not eating until you tell me what you've been keeping from me."

Cope walked into his bedroom without a word. I followed him, watched as he pulled two battered shoeboxes out of the closet. We sat on the floor in the tiny bedroom, backs against his bed, feet propped on the door. He took the lids off both boxes, then dumped the contents over my legs and his; I felt a twinge of fear, thinking that what he really wanted was to bury me. As if the floods of memory weren't already high enough to drown us both.

I met the dead girl then. Dell. In the pictures, she had thin, bright lips, high cheekbones, eyes an odd beige color; Copeland called it almond. She looked both delicate and tough, so tall and thin she was almost boyish, but with a girl's graceful back and shoulders. She had long, straight wheat-colored hair. It reminded me of Copeland's, except that she wore it down, a tortoiseshell barrette on either side, just above her ears.

Most people make sex into a secret, something they both hope and fear will distinguish them from other people. We lock away what brings us most together, render it taboo—which is why people never talk to each other anymore—really talk, I mean.

I'm different. For me, sex and secrecy aren't linked the way they seem to be for many people. But for Copeland, they were linked, more so than for anyone I'd ever met. Preserving Dell's memory let him preserve that link: she, his secret, became his sex. His sexuality revolved around his secret: the memory of a dead girl who, in life, must herself have been silent, cautious, unknowable, even to him.

Especially to him?

For nothing about her pictures was transparent. Usually, you can tell something about a person from photographs; the way they smile, stand, or hold their bodies gives you a clue about who they are. Dell's photos revealed absolutely nothing. Oh, you could tell a lot about the way she might have moved, how her body might have looked in motion. You could see right off that she mixed grace and roughness, liked it that way, cultivated ambiguity. But her personality? The depth or airiness of her opinions, her favorite foods, what she watched or listened to or read, how she fucked, who she fucked, who she voted for, what she most wanted? Nothing. You couldn't even tell much about vocation, money, education. And what I most wanted to know was nowhere to be found: Why Copeland? And for Copeland, why Dell?

He told his story while I looked through the photographs and mementos: a toothpick wrapped in plastic and a Clapton tape that had come unwound. I sensed from the slow spill of his words that he wasn't used to narrating, but he was a natural storyteller, and every word evoked an image. I began to see Dell, to hear her husky voice, to smell the inside of her cab: leather, menthols, Ivory soap. I didn't realize 'til much later that Cope left out his side of the story. Oh, he talked about what they'd done together, plans they'd made for the future. But everything was Dell, Dell, Dell; very little about what he felt, and nothing about how she continued to haunt him. I had to figure that out for myself. I had to see her myself to know.

It happened for the first time at the movies. We'd gone to see some Steve Martin picture. Cope admires the man, worships anyone who can make him really laugh. And he did laugh, and in the middle of the picture, he took my hand: not something he did often. But a little later his laughter slowed down. There was a half-serious bit to the movie; when I glanced over, I realized that he'd closed his eyes. Later that night, when we got back to the trailer, I poked him in the ribs and said, "Don't think I didn't notice the little nap you took midway through the movie." Cope rubbed his eyes; at first, I thought he was mimicking sleep, and laughed. Then I realized his thoughts were serious.

"I was seeing Dell."

I knew then that we were in trouble.

I made him explain the whole damn ritual. How he'd lean back in the brown chair, close his eyes, imagine her face. How he'd scan her face for changes, making sure he remembered every detail.

"Does anything ever change?" I had to ask. He didn't answer.

Once he'd explained his obsession, none of the details were enough for me. I needed to see him seeing her, to watch his eyes shift underneath focused lids.

"Let me see you," I said; he looked blank.

"See me?"

"Sit in the chair." My voice felt harsh; it hurt my throat, but the words forced themselves forward. He knew what I meant. Got up from the sofa, moved to the brown chair. Pulled up the old microwave box he used as a footrest.

I walked closer to him. "Close your eyes and forget I'm in the room." He put one hand across his face, but I moved it away, let it rest on the chair. "No. I need to see your eyes."

"Now what?"

"See her."

I began with my own eyes open. But as I watched his face twist, relax, smooth, brighten, I found my lids twitching, first in sympathy, then in curiosity. What did he see? What had he found there, against the skin of his own body, within the dredge of memory, what had he found to comfort and convince him? Would it work for me? I'd never met her. I sat down, curled my legs beneath me. I closed my eyes, and waited.

Mostly I saw black, or dark brown. Some patches of light, speckles that I assumed were from the TV or the lamp. It was hard just to sit with my eyes shut; it made me tired. It felt as if my eyes were pushing against the skin of my eyelids. But I waited. I needed to know. I had to see if it was true.

I tried thinking about her. "Dell," I thought, "who were you? What did you give him that I haven't got?" I wished I could talk to her; I wanted to ask her questions. Maybe I even wanted permission. "Dell," I thought, "you wouldn't want Copeland to be so alone, would you? Can't you let him go? Can't you see how ugly grief has made him?"

Something happened. I felt a chill across my lips. Then, for a second, I saw a picture: not her face, but the length of her, her tall slim self, shoulders sturdy and wide like a swimmer's. Her hair swayed slightly as she moved. She was walking, her arms moving gracefully in sync with her leggy strides. Took three, four steps, then she was gone.

"Cope." I shook him 'til his eyes opened. "Cope, what did you see?"

He looked at me, nodded.

"Tell me!"

"Her face. It's always her face. But I usually can't do it when anyone else is around."

"Cope, I think I saw her!" I took his hands, pulled him out of the chair. I tried to imitate her walk. "She was walking, like this…"

He bit his lip. "You're making fun of me."

"No, I'm not. I saw her. She was…"

"Nora, stop it. Cut it out." He turned away, but I grabbed him by the shoulders.

"Cope, I'm not making fun of you. I saw her."

"Stop it."

"I saw her."

He turned away from me, walked towards the door. "What are you saying to me?"

"Cope, I'm telling you I saw Dell." I came up behind him, put my arms around his chest; he kissed me, and we moved together into the bedroom. Fell on his bed, and he was there, it was the only time I'd felt him really present. We made love, but it wasn't just two of us.

"Pretend she's here," he whispered. I knew what it cost him to say it. I knew I'd never hear him say it again.

"Watch me," I said, and he did. I cleared a space between us. I let my hands run the length of a body that wasn't there, cupped my mouth around the memory of a dead girl's sex.

Don't ask me if it was real for me or not. I know it was real for Copeland. I didn't have to touch him. He cried out on his own.

We woke the next morning tangled in bedclothes; I tiptoed out to make coffee and found the door the way we'd left it: unlocked, the screen ajar on the outside. "Lucky nothing was stolen," Cope said, coming up behind me. I reached for him, took his hand, brought it between my legs, but he shook me off.

She was gone again, and he'd followed her.

After that, little things changed, and I let myself think he was starting to settle in with me. He'd laugh more readily. He'd flick the radio right away to my favorite station. Once, he brought home flowers, blue and yellow in a mug with rainbows that I still use to hold my toothbrush. But mostly he was gone, distant the way he'd always been. I don't know why I fooled myself; I guess I thought that loving him gave me the right to lie to my own heart.

It hasn't forgiven me.

Sometimes I still think things would've worked out eventually, if James hadn't found out about the two of us. One of Cope's pals was having a party; he asked me along, and I was right away flattered. He hadn't taken me out with his buddies before, so it seemed like a sign to me. I was eager to be with him in public, to hold his arm, to show his friends and all of Carlstown that I was the one woman who'd been able to tear his mind from Dell. It felt almost like a ceremony, that party. I dressed high, a beige mini and a lacy white blouse. I let my hair go in curls around my neck, unpinned. Cope whistled when he saw me; it felt like together for real.

I don't know why it hadn't occurred to me that James might be there. I'd worried so much about that our first month together, since Cope worked for James' company. But his name rarely came up, and we never ran into him; I was careful never to visit Cope at work. I wasn't sure if he ever mentioned my name to the boys, but I some-how thought he hadn't. He and James weren't best friends anyhow; fishing every other week, that was about it.

We walked into the hallway of Brad and Katie's house; Brad took our coats, asked us what we wanted to drink. I followed him into the kitchen, and bumped into a dark-haired man half-in, half-out of the refrigerator.

James.

His face went stoney for less than a second. Then he recovered, lit up with a smile the size of Detroit. Lots of teeth, James had. He shut the fridge door, and extended his hand. "Pleased to meet you. Don't think I know your name. I'm James. Brad's boss at Carlstown Yellow."

Margaret wasn't there. "She's sick," someone explained, raising an eyebrow, and pointing to a slim, pretty woman with curly hair in a yellow dress. "So sick that Jennifer had to come by with James to keep his mind off his poor, poor invalid wife." I lifted an eye-brow back; I make a point of acknowledging irony. Then I checked her out. She was quiet, slightly nervous, and looked suspiciously like me.

I thought Jennifer would make us even. We'd both moved on; James was here with someone; I was here with someone. Why hold a grudge? But he tailed me. He stayed within five feet of me the entire party, breaking off conversations mid-sentence to move behind or beside or in front of me, occasionally taking part in the chatter of whatever group I'd found myself a place in. I started off feeling sad—that moved rapidly into nausea, and finally into fear. He was stalk-ing me in a roomful of people, and there was no one to tell, no one to ask for safety. I didn't want Copeland to know, though looking back that was silly: after all, I knew everything about Copeland's past. But a man who's faithful to his dead lover is different from a woman who's slept with her boyfriend's Don Juan boss. I had a rep-utation to uphold, or at least construct. So we moved, James and I, to the queer choreography of a hostile romantic drama, skirting a wide circle, then moving closer and closer to the center of the living room. By the time I reached Copeland, who was standing beside Pit talking cars and eating Triscuits, I was exhausted. I put my head on his shoulder, and he put his arm around my waist without taking his eyes off Pit.

"Can we take off soon?" I whispered. Before he could answer, James clapped a hand on Copeland's shoulder.

"Good to see you with a lady, Copeland. Good to see you with a pretty lady handling your arm."

Handling his arm? So James knew that I was the one in love. That I was the one doing the clinging.

Cope grinned at James; I gritted my teeth through a smile. I could feel the cold metal of James' diamond against my skin, see the smokey circles of dancers at the Metropolis. How close to the surface did James hold his violence? Cope just kept grinning; I bent over to whisper in his ear again, but he shifted, shrugged my words away.

"Maybe you and your lady friend can come by our place sometime," James made a funny little bow in my direction, "have yourselves some dinner with me and the wife." I could just see it. Me, Cope, Margaret, James, and Dell's ghost. We'd clear the table, have an orgy, tie each other up in Laura Ashley curtain sashes and leave the mess for the maid. Jesus H. Christ. I felt my stomach churning, and took hold of Cope's arm as I pushed my way towards the door.

"Yeah," I said, looking James hard in the eye, "maybe on a leash."

Someone beside him gasped; I think it was Pit's girl Maggie. God, I thought, God these people are naïve. I was sick to death of the whole scene, sick of the men's hypocritical kindness, the women's false gentility. You people tie each other up at night but don't allow public insults? You cheat on each other behind closed doors, but can't stomach sarcasm? It infuriated me that no one seemed to see through James' cruelty. Why hadn't it occurred to anyone that we had history? But that was my fault, I thought, as Cope and I moved briskly towards the car. His hands were jammed in his coat pocket, and the set of his chin was sullen. There was no way for me to explain this one, I knew that. No way for him to understand unless I told him about my affair with James.

Should I tell him? Somehow I sensed that telling Cope would end things right away. He had no patience with infidelity. The few comments he'd made about James' affairs had been biting and cruel; I knew he was thinking about his fidelity, even after death, to Dell. Cope wore his loyalty like a badge. If he knew I'd been part of somebody's infidelity—even if most of it had been about talk, not sex (but had there really been a difference?)—he'd throw me over. Oh,

I could've lied, or played coy and simply hinted. But I figured if Cope even suspected I'd ever met James before, he'd automatically assume we'd been fucking on doormats all over town.

Goddamn double-standard. Times like these could almost turn a girl feminist, flag-waving and carrying on.

Cope took Westerly Road home; midway to the trailer park, he made a left on Smith Pike. I didn't say anything. It meant he was dropping me off at my place. And he did: foot of my driveway. He didn't even bother to drive me to the door.

Why did I stay with him?

Love's about masochism. I don't mean the fool games I like to play, rough stuff in bed. I mean emotional masochism. Forget banning whips and tit clamps, forget regulating porn. Somebody should pass a law prohibiting people from chasing after folks who just plain don't want them. No more running after anyone who treats you badly: now it's against the law! Imagine the propaganda: posters with an anxious looking puppy dog in a red circle, a big slash through the middle. Now there's an enforcement problem for you. I can just see the blue suits busting into the kitchen of Mrs. Jane Doe, handcuffing her wrists, stuffing her in the wagon without even allowing her time to take off her apron. Charge? Loving a shithead. Loving him too much.

I stayed with Copeland because I liked the highs and lows. It was a challenge: first I wanted to find out his secret, then I wanted to take Dell's place. But after making love to Dell's memory, I had another reason, as well. Her swagger, the bold way she walked, the fall of her long hair, the queer almond color of her heavy-lidded eyes. Cope wanted it to be about the three of us, and the idea of sex with memory made our bedding together strange. It was the way salt changes a dish, that extra, bringing out what's already there. I liked that, I liked Dell, and I didn't want to lose the girl I'd seen.

Even though I knew about Copeland's drinking problem, I wanted him to take me to the Metropolis. I wanted him to watch me dance, to see me lively under lights, to know the Nora I could be when I was surrounded by music. Too, I wanted to erase the memory of James' proposal from my breasts. I needed to have new memories about the place, so I could drop by with Susan again, enjoy a beer, chat with Alex, watch the regulars sway and loosen. One

night Cope got soft with me, then softer. "Let's go to the Metropolis," he said, watching my eyes for a response. I had to grin. That night
I wore a long skirt slit up the front just past the knee. A blue leotard
top, big hoop earrings, spikey-heeled boots. We drove in the cab; I
fiddled with the radio, trying to find something to tap my feet to.

I'd promised myself not to drink in front of Copeland, but as
soon as I walked in, my hands begged for a glass. And why not? I
thought. That's his problem, not mine. So I ordered two drinks: a
White Russian for me, and a club soda for him. We found a table
near the dance floor, nursed our drinks, watched the lights change
colors. When the mood hit me, I pulled him out of his chair. "C'mon,
bud," I laughed. He wasn't the world's smoothest dancer, but his awkwardness was charming. Usually there was tension about him when
we were together, a sort of sad tiredness I attributed to carrying the
weight of Dell's memory around like a knapsack. But that night things
were different: calmer, I thought. We danced song after song, until
the toe of my left shoe began pinching, and I needed to stop. So we
sat down again, watching the lights and movement; I swayed in my
chair, ordered another White Russian, and wished I'd worn better
shoes. Then I started worrying about my make-up: my mascara runs
sometimes when I sweat. I went into the bathroom to check; when
I sat back down, Copeland started talking at me right away.

"Nora, there's something I've been meaning all night to tell you."
I was half-listening, playing with one of those laminated drink cards
they leave on the table to get you to try specialty drinks. Our table
had one advertising something called the Pink Flamingo. With my
taste for sweet drinks, I wondered if I'd like it. Should I try? Would
it make me sick on top of the White Russians?

"I want to tell you about it now."

I was glad Copeland was feeling chatty. I put my arm around
him. "Tell Nora all about the thoughts running around that big old
brain of yours. Copeland, you just tell Nora all about it." It felt good
to be with him in public, to have my arm about him, to talk teas-
ingly. I gave his shoulder a squeeze.

"Nora, it's this. I don't think we should see each other anymore."

Even over the music, I knew I'd heard him right. My throat
ached. I wanted another drink. How could he? Then it hit me: so
that was what the calm was. He'd made the decision long before we

set foot in the door. Was that why he'd taken me here? As a good-bye gift? I pushed back my chair. I just wanted distance between us. I was afraid I'd hurt him, afraid I'd hurt myself.

"Can you talk to me? I mean, tell me how you're feeling."

"How I'm feeling?"

I stood up. His features blurred until they resembled James', and I remembered the feel of the ring, the eyes of the on-lookers. "Wear it!" James had said. That was the night I'd met Copeland. He'd rescued me from my drunken self. Who would pick me up tonight?

But it wasn't only self-pity I was feeling; it was anger. Oh, I'd known there was distance between us, that he wasn't in love the way I was. But I'd thought he wanted me, even if only to keep company with Dell, even if only to fill his house with chatter, to cook, to brew coffee in the mornings. When had he stopped wanting me? Had he ever? I felt anger fall across my body like a shadow, chilling me even in the overheated room. I wanted to shake him, but most of all I wanted him to want me back. So I used sex then, not because I thought it would work on Copeland, just out of habit. It's the only tool for revenge I know. I flicked my skirt open a little, teasing him. Then I felt my throat tighten, desire and anger rubbing my voice raw. I leaned across the table, took hold of his shoulders. "If I were a man," I said, and meant it, "Copeland, I'd rape you."

I left the bar, and set out walking; halfway home I took off my shoes and stuffed them in my purse. I meant never to see Cope again. How could I, knowing I was capable of brutality and love both? How could I look at him again, knowing that what I felt for him was something so ugly? I'd thought my love for him was beautiful; that night I saw my neediness in the mirror of his eyes and couldn't bear it.

But something happened to bring me back. I went home, threw up, didn't sleep all night. But I made plans. When the sky began to lighten, I called James at home, interrupting breakfast. I got Margaret's thin, watery words. James took the phone from his wife; when he heard my voice, he cleared his throat. As he said my name, I realized from his tone that I had him back. If I wanted him.

We met at noon at the Rockline Inn, where it was easy to talk without being overheard. I told him that Cope had dumped me. I told him I had no one else really to go to, which was true. And I told him that Cope was still in love with Dell. I didn't lie to him. I let James know that I wasn't interested in having him back for his own sake. But I was willing to do certain things to get at Cope, and if he could offer me any clues, any advice, well, I'd be thankful. More than thankful. And I'd show him how I felt.

James began talking. Told me stories. We sat at that booth 'til almost four o'clock, drinking cup after cup of coffee, ordering plates of food we didn't eat, just to keep them from throwing us out. James told me about Dell, things I'd never have guessed. He gave me ammunition, "if you want to fire," as he said. I held the secrets he gave me in my palm, pocketed them as we left the restaurant.

"I'll be in touch," and I kissed him, there on the steps of the Rockline Inn. "I owe you one. I'll give you a call."

Then I got in the car, drove home, paced around the bedroom. Got back in the car, drove to Copeland's.

Almost as soon as James told me Dell's story, I thought, yes, I'll use it. I'll tell Copeland. I'll hurt him the way he hurt me. More, even. I thought, I'll kill Dell for him. I'll kill her off.

That was what I planned to do. When I opened the door of Cope's trailer, I was armed, Dell's story tucked like a handgun in my pocketbook. I wanted to destroy the one thing he had. I planned to kill the dead girl a second time.

"Copeland," I could hear the woman's name echoing in my mind: Terry, Terry, as if she were a second ghost, another woman I might see when I closed my eyes. I readied myself to say her name. "I came by...do you know why I came by?" He couldn't, of course. I knew something he didn't.

But when I opened my mouth to tell him, when I prepared my tongue and throat and brain to force the story out, into words he'd have to hear, what came out instead was, "I love you."

"I want us to be together," I said. "I want you to let me into your life. You haven't given me a chance. I just want a chance. I want what Dell had."

I tried to explain to him about love. How you can love more than one person in your lifetime. How you have to move forward. How you can't just stop. I didn't tell him that Dell had kept secrets from him, that she'd been in love with someone else, with a woman, Terry Cintos. That she'd maybe died with Terry's name, with the taste of Terry's lips, on her tongue. Oh, I hinted a little: I couldn't hold that back. But it was more boasting than hinting, more wanting him to recognize me, to see me, and know that I could give him something Dell never could.

He went cruel on me anyway. Called me dust, pushed me away. Threw things, and clung to her ghost like he was drowning in my tears. Then he told me to leave, and I snapped. Because his voice said he'd written me off. This wasn't another fight. This wasn't even James, angry and humiliated and frustrated. It was something deeper. He was fighting for her life.

I did a cruel thing, then. I'd thought not telling her story was a kindness, and maybe it was, but I did the next meanest thing I could think of. I told him the truth. I told him he was haunted, that he was living with her as if she were still alive. Fucking her, eating with her, speaking to her. "You still live with her, you bastard!" I said, and then it was over between us, and we both knew it.

No reason to look back.

I won't ever kill time for a man like that again. A man buried in a room that reeks of a dead girl's history. He couldn't see me, Copeland, because his eyes were too full of her face. He couldn't see what might have been his future, because he was brow-deep in the past.

I wish him ill. I do. I'm cruel, and I don't deny it. What hurts is that I could do worse—could do real damage—but I don't. And there's no thankfulness for silence. No one to pat you on the back and say "Thank you, Nora, for not telling tales about the dead."

Some nights I rehearse those tales, rehearse what I'd say to Copeland if I ever felt ready. I'll never be ready, though, because what I have to tell would kill him.

It would kill her, too; Dell, I mean. And that would be a shame. A real shame. Even *I* see her now sometimes, when I close my eyes. When I reach out for the second pillow, pretending it's a body I've never seen. I don't want to be the one to send her ghost skittering back across the planet.

But I haven't told James. I'm not sure he'd understand about the two of us.

CHAPTER 3

Terry

SHE was bleeding, so she wanted to lie on the floor, but I refused. Sex is always about blood, whether it's visible or not. Why pretend otherwise? I've never understood lovers who try to make sex presentable. Bodies together generate chaos; you can't straighten it up, scrub it down, dust off its shelves.

"You're positive he's away?"

" 'Til at least six tomorrow. Sure of it."

Silly things: space, time, privacy. The room was so tiny that when we stood, my legs touched the bed, and her back touched the wall. I put one hand on either side of her shoulders, she bent her head, and I could smell her hair, like cinnamon. I undid the first three buttons on her shirt, slid my hand along her bra. Snap front: that made me laugh. She asked me why; I said, "Remember high school?" and she laughed too.

But she stopped my hands then, held them, kneading my fingers. "I need to ask you if you're safe."

"I've taken the test, yes." I looked into her eyes without blinking. "I don't have it."

"Then that," she loosened the weight of her hands against mine, "makes two of us." It felt lucky, and I whispered just that into the hair falling tangled across her ear.

It seems funny now to think that I was so incautious. Odd, isn't it, the way *safe* has come to refer almost exclusively to the immediate danger of disease? If she'd asked me that question a decade back, I might have interpreted it differently. Once, "Are you safe?" might have meant, "Will you stay with me? Will you feed my heart, or break it?" Now it means something clinical. We need new words to speak of heartbreak.

She wasn't really safe. But she lied, and kept the meaning of *safe* corporeal. Kept it encased in a clinic, where the only blood exchanged is in tubes, where skin meets latex, and needles gleam like bedroom eyes in darkness.

But what does it mean, *safe*? How can love ever be safe? Safety and love are mutually exclusive. And besides (I reminded myself, almost saying it aloud), this wasn't love. This was sex, no more or less. My hands on her breasts. My leg between her legs. Her voice, sighing, not calling my name, but singing.

Singing?

It went low and sweet, her voice. I didn't realize. "I didn't realize you could sing."

"I just talk to my radio for company."

I tried thinking back to the day we met, that first ride into Carlstown. Had she been singing then, too softly for me to hear?

She shook her head. "Never with strangers."

Odd to think I was a stranger once. I remember stroking Kyla's cheek good-bye; I remember buttoning my yellow coat as the plane dived down; I remember coming out of the airport, shielding my eyes against the staggering snow. But I can't get back to how anything really felt before Dell came round: before I hailed her through white weather outside the terminal, her face covered by a sign like a scarf, a sign that read *Parker's*, the name I called out before I knew her as Dell.

I shook off memory. Put my mouth to her throat, let my lips travel. Have you ever eaten someone else's breath? Let your mouth close around air that's spun through the sponged crevices of their lungs? How close how close how close is close. How painful it is not to travel with her breath, to be limited to the outside of her body.

"No." I stopped her palm. "No, I'm touching you." My words sounded corny as soon as they hit the air; she laughed, but slid her fingers out from underneath my shirt.

"Is that how you want it?"

"It's what I've imagined."

She laughed again. "This isn't about what you think you know."

And it wasn't, because what I already knew receded, the way a red light goes dim and you forget its presence once the green goes on. We were very much two people, not one. Never one, but two, each pulling the other in a different direction. When one of us let go, the other fell fast forward, saved by a hand or leg or eye at the last minute. We used no net. There was nothing easy about it.

I wasn't interested in loving her. That happened by accident, the way most important things do. Sex came first, and love tagged after. The way people say sex and love are inextricable? Foolishness. She took them apart, let me examine each.

Once or twice I thought she'd stopped breathing, and had to check, put my ear to her heart.

"I need to know you're still alive."

She answered with a gesture I can't describe. She said, "This isn't something you already know. Don't follow rules. Don't think you've been this way before."

She lay on her side along the bed; I placed one hand on the flat between her breasts. My favorite part of her body, the wicked point of departure. I lapped my tongue across and down. She took my head with both hands. "Do this." It was a slow sort of something. Oh bid me bid me bid me, and I did what she showed me. Outside I assumed it had gone dark, and people were locked in houses, hoping they were safe. Her breathing ranged from fast to slow, then ebbed to steady 'til she went still. I couldn't see her eyes from where I lay, but knew they'd gone glassy, or closed, or fluttered lightly. She wasn't seeing me, but bright lights, or simply darkness, and I let my hand move a little faster, but softer. You learn what to do, and then there's inspiration, and when it's good, they meet and mingle, like a little party, some gala, right there across a woman's open body. I want to say she came, but how I hate that word: *come*, as if you ever really arrive. As if you find your destination, drop the suitcase, too tired to unpack. What her body made was motion, circles without start or finish; I liked watching this woman's body unroll, and reading the history I found written there in coiled script. She had stories. Her hips were sturdy, and I put my mouth to the bone that crested there.

Bliss knows itself, and its location.

Bliss is a map.

Why is sex tied to movement into and out of this blue world? She bled, and, bleeding, reminded me of what comes after and before. I went selfish, begged her never to have children, to reserve access to her body for me alone.

She laughed at my fascination with origins, mocked my desire to stake some sort of claim. "You've forgotten sex with objects." She forced on me a litany of desire and the daily body: dialing the telephone, sealing an envelope, putting in time behind a wheel that knew her hands better than any lover.

I took to the floor. Tried twisting my body into shapes that could replace any ordinary object her long fingers and rough palms might ever need. "I'm a telephone," I said. "I'm an envelope."

She believed me, and I became all ordinary things.

What's sex, but surface meeting flesh?

What's desire, but needing to become someone's necessities?

When I glanced back at the bed, I could see her blood on the sheet. It was scrawled, shaped like a letter. "Dell," I said, letting her name rest on my tongue for the hundredth time that night, "what do you see?"

She touched my lips. "You don't mean blood." Then I knew she understood.

"I mean that *T*."

"It starts your name, of course. My blood starts your name." She lifted my chin. "Terry," she said. The syllables seemed to go on too long, drawn out almost into three.

CHAPTER 4

James

IF anyone ever tells you that you can only love one person at a time, tell them no. No no no no no no no. Tell them that's how our parents did it, and look where it's gotten us. Say to them, "crack babies and MTV." Say, "light beer and gun control." Tell them to get on a freeway some night and just drive, without any destination in mind. Then ask them about the nuclear family. Then ask about monogamy, sex as an expression of pure love and mutual fidelity.

The way I see it, each heart has a number that sets its love ticking. Maybe for most folks that number is one, or maybe that's just a myth they follow blindly. All I know is, my whole life long my love's been split in two. Two parents, two brothers, even two dogs, a Shep and a mutt who ran each other half-crazy with jealousy. It seems two is my heart's best number, and there isn't anything I can be or think or feel to change that. Of course, I didn't always know who I was; love knowledge came gradually. For a long time, the number two seemed so natural I didn't notice its presence. Not for some time did I learn the name for what I'd felt inside all along: fracture. My heart was split straight down the middle. Not for some time did I realize what this meant: that I was destined to betray one person whenever I loved another.

Everything hurt the winter I did my learning. The ice stung and the sun grimaced as if even the elements had divided themselves against me.

I'd gone foolishly confident after meeting Margaret. I thought she could cure me; her love was so singular, so precise. She would've made a great fanatic, but she met me instead, and became a wife. I felt sure whatever I offered in return would have to be straight, clean, safe. For a time it was. We'd go to movies, to dinner, hold hands in the park the way young lovers do. We even went to her church a couple of times, gazed at each other through the incense, bowed our heads together while our knees touched. There wasn't another lady in sight. So I got cocky. Thought, the worst is over; steady times are up ahead. I took her to a fancy Italian place one night. Had a waiter bring a rose and tiny velvet box on a silver tray. I got down on my knee (my bad knee, too), murmured, "Will you marry me?" But inside I was thinking, "Will you save me?"

Margaret was as sweet as a woman comes. Buttered me up with her toast in the mornings, told me how high her love was even after I'd done something ugly or stupid. She was sweet like fudge sauce on chocolate-chocolate cake. But somewhere along the road, the sweetness started adding up, the way too many desserts hurt the back of your throat, and I went sick with it. I began pushing her, to see what was underneath the sugary gloss. I'd go cruel suddenly, or turn away from her arms, or simply clam up, pretend she wasn't in the room. But nothing happened. She stayed the same Margaret I'd married. Cleaning and cooking and smiling and stroking my chest in bed at night. Not asking for anything back. My cruelty fell flat. It was like punching a fist through a big fat angel food cake.

Then the old ticking began. It'd been so long that at first I didn't recognize the number two in its widow's weeds. But soon my heart's number began showing itself, first shadowy like a spy, then neon-bold. My license plate number that year? Two two's within it. The number on my daughter's softball jersey? Twenty-two. I got two phone calls in one day from an old friend of mine from college. Wore down two pairs of running shoes; lost two pairs of contacts. One January morning, I woke to find a pattern in the frost on the bedroom window. The ice was swirled in a giant number two. It was a sign; sooner or later, I knew I'd give in.

I held off my demon arithmetic all through the early years of our marriage. Oh, I cheated on her now and again, but always only one-night stands, nothing serious, nothing to shake the number one. Then Margaret got it in her head to visit her mom, take Art and Emmy with her. Sure, I said. Good idea. Here's money for the ticket. Me? No, I'll stay here. Business, you know. Cabs gotta run on time. Cabbies don't get no rest.

I felt like a shit, lying to such a snooky-honey-muffin-baby like that. But I was sick of being buried in sugar all the time. I wanted to experience Margaret's opposite. I wanted to find a woman who'd be cold and hard right back to me. My number was up. I had to find a lady to play twosies with.

The night I went to the Metropolis, I was looking for mean. I'd gotten the taste on my tongue and had a craving, the way a pregnant lady wants horseradish on vanilla ice cream. When I saw Nora, I knew right off. The girl she was with wasn't the type I wanted, some Sara or Sally; she was too nice, too ordinary. But I thought Nora would do, and I was right. While we tossed basketball stats back and forth, I watched, waiting for her to tap her foot against the metal legs of the bar stool, the way women do when they're ready to let you in. That was the first sign. The second was when Sunny or Sammi began fiddling with her lady accessories: puffing powder on her fat cheeks, outlining her flat lips in sticky red paint. It's a signal between girls, you understand. They come to places like the Metropolis together, each hoping she won't be the one to leave alone. I waited to see where Nora's loyalties lay, and what she was willing to give up for a drive home with a stranger.

When Sandy came for her, Nora shrugged her off.

How did I know Nora had what I wanted? It was obvious, nothing abstract or intangible. Her mouth: bow-shaped, full, with a fleshy underlip and a top lip like a sentence. She wore passion-colored lipsticks, not shiny but dull-looking, as if she'd put powder on top to blot the slickness. I only saw her without lipstick once; her face seemed blank, her expression stupid, as if someone had asked her a question she couldn't answer. Nora's lips signalled meanness because they were selfish: they opened for her pleasure alone. All the drive home I thought about her lips, and how to control them. A woman's mouth is a dangerous thing.

I slept with Nora once, that first night, and never slept with her again. That was because I discovered that I didn't like the feel of her mouth against mine. I didn't want it to touch me; I just wanted to watch it move. Her lips in motion were like birds, flying low over a lake. But they were also sneaky, plump with desire and stubborn to relieve it. As she undressed, I watched her. We were in trouble then, and I knew it. I had to find a way to contain her before her lips consumed me.

Curtain sashes. A lady's wrists and ankles, delicate as chicken bones. What happens to a lady's lips when you tie her down? Do they move in symmetry, opening and closing like the smooth faces of choir boys? Or do they tighten, taut circles like rings, rosy and patient? Do they wither like scars, wrinkled left-over wounds? I never entered her. I let my tongue rest once on the hairy inners of her thighs, that was all. I didn't want those lips to touch me. I wanted to hear her speak, so I could take her words and handle them, refute them, address them with the safety of air between us. I tied her wrists and ankles to the bedposts; I gazed at her mouth, open and at my mercy. Oh, I could enter her, but I chose not to. I made her open herself to me, made those lips speak, then joyed to leave her dry, and in silence.

I gave her my phone number for kickers, though I knew she wouldn't call.

I called her.

I only wanted to watch her lips move, leaves shifting restlessly on a brooding tree. I wanted someone to listen to me while I rolled the big questions around like pebbles in my palm. When she answered, when she asked, I could hear her voice especially clearly because I'd marked her mouth for mine. She'd had her voice taken away and returned to her. I didn't want those lips near my face but I liked watching the way their reds and pinks and violets blurred and stuttered.

No one suspected that I controlled Nora, except Nora herself. We'd talk for hours, and she'd pretend she controlled her own voice. But I contained her, I bound her to me with circles, and I knew, even then, that someday I'd have her as my own permanent thing, fulfilling my heart's number. When I gave Nora the ring, I made it all visible. I wanted to let the world know that I had tied this woman to me. Oh, she denied it. Said it wasn't "legal," as if the law has anything to do with what a man can take from a woman's body. I don't need law; I am law. No one can control me, because no one can enter me. I said, "Wear it," and my voice was my own. I said, "Wear it," and she tried to run away, tried using her body as a weapon against me. But it didn't work, she merely advertised what I already knew: that she was only circles stacked one-on-one, circles and holes, nothing solid. Just like a woman, to be smoke and think she's wood. I watched her shimmy and knew she'd come running back when she got tired of competing with a ghost. And she did; she ran back. The first thing I did was to tie her down again.

"My Nora." I watched those lips move, a nest of feathers in a windstorm. "Will you wear it now?"

"Yes," they said, "yes. Yes. Yes."

I know a few things about the ladies.

In between her first lesson with me, and her second, she tried escaping with a man whose hands were always too gentle. It hurt her to see him turn his back; I don't know what Dell did, but I suppose ghosts have their cruelties, also. When she crossed Cope, she crossed the white girl, as well. But then, Cope and Nora should never have gotten involved with each other in the first place. They were wrong, so wrong, not in the ordinary "honey, I love you a lot but please leave so I can find somebody better" way, but in a damaging way. They drove each other crazy without even wanting to, or getting any pleasure out of it. You know love at first sight, how it works, what they say about it? Like everything else, it's got its own opposite. That was Cope and Nora. The opposite of right away, and just right. What made it so sad was that they couldn't see why, so they couldn't see what was happening. Other people saw it; they were the town's best talk for a good while, and everyone said the same thing: "That match-up is a big huge mistake." But they couldn't see it themselves, could only hurt each other and break inside, shards and shards, 'til they each looked sick and dog-down all the time. It was what you might call a catch-22: the reason they couldn't see why it wasn't working was the reason it wasn't working.

Cope and Nora had very different eyes. Oh, everyone sees the world differently, I suppose. I look at pretty girls a lot, but Pit? All he ever sees when he walks around are cars. My wife likes colors. We'll be walking the dog down the sidewalk and she'll stop suddenly, draw a deep breath; I'll think she's experiencing angina pectoris. But it'll be flowers. "Look, Jamey, look at that ocher. And with the violet three rows behind, my goodness. Will you look at that. Just look." And our dog Pizzaface? He looks for places to pee, and greasy dead things to chew on. So everyone has their own little world, but with Cope and Nora, it was more than just liking different parts of the same big picture. They didn't even see the same big picture. It was like they lived in totally different countries, with different languages, rules, religions, morals. But they were somehow each caught up in thinking that the other person was really living in their country. It reminds me of this movie I saw once with Kathy, about this scientist who's trying to fly an airplane to Cleveland to visit his mother but accidentally winds up on another planet. Only he doesn't realize it until the movie's almost over, because the planet looks just like Cleveland. Same buildings, decor, weather, so forth. So most of the movie is about this poor bubba stumbling around Cleveland—only it's not Cleveland—looking for his mother, who of course isn't there, wondering why everyone takes everything he says the wrong way and why he keeps doing the wrong thing. Cope and Nora were like that: mistaken foreigners in each other's countries. It made me sad to see it; it's godawful to watch two members of the same species utterly unable to communicate. I get scared when language fails. If we can't talk among ourselves, what have we got left to do but up and shoot each other?

It was harder on Nora than Cope, because Cope had Dell. He's a funny man, Copeland. What a name: Copeland Emory Smith. Fancy, and then plain. That's Baptists for you. When Dell died, Cope just got stuck. It was like he set up camp at the scene of the accident. Copeland's Church of Dell. He'd drive out every day to put flowers by the side of the road where the semi swerved and took the top off Dell's cab. I went with him the first time, just to show my respects. But after that, I refused to do it again. Things need closure; you need to go through certain rituals so you can finish up with sad and move on. Even though I went through a time of envy for the things he took from Nora, I feel mostly pity. Sometimes his heart's number seems more troublesome than mine.

For Cope, the affair with Nora was just a distraction: a papercut on the finger of an arm that'd been shot in the shoulder. But Nora. For Nora, the thing was real. She fell, and you could see her falling: arms flailing every which way, skirt ballooning. Much as I feel sorry for Cope, I hated him when I saw what he'd done to Nora. After Nora's meanness showed itself in the dance, after she'd let my ring fall, after I'd left her stranded at the bar, I'd hated her with a bitterness I'd never before known. It even pleased me a little, it was so singular. No question: for once I wasn't split, but steady. I tried for a while to get over her; I really thought I could. Then I saw her with Cope at Brad and Katie's party. That night, her memory began rubbing its pretty self up against my body, and I had to admit that I wanted her back. An odd thing happened to my anger then. It transformed itself, turning mid-flight like some crazy boomerang. It doubled back, towards Cope. I started hating Cope instead of Nora. And I cooked up a plan, because I'd already realized just how wrong they were for each other, how deep she was for him, how little much he cared. Sooner or later, he'd leave her; when he did, there was a chance she'd cry to me. She didn't have many folks around for her, Nora. A good-time girl whose apartment was empty on her off nights. So I wanted to be ready, just in case. I wanted to know things about Cope that I could divvy out if Nora ever came asking, ready to bargain.

I found stories unexpectedly: "serendipitous," as Emmy would say. Not about Cope: his life's too clean, too safe. He should've married Margaret; they could've painted the house blue, and the fence white, raised bunches of prissy children. No, nothing to find on Cope. But Dell? All the while, I'd suspected something was different about her. But a queer? Makes me sick to think about it. Oh, I like a little tussling in the sheets myself, everything doesn't have to be soft and sweet. But two girls together? No place for that but the porno flicks. Don't even get me talking about two boys together, because it gets me sick. If some man tried to get the wiggles on me? I'd shoot him up, straight between the eyes. Now, Art and Emmy are good kids; I love my children, don't get me wrong. But if I found one of them messing around somehow queer? I'd kick them out of the house. It'd be the end. Nobody has a right to love someone of their own shape.

Arthur, he takes drama lessons at school. Got a part in a play, something small, but it excited him. I like to see the kid excited, watch his eyes when he's talking about acting. It means something to him, you can tell. He likes the drama teacher, too. Miss Cintos. But there's a funny story about this Miss Cintos. To start with, I pay big bucks to send my kids to Wylie. Keep them out of the public school, 'cause it's going black, and I don't want them getting that kind of an education. The past few years, all Arthur can talk about is Miss Cintos this, Miss Cintos that. Finds out her first name is Theresa, insists on naming the kitten we picked up at the pound after her. So he's got this crush, see, and we've got this cat named Terry, and everything is fine and dandy, I'm thinking at least he's not a queer, and then comes time to give up a Saturday night playing pool or drinking with the boys to go see the kid strut his stuff. Margaret and I get fancy, walk in together, find seats up front, because we figure since our kid is in the damn thing, we ought to be where he can see us smiling. Only we don't do a lot of smiling, because the play is very sad, very tragic, all about a man who kills his father without knowing it, and what's worse, sleeps with his own mother. We were kind of shocked, me and Margaret, to tell the truth. I mean, I'd heard of having an Oedipus complex, but I never really understood what it meant. It was pretty scandelous stuff, and we don't even consider ourselves half as conservative as some of the Wylie crowd. I felt relieved that Art was only a messenger. I wouldn't want my kid pretending to do all kinds of immoral stuff, acting or no acting. You never know what a kid'll pick up.

The play ends, very sad, very tragic, and everyone is drying their eyes, or pretending to, because the acting wasn't very convincing, so the tears weren't either. Then the clapping starts, the actors bow, the actresses too, everybody's bowing, clapping up a storm, when Joey Cleary, Arthur's best friend, comes up to the microphone like it's Oscar night or something. Everybody quiets down right away; he's very intense, that Joey, like his mother. He takes the microphone and says that there's someone all the actors and actresses and stage crew and even the audience ought to thank, and that's Theresa Cintos. And then everybody starts clapping like crazy all over again, and I sneak a look at my watch because I'm getting up at five on Sunday to go fishing with Brad and Cope and when I look up, there she is. Miss Cintos. Theresa Cintos. Terry, for short.

Only thing is, she's black.

And my jaw just drops open, because here my kid's been following her around this whole time like she's got something to teach him. I guess Margaret noticed me shifting in my seat or something, because she leans over, whispers to me, "They're all over, just everywhere, aren't they?"

I nod, and whisper back, "Yes. But what can you do?"

This country isn't what it used to be.

The really weird thing was that as soon as I saw her, on top of feeling shocked that she was black and all, I also had this strange feeling like I'd seen her before. Deja vu, as they say. Only I couldn't for the life of me remember where or when. So I put it out of my head, because it didn't make sense at the time.

When we got home, we sat with Art in the kitchen, and talked about the show. Joey came over too, because they're practically inseparable. I had a friend like that at Arthur's age. We were so close, we were like brothers, only better, because we didn't fight. It was just the two of us, me and Darryl. We went fishing and bowling and snuck smokes together and drove too fast up to Swallen Hill, where we'd watch the couples steaming up the windows by the Pointe. Sometimes, when we were feeling feisty, we'd sneak up to a car that was especially smoking and fire off his brother's BB gun, just to watch the boy fumble with his belt, and the girl cross one arm over her chest while she grabbed for her shirt. Darryl was my best. But he liked guns too much, and one day when he was cleaning one, he fucked up and that was the end. I hardly think about him anymore. I suppose it hurt some then, but that was a long time ago, and I can't even remember what he looked like unless I close my eyes.

That night, Arthur and Joey were just babbling, they were so revved up from the play. It pleased me to see them happy and all. But I wanted to get in a word or two about Miss Cintos. I like to explain things to Arthur straight out, so that he knows what's what. You need to show kids what parts of the world are worthy of their attention. Otherwise, they look in the wrong places, and then what happens? I coughed when a silence finally came around. Margaret was clearing the ice cream bowls from the table, getting ready to do dishes. But she knew what I was going to say, and gave me a quick pat on the shoulder.

"Boys," I began, "I'm glad you had such a fine time acting in the play. You did an excellent job. Arthur, we're very proud of you; Joey, we're proud of you too, and I know your mother will say the same. But I think it'd be a good idea if we talked some about Miss Cintos."

Art was folding and unfolding his paper napkin, like an airplane, only he kept undoing the wings.

"Art, I realize that Miss Cintos is someone you admire; maybe you, too, Joey. And it's a pleasant thing that you've had the chance to work on a play like this one. But it's important to remember something, boys. Miss Cintos—Terry—is black. That means that she comes from a different background than yours. Sometimes, there are things black people don't understand about the kind of education a white person needs. Arthur, son. Why didn't you tell me that your teacher was black?"

Art began tearing the corners off the napkin. "Look, Dad." His voice was dull, as if he were getting sleepy. "I know what you think. I've heard it, OK? But Ms. Cintos is different. Me and Joey...we talked about this some and we even went to talk to her once and then Maureen..."

"I'm not talking about Maureen, Arthur. I'm asking you a question. Why didn't you tell your father that you had a nigger for a teacher?"

Margaret finished with the dishes, and stood next to me, drying her hands on a towel. She put the towel back through the door handle of the refrigerator and sat down beside me.

"My mom says not to use that word." Joey took off his baseball cap, turned it around, put it on again backwards. "She says it's a trouble-making word."

I laughed. That kid's mother sticks words in his mouth as if they were candies. He'll be a mama's boy if he doesn't watch out. "Joey. Arthur. I'm certainly not a man to make trouble. Trouble's the last thing I want. But I'd like a straight answer from you, Arthur. Tell me why you kept this from me." Nothing. No one spoke. I could hear the refrigerator humming, way loud like usual; it sounded a little like that song—I can't remember the name of it—that song about 1963. *Oh, what a night, what a lady, what a night.* Then I had an idea. Maybe letting Joey spout off at the mouth would be a good idea. "Joey. Tell me more about what your mother says about Miss Cintos."

Joey took his cap off again, put it on forwards, and stood up, almost knocking his chair over. "My mom says that it's about time Wylie had a black person as a teacher. She says the school is like Wonder Bread Academy and that the whole world is changing and that it's a damn good place for me to be getting a textbook education but she wishes they'd give me more of a practical one. And you know what else?" Arthur was watching Joey with the oddest expression on his face. "My mom says that Ms. Cintos can sleep with whomever the hell she wants to and she doesn't care to hear one more word about it!"

Margaret tapped her fingers on the table: tap-tap-tap, the way she does when she's got nerves. I put my hand down over hers, pressed it firmly against the table. "Stop it," I whispered. Then I turned to Joey, and made my voice go warm, like syrup on hotcakes.

"Joey, your mother sure has a lot of opinions. Tell me more about that." But the moment had passed. Joey clammed up; I guess it hit him too late that he'd said something he shouldn't have. He was squirming a little in his seat, and then I felt sorry for him. Poor kid, growing up without a father. No one to take control. Following Miss Cintos around like she could give him what he wasn't getting at home. Don't get me wrong, I like Maureen Cleary well enough. She's pretty, very pretty. She takes care of herself, of the kid, their house. But she's got some wacked-out ideas about the world and who should run it. She needs a man around to show her who's who and what's what. Kid needs a father, too. That's why I figure it's good he hangs out so much with Arthur. Maybe some of my ways will rub off on him indirectly.

After that night, I kept my eyes and ears open just for my own amusement. I like gossip the same way I like puzzles: fitting the pieces together until you can see the whole big picture. I knew Miss Cintos was a black person, and I knew that she had something funny going on back home in bed. But I didn't know what, exactly, or why any of that might be useful to me until the second serendipity happened. Of course, there were two of them. It's always so, for me.

The next morning, I went to pick up Brad but when I got to the house, Katie came out in her robe, motioned towards her stomach from the doorway. I didn't get it: she's pregnant, so Brad can't go fishing? Katie's kind of ditzy sometimes, one of those girls who can't stop trying to be cute. So I got out of the car and walked up the front steps.

"Brad's sick. Stomach flu. He said to tell you he was sorry; maybe next Sunday."

"I guess this means he won't make it into work tomorrow, huh?" I could tell what was coming next.

Katie's face went funny. She has nervous spells, Katie does. Looks pale, like she's going to faint. I don't know what Brad sees in her, except maybe her breasts. Big fat things.

"I can't say about that." She crossed her arms. "You'll have to call him later today."

"Honey, you tell him to call me." I headed back to the car. Their door slammed behind me right away.

At the trailer, Cope was wide awake. Climbed in the front seat with a thermos full of coffee and a brown paper sack full of sandwiches. We broke into the sandwiches while I was driving. We didn't talk at all, just listened to the car making its morning noises. That's one thing I like about Cope: he knows when to keep quiet. He's not chatty, Cope. That's one reason I like going fishing with him.

We set up shop on the east side; for about an hour, there were no more words between us than "Biting over here," and "Pass the bait." But as it came towards sunrise, we got to talking. Small at first. Then a little bigger. Cope mentioned Nora's name a few times, and I had to bite my lip to keep from saying anything. He didn't know about my affair with Nora, and I didn't want to be the one to tell him. Why? Because I wanted Nora back. I knew if I told Cope what was what, he'd drop her like a hot potato, she'd blame me, and I'd never see her face again. I was waiting for him to do the dirty deed himself. When it happened, she'd come running to me, she'd wear my ring, and be happy about it.

I know a few things about the ladies.

After Cope talked some about Nora and I bitched about Margaret for a few, he started tossing Dell's name around. Now, I've gotten pretty darn sick of hearing about Dell. I figure six months, a year at the most. Then you move on. You don't dwell in death like it's a house. I tried to find a way to move the conversation onto something else. That's when I mentioned Oedipus, the guy who killed his father and married his mother. I joked with Cope that things could be worse.

"But you know what?" Cope had a tug; I waited until he reeled up. Nothing, but the worm was gone, so I passed the bait bag. "Art's been following his drama teacher around like she's the queen of somewhere, talking about Miss Cintos this, Miss Cintos that. But last night? When she comes onstage to take a bow? Turns out Miss Cintos is black as dirt. Darn if we didn't name our cat Terry after a nigger!"

I laughed, but Cope stayed quiet. Looked over at me. "Terry Cintos?" he said. "She's your Arthur's teacher?"

"Do you know her?" Cope didn't have any kids, so I couldn't think where he'd know Terry from.

"Naw." He put down the bag. Coughed. Looked out over the water. "I don't know her, not really. But Dell did. She and Dell were friends. They'd go drinking, ladies' night out, that sort of number. She came to the funeral, Terry. Shook my hand."

Then Cope went back to talking about "what if" and "how come," all that same old crap, and for a minute, I was so annoyed that the subject had gone back around to Dell that I didn't think about what Cope had said. Then it registered. Friends with Dell? Far as I knew, Dell didn't have any friends. Much less black lady drama teacher friends who had something funny going on at home in bed. My curiosity went up like an antenna. And then, very sudden, I had this memory flash, kind of like news flashes on prime-time TV, and I knew where it was I'd seen Terry Cintos. One night when Margaret was getting especially on my nerves and I had to have something to drink, I went down to the Metropolis by myself. Not to make trouble, not to find someone. Just to drink, chat with Alex, watch the kids dancing and the oldsters playing pool. Now, one thing I noticed a while ago about the Metropolis is that it's starting to go queer. Sometimes when you go in, it's normal: guys dancing with girls, lots of scoping going on, a pick-up if you want it. But a couple years back, it started that sometimes, every so often, you'd see something funny. Two girls dancing, not just friendly, but close together. Or two guys hanging on each other's arms in the back by the pool tables. That night I went by myself, there was some of it happening. I'd taken my beer, gone to sit by the dartboard. I was watching the dancers, something I like to do. One girl especially, moving her hips like they were on fire. I was watching her going at it, taking up space on the dance floor, her breasts all high in her shirt and her skirt slit, when out of the corner of my eye, I realized that the table beside me was going queer.

It was two ladies. One had her back to me; the one whose face I could see was black. I tilted my head just a little, so I could eye them, but pretend I was watching the dancers. Then the black one reached across the table and kissed her girlfriend's face. I had to turn away, it made me so sick to see it. I wiped my mouth on my napkin, and walked out of the Metropolis. Didn't even finish the beer I'd paid for. But the odd thing? The girlfriend, the one whose face I couldn't see, had been wearing this backwards cap. It was some dark color, very worn down, with words on the front, like they often have. *Foster*, it said. The letters were white, or yellow, something bright. As I drove home, fast because I was angry at the stupid queers for taking up space in my bar, I realized that Dell had a cap just like that. Dark, worn out, with *Foster* in light letters across the front. I remember, because every so often after we'd gone fishing Cope would invite me in when we got to the trailer, and we'd sit while Dell fixed coffee or opened a can of soup. She had that hat on a lot back then. Usually wore it front ways, but sometimes backwards, too.

But it never occurred to me that it was Dell sitting there being queer with a black girlfriend at the Metropolis. My brain couldn't even think the thought. At the time, I just remember deciding that it was a weird coincidence. But as Cope and I stood by the water, the girlfriend's face came back to me, and I knew it was Terry Cintos. Dell's friend.

I've always felt both blessed and cursed because of my heart's number; sometimes, I wonder whether there's anyone else in this town, or even this country, who has the same kind of torn-up feeling inside. When I first met Dell, I liked her. I mean, I really liked her. She had nothing on her resumé, no experience, but I hired her for Carlstown Yellow because she was fine. Strong girl, sturdy, sexy walk, eyes this weird light brown color, all this long hair, practically blond. But it was more than just looks with Dell. It was something she said during the interview. I was talking about my family, about Margaret—didn't want her to think I was hitting on her or anything—and I dropped a hint, like I sometimes do. I want to find my people, you understand. I know there must be others out there, so I drop hints sometimes, just in case.

"Got two children," I said, "Arthur and Emily. Great kids, both of them. But you know what?" Looked her right in the eye. "I hate feeling split between loving the two of them. Isn't that always how it is, though? Got yourself two things that matter in your life. Nothing ever comes singular."

Most people would just nod and say "uh-huh," something of that nature. But Dell? Dell looked at me like she'd really listened.

"Yeah, I used to feel that way about my brothers. Two of them, twins. I could never decide which one of them I was supposed to love best. Everybody else played favorites, even my ma and dad. But I couldn't. They were the same to me. I had to love them both the same." That set me wondering. Was Dell like me? Was she split, did she know the feeling of fracture? I filed the questions away in my head to ask them later; when things took off between Dell and Cope, I watched especially carefully, waiting to see if she'd take a second lover. Truth be told, I was hoping it might be me. Talked it over some with Dennis. Neither one of us could understand why Dell picked Cope, and I still can't. Cope's a nice enough guy, but not much of a talker. So I flirted with Dell, teased her up some, like the rest of the boys. But she never took the bait. She surprised us all by packing up one day and just leaving. Took a job with Parker's, pay cut and everything. I was insulted, but also disappointed: looked like Dell's number was one, like just about everybody else's.

That day by the lake, fishing with Cope, I put all the pieces of the puzzle together, and realized I'd been right about Dell from the beginning. Dell's heart's number was two, just like mine, only she had it even worse: split between men and women both, half-normal and half-queer. Thank you Lord, I said silently, as Cope reeled in his third, another small one. Thank you Lord for making me normal, not making me split like a sick queer faggot. I felt sorry for Dell then; it was the first time I'd ever felt sorry for a homosexual-type person. I felt sorry for her, because being split that way was a whole lot worse than anything I could ever even imagine.

Dell and Terry Cintos.

Queer.

After I dropped Cope off at the trailer, I drove around some. I couldn't go back to the house, couldn't face making small talk with Margaret, listening to lovey-dovey crap, or having Art and Emmy tug all over my sleeves, asking me homework questions they could find in any library book. I drove in a circle, all around Carlstown, just thinking. Wondering if it was true. Wondering how I could find out for sure.

Came three o'clock, and I got hungry. I still wasn't ready to head home, so I stopped by Sam's Deli for fries and a Coke. That's when two things hit me hard. First thing was, Cope's Dell was a queer. I couldn't get over it. Dell? That pretty thing? All that long hair? Besides, James, I said to myself, if Dell was a queer, wouldn't she have more sense than to go around finding herself a black girlfriend? I began to doubt myself, then; after all, only thing I had to go on was the cap, and Dell's being friends with Terry. When I went to pour ketchup on my fries, my hand shook, and I dumped half the bottle out by mistake. Had to send them back, ask for another order. That was the first thing. But the second? The second was that Dell was dead. Dog-dead, cut in half neat as a lock of baby's hair. When a semi takes a spin, not much you can do; I've seen it happen, and it's not a pretty picture. The girl was dead. I had to ask myself, James, why do you have to go messing around with a dead girl's memory? Why can't you let her rest in peace? Hell, she's got enough trouble what with Cope calling up her ghost every five-and-a-half minutes. She doesn't need you to go poking into her life-that-once-was.

But there's that old flame curiosity.

"You're so curious, you'd open the devil's coffin to count his teeth," my mother used to say. She'd hit me when she thought I was being too nosy, but it didn't change a thing. I like knowing things. I like other people's secrets. Turns out it wasn't hard to find the information I wanted, all it took was keeping my ears open. Didn't even require any sort of real poking around; I just kept still, let someone else talk the information into my head. A woman will always do everything for you herself, if you wait long enough. That's my motto: wait, and she'll come.

It happened while I was watching Emily play softball; her team is sponsored by Sam's Deli but just called Sam's Girls. She's good, my daughter: second base, sometimes shortstop when Abby Micheals has to miss a game. Strong swing, left-handed, which kills them in girls' league, because those right-fielders are always prissy Christines who can't catch. She surprises them every time. Finds them staring at the sun, thinking about their boyfriends or their tan lines. And then she runs. Like a blur, Emmy. It makes me proud; I only wish that if it had to be just one of them good at sports, it was Art. I've said it to their faces, and I'll say it again. Nothing against girls' games, I just think a boy should know how to hit, that's all. And then Emmy always wants to wear her team t-shirt to school, instead of a regular blouse. I've said to her, I've said, "Emily, you're a pretty girl. You've got a nice shape and you should show it off." But she won't hear me. Sometimes they go their own ways, and then it makes me wonder. Makes me think maybe I did something wrong, way back, when they were little. Maybe my strange way of loving made them so. I think my kids are great, don't get me wrong. But I worry. I want them to be normal so that they can be happy.

Abby Micheals is Emmy's best friend. They call each other "Ab" and "Em," practice batting and catching, study and go to parties together, sleep over almost every weekend. Couple months ago, Wylie had a dance for their grade. The theme was "Planetarium," and the kids had to dress to match. Most of the boys wore suits with stars on the lapel, and most of the girls dressed in silver or gold, called themselves moons or suns. Abby and Emily? Spent weeks planning. Raided my closet, borrowed from Abby's older sister, Maura. The night of the dance, I barely recognized them. Abby had on one of my dark suits, but tucked and tied and pinned so that it almost looked as if it fit. Fake mustache, big red bow tie. And Emmy? One of Maura's dresses, yellow, loose, very prim and plain. Only thing that didn't match was their shoes. They wanted to dance, so they'd just worn their Reeboks and pom-pom socks.

"Let me guess." I scratched my head; I was really stumped. "Hmm. Abby, you're night, and Emmy, you're day." I thought that was a pretty good guess myself, but they just looked impatient.

"You'll never get it," Abby smirked. Now, Karen Micheals is a friend of Margaret's. They shop, drink tea together, lady-type things. Karen's pretty, a real nice kind of lady. Southern, because the Micheals are from one of the Carolinas, I can never remember which. Bob got transferred up here four years ago; Karen still hasn't adjusted properly. At least, that's what Margaret says. I say it's Abby who hasn't adjusted. I know Emmy needs her friends, but Abby Micheals isn't the kind of girl I want my girl taking after. Too tough to suit me; usually a little grimy around the ears. Sometimes when she talks to me, I feel as if she's secretly laughing inside. This was one of those times. So I tried just throwing my hands up in the air, acting like it was all a big joke. Privately, I was miffed that I didn't know what the hell was up. I don't like feeling as if my kids have the what's what on me.

"It's hard, Daddy." Emmy tugged on my jacket. "It's not your fault you didn't get it. I'm Caroline Herschel, and she's William Herschel, my brother. We're astronomers. We read about them in a poem at school."

"Well," I slapped Abby on the shoulder, "that was going to be my next guess."

"Do you want to hear the poem? Abby has it by heart." Emily

looked at me and made her eyes go big, so I nodded. What the hell.
It bored me, though. Poetry always bores me. What was weird was
how into it Abby was. Seemed like she'd recited it a hundred times
before. And Emily? Emily just stood there and grinned, like Abby
was some famous TV star. I didn't like it. Why couldn't they just
wear party dresses and put silver moons in their hair, like the rest
of the girls? Sometimes I joke with Margaret, ask her, "You sure
Arthur and Emily are mine? You sure they're both mine?" Makes
me laugh, but she doesn't like that one. Sometimes I wish Margaret
had a better sense of humor.

Margaret doesn't go to many of the Sam's Girls' games. She's not
a sports fan, doesn't like being out in the sun. But I go to quite a
few. Usually, I sit next to Karen Micheals. She's always there. Brings
ice tea in this enormous thermos, wears a big straw hat, and—what
I like—these little dresses with all this windy material that blows
and fusses. They usually make a straight line across her bosom, and
have these thin, thin straps, like spaghetti. You can see pretty much
right down between her breasts and I like sitting next to her, watching her shade her eyes with her hands, smelling that salty smell that
women get when they're out in the sun for a time. This one particular day, Karen and I were chatting during the second inning. I mentioned Art, how I wished he'd get involved in a sport instead of being
in drama club every semester. Every semester! Since sixth grade.

"Seems kind of sissy to me, tell the truth."

Karen Micheals just nodded. She was watching Abby in the dug-
out. Abby paces back and forth when she's upset with where the
game is headed; she was just getting started. Emmy came up to her,
though, whispered something in her ear, and she sat back down.
Emily calms Abby; that's why they're friends, I suppose.

"I just wish he'd try something. Doesn't have to be baseball.
Maybe track. Hell, tennis or golf, even. I just wish he'd do something besides follow Miss Cintos around like a lost pup."

"Terry Cintos? The drama teacher?"

"That's right. She puts on the plays each year. Art was in the
last one. Got tryouts for the next one coming up soon."

"Terry Cintos." Karen took off her hat, fiddled with the scarf tied
around the band. "I met her at a Wylie social last year." She tucked
the scarf in her handbag, then put her hat back on again. "She's

black. Did you know that? It surprised me. Down South, you would-n't find some black person running the drama department at a school like Wylie."

"Yeah, but what's the world coming to, right?"

"Sometimes, I just do not know." Karen Micheals gave a little laugh. She has a prissy laugh, Karen, but there's something under-neath the prissiness that makes me excited. Hard to say what, but you can tell she knows you're listening to her.

Sam's Girls went out into the field. The first batter hit right to Emily; when she caught it, she jumped into the air.

"Yes!" She made a fist, pulled her elbow into her waist.

The next batter hit way out to left center; Sue Bucky missed, and all the outfielders gave little push-off jumps and ran back on the diagonal towards the fence.

"James," Karen Micheals tapped me with one fingernail on the forearm. She has really long nails, red or pink. They change. "You know what else about Terry Cintos?"

"What else?" In the sun, she was pretty. There were freckles on her skin right before her breasts started. I wondered if the freckles went down around to her nipples.

"Well." She took a breath, like she had a long story to tell. "At this parent-teacher social? Bob and I were sitting with Ed and Paula. And when Terry Cintos got up to speak, Paula started whispering to tear the roof down. You know how I like gossip?"

I nodded. She did, it was true.

"Well. I leaned right over, and told Paula that if she had some-thing to say, she ought to share it with the whole class!" We both laughed. "So she did. Right there and then, can you believe it? Said she'd heard things about Terry Cintos."

I could tell she wanted me to ask "What things?" so I did.

"Mmmm." She got this little mysterious smile around her lips, and her eyes scrunched up. Pretty. In the sun she was pretty. She tapped my forearm again with one of her colored fingernails.

"Paula said that Terry Cintos is a goddamn lesbian." The way she said it, the final word came out funny. It came out "lez-bean," the last part sounding like "bean." Green beans, I thought. Red beans. Snap beans. Little bitty yellow beans.

"That right?" I was shading my eyes with my hands, staring out across the field as if what Karen Micheals had just said didn't matter much to me at all. "A lesz-bean, huh?"

Soon as I said it, I felt bad, worrying that maybe she'd think I was making fun of her accent.

But she didn't seem to notice. She just kept right on, as if talking about Terry Cintos was the most natural thing in the world.

"When Bob heard that, he practically knocked over his water glass. Said somebody ought to tell the headmaster and the board of trustees right then and there. But Paula said they already knew. That they knew when they hired her, and told her it was OK by them. Can you believe that? OK by them. Now, Bob says that we, the parents, should have some say in this. We're the ones whose children are affected. We're the ones paying bundles of money to send our kids to Wylie Academy." Bundles came out like "bun-dulls." I wanted to ask her to say it again.

"That sure is true." Funny thing is, whenever I talk to her, I start having an accent, too. So "sure" sounded like "show." I wondered why Abby didn't have much of an accent. "Did anyone think to do anything about it?" What I really wanted to ask was, "How did Paula know?"

"Seems like there's not much we can do. Paula and Bob talked some about circulating a petition. But Terry Cintos is very popular with the kids, and she teaches middle and upper school classes both, runs all the play productions, drama club, so forth. Paula said not many teachers would do all that. And besides," she bit down on her lower lip, sort of lifted her shoulders and her eyebrows at once, "she's black. What'cha gonna do?"

"How did Paula know?" I couldn't help it.

"You mean that she's a lesbian?"

"Yeah. She doesn't look that way."

"Paula heard it from Veronica Smythe, who got it from her husband Mitchell, who's on the board of trustees. But you know what?" She took out her thermos and a little white plastic cup.

"What?"

"Paula said she saw her. Terry Cintos, I mean. With one of her girlfriends."

Dell, I thought. Was it Dell she was with? "What was her girlfriend's name?"

"Oh, I don't know. It was about five years ago, maybe six. Paula and Ed had gone out to Cryer's Lake to give the dogs a run in the woods. And they said when they were walking the path, you know the circle path you can take up around the lake and through the woods, the one that goes over that little bridge?"

I nodded.

"They saw her up ahead of them when they came around a corner. She was holding hands with this girlfriend. But Paula said Terry Cintos and her girlfriend heard the dogs and dropped hands, started walking apart, like they were just friends and not lesbian perverts."

Dell, I thought. Was it Dell she was with?

Got home around six-thirty. Margaret was watching some dumb TV show. I had a beer, sat down next to her on the sofa. We watched 'til eight-thirty, four whole dumb shows. Then I got hungry, had her make us some sandwiches. We ate in the kitchen; I read the news-paper, and she flipped through one of those decorating magazines. After I'd finished eating, I put my arm around her shoulders. The kids were in their rooms, doing homework, or talking on the phone, or just staring up at the ceiling like teenage kids do.

"You ready?" I said to Margaret. That's kind of a code phrase with us. Because it can mean, "You ready to get the hell out of this joint?" if we're at a bad party, or "You tired, ready to sleep?" if we're at home. But it also always means, "Because I am, and I also want to fuck." Or "make love," as Margaret puts it. I like "making love" but I also like "fucking," and it irks me that Margaret doesn't know the difference.

That night, I wanted to fuck.

Margaret shrugged, which meant "I'm not really into it but if you want to, OK." So we said goodnight to the kids through their doors, went to the bedroom, undressed. While Margaret put in her diaphragm and brushed her teeth, I lay on the bed on my back with my eyes closed. I was tired, and my mind was still on my conver-sation with Karen Micheals. I remembered the way Karen had said the word "lesbian," and what she'd said about Paula and Ed's trip to Cryer's Lake. I kept wondering if the woman Terry Cintos had been with was Dell. Dell, whose long hairs were always lying on the sink in the office bathroom. Dell, who'd chain smoked on the stoop, who'd been divided in love for her two brothers. Dell, who'd chosen Cope instead of me.

Lying there with my eyes shut, I forgot all about waiting for Margaret to hurry up in the damn bathroom. I forgot all about Karen Micheals and her flowered dress, and Paula walking the dogs with Ed up by Cryer's Lake. Instead, I had this dream—sort of a dream anyway—only I'm pretty sure I was awake the whole time. I imagined that I could see Dell, with Terry Cintos. And it was so real, I nearly reached my hand out to touch them. So real I wanted to say, "Dell, wait. Don't drive when it's icy. Stay home, take those days off."

"Honey, I'm ready." Margaret had on her white nightgown, with the high neck and long sleeves. She sat down on the side of the bed and let me unbutton the top few buttons. She always wears the dumb thing on nights we have sex; I've never understood why. I mean, I'm just going to unbutton it anyway, so why bother? But Margaret likes to do things in a very orderly way. When we first met, it seemed sexy to me, because there were all these obstacles. We had to kiss for months before she'd let me touch her breasts. Then we waited another month or two before I could take her shirt off. And so forth, and so on. Now, it just seems tiresome. We're married, right? Two kids, right? Who does she think she's kidding by trying to act all virginal and pristine?

We got beneath the covers, and I rubbed her belly for a little while, then put my hand between her legs. She was really dry, so I tried kissing her for a while longer, very soft and patient, but every time I checked, there was nothing happening. So finally I went ahead and went in. It was just fine.

Only I kept seeing Dell.

I had to know.

Monday afternoon around one, I called Paula from the office.

Now, Paula Chesley and I barely know each other. She and Margaret aren't especially friendly. I don't think they dislike each other, they just don't talk much, or do things together. They look a little bit alike, Paula and Margaret, so maybe that's it. Women who look alike always try to act as if they don't see each other. So I had to come up with some reason to be calling Paula Chesley on a Monday afternoon. I'd thought about it all morning, while I was taking calls and booking drives, sending drivers this way and that. Cope had driven a night shift, so when I came in at eight, he was just leaving. He looked pretty worn out; this was when Nora was still running him ragged. I waited 'til he'd gone, and 'til Pit stepped outside to smoke. Then I looked up Chesley in the book, wrote down the number on a little slip of paper, played with the phone cord some, finally dialed.

I still had no idea what I wanted to say.

"Hello, may I speak to Mrs. Chesley, please?"

"Speaking."

Paula Chesley's daughter Dawn is one year ahead of Arthur at Wylie. So I started off slow, said I was calling to find out about Dawn's classes, see what she thought of her teachers, if she had any advice I could pass along to Arthur when the time came to choose classes for next year. Paula was more than happy to talk to me about Dawn, talked my ear off, in fact. I had to put her on hold five times to take calls from customers; Pit came and went, Brad stopped by, it was a regular hoe-down, and there I was, nodding my head, saying, "Um-hum" every five minutes. It took forever, but finally Miss Cintos' name came up.

"Dawn also enjoyed the drama class she had this year."

"Is that right?" Very casual. "Who taught that class?"

"Miss Cintos."

Then I had an idea. "Terry Cintos! What a coincidence. I was just talking about Terry Cintos today with a pal of mine."

"Is that so?"

"Yes, Terry Cintos hung out with a mutual friend of ours, name of Dell Richards. She drove for Carlstown Yellow for a while, then went to work for Parker's. I know she and Terry were supposed to be close." I paused. "Really close. Don't suppose you ever met Dell Richards, did you, Mrs. Chesley?"

"Richards? You say she drives a cab for Parker's Shuttles? I don't believe so, no. Does she have any children?"

"No, she didn't have any kids. Dell passed on about four years ago."

"I'm terribly sorry."

"Thanks. Anyway, she was supposed to be buddies with Terry. I've even thought to call Terry to talk to her about Dell."

"Now, why is that?" I couldn't tell if she knew I was playing her, or if she was genuinely that naïve.

78

"Mrs. Chesley, I miss the girl. You could say I'm collecting memories. Sort of like collecting photographs for an album."

There was a pause; for a moment I thought I'd lost her. She cleared her throat.

"Well, I may have met Dell on one occasion, several years ago. But I'm not sure of it. What did she look like?"

I closed my eyes. I detailed Dell's face, body, gestures. Tried to include the little things that made her Dell.

"Dell Richards." She made the name sound like a question. "Yes, I think Ed and I met a Miss Richards once with Terry Cintos."

Call waiting clicked twice, and I had to put her on hold. When I pulled Mrs. Chesley's voice up again, I repeated her last words back to her.

"Yes, come to think of it. Her name was Dell; I remember because it's such an unusual name. I thought perhaps she'd said Kelly, but she shook her head, and spelled it out for me. 'It's Dell,' she said, 'D-E-L-L. *D* as in dog.' That last bit made my husband laugh."

I could see it, hear it, too: Dell's impatience making her voice go rough and quick. Dell didn't like prissy ladies like Mrs. Chesley.

"Did you meet them at a play?"

"No, not at all." She giggled, a high-pitched giggle like a little kid's. It didn't match her voice. "Ed and I were walking the dogs down by Cryer's Lake, the way we do every now and again, when we saw Miss Cintos and her friend ahead of us. They were walking over by the bridge, you know, the one on the west side? At first they didn't see us, but then they heard the dogs. Hamilton, our Golden Retriever, just took off, and wouldn't listen to our calls, not even Ed's. But Miss Cintos got his collar, I'm not certain how she did it. We stopped for a moment to thank her, and she introduced us to Dell Richards."

I was suddenly beyond bored with Paula Chesley. I practically set off sparks, trying to wind down and hang up. I knew what I needed to know.

And I had a secret.

Some people think having a secret is like playing basketball. They wait for the thing to come to them, scope around some, then toss it where it'll come closest to scoring. Me, I like secrets in and of themselves. Don't need to share them to take my pleasure. This secret of Dell's? I cupped it in my hands like it was water, took a long drink, and thought that would be enough.

But it wasn't.

I like stories too much. I like stringing happenings together, asking why, what for, what if. I like the big questions; when I can't answer them, or when I've got no one to talk them over with, like I could with Nora, then I lie in my head and my eyes invent things when I shut my lids. Without wanting to, I brought Dell back to life. I watched her walking the bridge at Cryer's Lake with Terry, watched them clasp hands, untangle quickly at the sharp cries of the Chesleys' dogs.

But there was more, a little movie in my head with flashbacks, close-ups, pan shots. They'd met at a gas station. Dell left her wallet on the counter when she paid, and Terry ran out after her. Dell practically ran Terry over by mistake, but then they got to talking, and Dell thought, why, she's perfectly honest and decent, not like those black people on TV. She didn't know Terry was a lesbian. And Dell said, let me take you to Burger King to thank you for returning my wallet. Then, over lunch, Terry must have looked at Dell while she was opening one of those little mustard packets, and whispered, "You have the sexiest eyes." Dell knew right then and there that she was doomed to love two people at once.

I just had this intuition about it, like ESP or something. Why? Because Dell and I were kin: her heart's number was two, just like mine. Only she was torn between men and women both. Even though she was a pervert, I still felt sorry for her. I know what it feels like to be split, always wanting something more than what you have. To act differently with the two people in your life. To know you'll never feel whole or final. Dell's life was secret, just like mine. She must've lied to Cope, telling him Terry was just a buddy, someone she went shopping with, girl talk, that stuff. And she must've lied to Terry, telling her she lived by herself, not letting her in the trailer because she said she was ashamed of how dirt poor it was inside. But she was smart, Dell, because chances were, Cope and Terry never would have met. No one knew enough of the story to tip them off except me, and I had no reason to tell either one of them, no reason to bother with either Cope or Terry Cintos.

So I would've left it all alone—honest, cross my heart and hope to die, all that crap—if Nora hadn't come running back to me, crying over Cope, whining because she'd fallen for a man so bogged down in mourning he couldn't see his own two feet. I wanted to say "I told you so," but I did something smarter instead: I told stories about Dell and Terry. Everything I knew, everything I'd imagined, and then some. It was never that I wanted to spring something on Cope; I'd never have thought of that if it hadn't been for Nora. I only told her because it seemed like one way to get her back.

So when she came crying, I gave her a loaded gun and taught her how to shoot. I sent her flying back to Cope, but I tied a string around her finger, too. Because whoever starts the story controls the ending. And I left things dangling. Nora's a finisher; she needs to put a finale on everything. I knew she'd have to come back, to hear how the story ended: Dell and Terry's, and hers and mine, as well.

I don't know what she told him, if she sifted my lies from truth, if she left them mixed together, if she could even distinguish between the two. I wish I'd been there, because Nora's meanness in its full colors is a sight to see. Even though I have nothing against Cope, it'd have been a sight to see his body giving up the ghost.

Good for him; that's how I see it. He's held onto Dell's cold body for too long. He needs to hear the silence of the trailer when it's just him, feel the hollow sleeves of Dell's jacket, the one he keeps trying to fill with his own arms. She's gone. If Nora can make him see it, she's doing him a favor. Comes around to kindness after all, the way meanness often does.

After Nora left Cope's trailer, after the scene she won't describe to me, she drove to the nearest phone, dropped me a quarter. I told her, I'll come by your place tonight, around sixish. I'll tell Margaret I have a late call.

I drove home and picked up the ring, which I'd hidden inside a box of dental floss in my shaving kit. I want to watch her try to take this one off. I bought it snug; once it's on, it's on for good. She can dance all she wants, but the circle never changes. She'll wear my ring like lips around her finger, making her hand another mouth that I can enter, or not, as I choose.

CHAPTER 5

Terry

LOOK closely, squint a little, and you'll see her. The face in the far left corner, behind the balding man with the machete and the skinny girl in the leopard print bikini? That's me, with my back turned, my head in a turban. Now surf a while...stop. The woman at the table with the blue paisley scarf, sipping tea and reading the *Times*? That's me, too. Likewise the face, unfocused, in the ad where the Jesus look-alike douses the eyes of a blind man with contact lens solution so he can see again. Likewise the legs on the pantyhose commercial where everyone is tap dancing on a giant egg.

I lost my last audition because I couldn't cry on cue.

"Your dog was just run over by a recycling truck," the casting coach explained. "You loved that dog. That dog loved you. You had a special bond. Start with a sniffle, and lead up to a medium-sized bawl."

I got the sniffle, but the bawl eluded me. A sort of a snort happened instead; I heard "Next!" and my identical twin waltzed through the "In" door as they shuffled me out, into the minus temperatures of a Chicago winter.

I bawled plenty on my way to Kyla's.

Where does "aspiring" end and "has been" begin? I'd promised myself to take this audition as an omen; with twelve flubbed auditions behind me, and three year's worth of nearly nothing on my resumé, my chances of getting the scantiest of parts decreased exponentially with each job lost. When I moved from Chicago to Carlstown, I knew my acting career was over, but I blithely assumed that I could keep my hand in, taking bit and background parts, a commercial here and there, just to ease the transition from acting to teaching acting. My first year in Carlstown, I flew or drove to Chicago regularly, and won several small parts; the pantyhose role was a special coup, since they'd originally wanted a white girl's gams. Then things slowed way down; I made it into a crowd scene in a peanut butter ad, and almost got a one-line speaking part as a nurse in *Days of Our Lives*. But that was it; there'd been nothing since then. Agents and directors who'd promised to keep in touch hadn't; I was out of the circuit. It was expensive to commute; and even though I stayed with Kyla, there were still food and transportation costs, not to mention pre-audition expenses: a good haircut, dry cleaning or new clothes, voice lessons when I was trying for a singing part. With all the money I channelled into my nebulous acting career, I could've made a down payment on a new car, bought my parents a decent stereo, or helped my sister Sukey pay off her college loans. So I decided to give it one more shot; if I flubbed my next audition, I'd call it quits, and focus on teaching. I even wrote myself a note and tacked it on the fridge:

I, Terry Cintos, being of reasonably sound mind and body, hereby declare that I will quit professional acting and settle down to serious serial monogamy if I fuck up the Tuff-Puffs audition.

I meant to hold myself to it. But as I climbed the last flight to Kyla's apartment, I found myself wishing I'd taken the note down before I left. Just in case I changed my mind.

"Did they make you cry?" Kyla was stirring something bubbly with one hand, and poking her mouse around with the other. She never stopped working; now that we weren't together, I could admire her ambition. She carried a pad of paper and a pen in her back pocket, even to bars and restaurants; periodically she'd get this spacey expression on her face, whip out the pad, and scrawl. Why she found Medieval art so compelling, I couldn't fathom; the dead don't fascinate me. I like live things, motion and music more than memory. But U. of Chicago loved her, and her book, *Medieval Madonnas*, was nearly complete. She was on track for tenure.

"Ask me about my dog."

"Not the dead dog bit again?"

"I didn't get it."

"The dog, or the audition?" When I didn't laugh, Kyla stopped stirring and computing long enough to wrap her arms around my waist. "Sweetie, they don't deserve you. You're too good for toilet paper."

"Facial tissues."

"Big difference. Here," she held out a spoonful of something yellow, with green bits in it, "try this. Couscous with frozen peas."

For the first time since leaving Carlstown, I found myself missing Jane. Or at least her cooking. The couscous needed more than a little seasoning; I told Kyla to finish her paragraph while I took over as chef-in-residence. But by the time dinner was ready, Kyla was deep into her work; I waited, watching snow collect on the sill, and listening to Billie Holiday low on the stereo. I angled myself on the sofa so she wouldn't think I was watching her, but her concentration intrigued me. I like observing people do whatever they do best: Jane cooking, Kyla writing, Naomi debating politics. When I see clips of my best performances, I'm not myself but someone else entirely. If Terry shows through the character, I know I've done something wrong.

I watched Kyla bite her lower lip, cross and re-cross her legs, wiggle her fingers, dart the mouse across the pad. Writing is physical for her, chair-dancing; as I watched, I remembered loving her, as if from a distance, not the feeling but the function. After we split up, she dated around some, but nothing took. Her work is more important to her than any lover; she has a hard time finding someone who'll accept that. Never much of a problem for us; I like being with someone who's passionate about something other than me. Takes the pressure off, leaves me energy to pursue my own stuff. Though I admit it's a fantasy of mine to find a woman who'll pull me so far out of myself that I can't find my way back. I've never been in love that way; hard to say if it would be wonderful or horrifying. Maybe romantic love is just another het myth.

In photographs, Kyla looks white; her skin is pale, hair and eyebrows a deep reddish-brown. The creamy undertones of her skin flatten out in even the best color shots, and she passes for cheerleader, a sweet straight WASP from Connecticut. It's only up close that you can see the luminousness beneath skin that looks dull-white from a distance. I like holding her face close to mine and trying to read the color beneath the surface: hints of pale yellow, beige, strawberry-gold. Or silver; there's something blue about Kyla's body in dim light; red washes away, and the violet of her chestnut eyes takes over. I didn't realize she was black until she told me; I'd never have guessed, and yet there's something about her that isn't white, and

84

I noticed that immediately. She teases me about it. Says my radar's weak, and maybe it is. But I knew she was a dyke right off, so that partially redeems me. We sat at adjoining tables one night at a blues joint, and I wrote my number for her on a matchbook; a clichéd start, but it took off. There was a lot between us, and if she hadn't been so scared, we might've worked.

Chloe's is where we go nights I'm in town, for old times' sake, and because Carlstown is such a berg that it doesn't even have a gay bar. The Metropolis is mixed, but that just means you won't get booted for kissing; hets still stare, and the bartenders avoid queer tables. I take weekend trips to Chicago to remember what it feels like to be comfortable: to grind in an all-girl bar or walk hand-in-hand through a gay ghetto. I can't get used to the closeted dyke scene in Carlstown; everything's about secrecy. That's why I insist on being out at Wylie. I don't want to contribute to the deafening silence.

Kyla snagged a table next to a strobe; I watched her face burn red, blue, green, and red again. Girls everywhere. It made me happy, seeing so many breasts and so little hair in one room. The music went on and on, "wannawannawanna" and suddenly I did, I wanna'd, and I grabbed her hand, took her for a circle: swing swing swing, shag dip swish, she laughed, scooped her hair off the back of her neck, held it up while her hips did the back-and-forth, back-and-forth, wide arcs, little S's, C-circles. What I love best about dancing with Kyla is that her cool reserve vanishes. Mostly she's closed off, a window that won't open far enough for a breeze.

I scanned the dance floor for familiar faces; a few old friends did hello, and I spotted two exes, one whose name I honestly couldn't remember ("You are so cold," Kyla said later, but I swear I blanked), and Pam, a barfly I slept with a few times before I met Kyla. I get embarrassed when I see her, because the sex was so intense; she was a talker, got me sounding like a nine hundred number. I liked the raunchiness of it, the way she'd stare me down, the way she made everything seem illicit. But she did simple things badly; I didn't even like the way she kissed: pressing too hard with her teeth, curling her lips over in what felt like a snarl. I was never able to figure out a way to tell her. I believe in working things through in bed, I don't expect everything to come naturally, but kissing? Isn't that supposed to be self-explanatory? Pam waved stiff fingers, a butch version of the Princess Di, then went back to rubbing up the navel of a round-faced femme with a bare midriff and multiple piercings. A skinny fag with ballerina arms swayed beside them; as the music spiraled higher and higher he raised his hands in the air and wound his whole self into a gleaming corkscrew; when the strobe started he unwound, arms and torso in lithe syncopated swirls. Then as if on cue, every single went coupled and every couple did three; as Pam pressed the femme backwards, a bold girl in jeans and a white men's T lay across Pam, breasts to back; the femme pushed up, it was hasty, made me happy. I tapped the table with my right index finger, impatient and hungry.

"You're a married woman, Terry."

"That so?" I leaned across the table and kissed Kyla's forehead; the music went slow, something sappy, and she extended a hand. I'm no good at slow, but Kyla's patient. Puts up with me when I insist on leading, and then do it badly. I'm glad she's taller, because I can bury my face in her shoulder without getting neck cramps, and I did, I nuzzled, and she bent her head over me, and we slowed to a sway and then a stop and somewhere along the line the music switched over to fast again but the dykes around us could see we were having a Moment and wiggled respectfully without breaking it up.

"Terry?" Someone tapped my arm, interrupting our swaying; Dana and Kit, and we hadn't talked in how long, and they went on, and we went on, and Kyla winked because it was clear that they thought we were back together so we played along for their benefit and then played pool and as I leaned over the table, calculating an angle, Dana pressed up against me from behind, pretending to point out an easy shot.

"What's up?" she said, pointing, not towards stripes but what might be solid: Kyla, her back turned, chatting Kit.

I winked back. Let Wicker gossip as it will.

We went home to Kyla's after a single game; wanted to be in bed before we were both too tired.

Oh, Jane knows. So long as you're safe, she says. So long as you're not in love. What Jane doesn't know is that Kyla always leaves me wondering. Because our breakup wasn't about an end to loving, but about mutual stubbornness: we split because I refused to do long-distance without long-term expectations, and Kyla refused to commit to anything serious. It's no longer any of my business, and I don't say it to her face, but I suspect Kyla's refusal was more fear than anything else. In the beginning, she wasn't afraid, maybe because I asked so little of her. When I finally started making demands, she backed away; I called her on it, and she bailed. But I know I mattered to her; on my last visit, she confessed that she was worried she'd never meet anyone else she could open up to so easily. What depresses me is that I never felt Kyla had opened up to me at all. I always sensed that she was holding back.

I can see now that we weren't good for each other, and it's a relief not to have to live with constant insecurity. Kyla's moods are opaque as milk, changeable as traffic. She can be as affectionate as anyone, but that warmth switches on and off, a glitter-light: fine to dance to, but hard on the daily eyes. She goes cold and abrupt without warning or explanation. I want my next lover to be someone who'll let me in all the way, without fear or hesitation. I can't say what she'll look like, or how it will feel. But I know it's what I want, and I know it's what I've never had.

Oh, I love Jane, and Jane loves me.

K-I-S-S-I-N-G.

"But you're bored."

Why do I have such honest friends? Naomi says I'm settling; maybe I am. But I worry that things with Jane are as good as they'll get. Naomi says when you're sure, you know, that certainty has a distinct flavor, like cinnamon or garlic. Her life is testimony; she's got one of those picture-perfect dyke marriages: two kids from the same sperm donor, a renovated house in the burbs with Republican neighbors they've charmed into tolerance, P-FLAG parents, the whole shebang. When we first met (she and Katelyn were the LC contacts for Carlstown; we hit it off, and started up as friends), I was still moping over Kyla, and openly jealous of their blissful Luppie union. But I always secretly wonder about my settled-down friends. Does the right girl ever really come along, or do you eventually get tired and give up the chase? And how can you tell the difference?

Hard to think back to how I felt when Jane and I first met. She stood two heads behind me in line at the Carlstown post office, and we noticed each other right away: the only black faces. Short and very round, with skin so brown it was nearly an honest black, she wore a deep red skirt and blouse, a hat made of thick purple cloth, and matching beaded bangles. I smiled my "Hi, I'm black too" smile; she smiled back, adding "Hi, I'm gay too," with her vast green eyes. It was smooth from the start, like a song you've heard so many times that the lyrics and music become inextricably connected and fade into each other. The closeness that developed felt new to me after Kyla's distance. Midway through our second month, Jane re-named me, or at least a part of me: St. Theresa, for when I'd go distant and demure, when I'd cease to be Terry, and become the conventional, selfless girl my parents always wanted me to be. It was a mask I didn't realize I owned; Jane demanded of me an honesty that came to season our talks, 'til speech between us felt as simple and complicated as thinking aloud. The only thing I censored was the thing that mattered most: my doubts about what we could have, who we might be together. Because for all her work at unpeeling, and all her success, the depth of emotional intimacy didn't translate for me into a kinesthetic response.

Kyla's so closed-off that sex is mostly physical; I can never tell what she's thinking, or what she really feels. As we climbed the stairs to her apartment, Kyla tugged at my shirt, but waited 'til I'd finished locking us in before taking it off. Once, when we were living together close to the university, we mistakenly left the door unlocked after stumbling home late and falling into kissing. When we woke the next morning, the newspaper was unfolded neatly on the kitchen counter, two mugs and two spoons beside it, and coffee was percolating in the machine. Nothing stolen; we searched the apartment, but no one was hiding in the closet, or beneath the sofa. Our friends were divided: those who'd lived in the city for less than ten years were freaked and bought new locks; those who'd been in town for over a decade thought it was funny.

Safety's one nice thing about suburbia.

"Are the windows locked?" I checked, checked again; next door's commercial neon crackled through slatted blinds and Kyla appeared to me divided, alternating glow light and blinds' shadows. As I reached over to blend the difference, my own flesh went under and came up striped. What sets two skeletons in sympathy, and where do their minds get to in the meantime? Tugging at cuffs, unbuttoning collars, slipping off socks with anxious toes: through the silence of city traffic, through the light of post-midnight pitch, we set ordinary motions to graceful measures. Or nearly graceful; standing, she tried to slide a foot out from her slacks and lost her balance. What makes an accident a dance? I pulled her towards me on the rug and we sprawled, one sloppy belly sucking one supple back, 'til she flipped me and we kissed, mouth to breast, rib to waist. Held inside her mouth was the taste of my cunt, and the pale, smoky flavor of cigarettes; held inside her belly was memory, and I lipped 'til she unloosed it. It was a pleasure like reading, my eyes moving to catch coded messages, her face open, lashes like pages. I wrapped my hands around her back; more cries and sharp intakes of breath, 'til finally we remembered sleep; too tired to find the bed in darkness, we tugged pillows down from the couch and swerved, back to back, dreams careening.

When I woke, she was already writing: her hair loose, falling over her face, screening me out, connecting her to a keyboard that looked, from where I sat, like an extension of her wrists. Do her fingers dream of keys when they rub over me? When she touches me, I don't produce; she can't save the words she spells on my back and ankles, or the words she makes when she tongues my shoulders. Nothing to be controlled or altered. Is that why she loosens underneath my hands: because there are no revisions to be made, only one automatic line without punctuation that goes on and on until body connects with clock and reenters the day? Is she saving herself for the words she loves?

I said good-bye, but she didn't hear; I leaned over and stroked her cheek and still she didn't hear, even as I tugged my suitcase out the door, my key in the lock, metal meeting same, my soles on the creaky stairs five flights down. With each step, I tried to vanish from my throat the soreness that always rose when Kyla iced over, tried instead to think of ice as something beautiful: its dissolute edges, opaque whiteness, indiscreet temperatures. On the street, it was beautiful: the roads slick with it; the clouds, which hung low for a Sunday, heavy with it. I caught a shuttle to the airport, and as the bus droned and stuttered over the sloppy roads, I tried thinking my way back to what was coming next: Carlstown airport, and a highway's ride home to a good woman waiting.

I love Jane, and she loves me.

Sittin' in a tree.

I-N-G.

Oh, I could fracture the rhyme, make it into rap or womyn's music, sing it backwards, work up a dance party remix. But without the right beat behind the lyrics, what would the words mean? "I love you."

The last thing I'd said to her on Friday before I left. If I crossed my fingers, did it still count?

Because I wasn't sure. I cared about her, thought she was smart and witty, beautiful and strong, yeah yeah yeah, and a fine cook and a sharp dresser, yeah yeah yeah, but there was something missing, woe woe woe, I could just see the video: "Ambivalence," by T-C and the Trailing Exes, lots of tattoos on the drummer girl, the lead vocalist a sassy chickie with a bald pate, her boots glossy, cut-offs tattered at the seams.

Jane was starting to count on me, in ways that looked Lego but felt like concrete blocks. Take transportation. She was beginning to drive my car, and to assume she'd chauffeur me to Wylie round-trip on her days off. It was a little too "Love Makes a Family," everything so neat and tidy. We exchanged lots of sympathetic looks, but few lustful glances; we expressed concern, but rarely desire. Things felt static. And stillness is something that's never interested me. I like easy motion: dancing, and the way a woman's thighs chafe when she walks; stretching, and the way a woman's shoulders vanish when she raises her arms above her head, reaching for something she'll never catch. Jane finds stillness sexy; sometimes when we kiss, she'll pause and wait, her tongue in my mouth, as if the music of her bones has momentarily stopped. My hands are always going, going; she'll clasp mine in hers and place them on her belly, but instead of connection it tugs like constraint. I don't like feeling held back, held onto; I need a woman who'll move faster than I can follow.

I like the chase.

Yet I know myself well enough to say that I won't leave her until I find another. I'm not good at being single; my solution is never to let it happen. The longest I've gone without a girl since coming out freshman year at Foster is five months, and that was too long. It's not even that I need someone around constantly; I don't like clinginess. It's more that I need to know there's someone out there thinking my face, seeing my name. I feel whole when I know someone else has their part of me. So yes, I'm thinking about leaving, but I'm also waiting.

From the airport window, I watched the sky shed snow, holding up a steel-blue ridge where it met the landscape; I watched orange overalls scurry over asphalt, carting off staircases to nowhere; I watched, until a disembodied voice announced that my flight was held up and I walked to the nearest Airport Shoppe, where I bought copies of *Seventeen*, *Sassy*, and *Mademoiselle*. I try to stay in touch with mainstream teen culture; difficult, since I was never much a part of it myself. Flipping through the glossy pages, I thought, so this is why my students are completely confused. The girls, so skinny, their faces are clownish and narrow; the men on their arms, ten years older at the very least. And white: even the black girls have Caucasian features. I never subscribed to this shit; I wasn't anything so innocuous as a tomboy. I took a rebel pose and held it for several years, as if poised for a photograph: sullen eyebrows crowning a smirk.

I used to think that my distance from het white girlie culture explained why my female students rarely see me as a mentor. It's the boys who fall under my spell, especially the faggots; the girls hold themselves back, shrinking into their bodies, smaller and smaller, 'til their hairbows are the only sign of life. Usually by year's end, I've forgotten I have girls in class at all. True, the rumor's out that I'm queer, so maybe the girls are frightened of contagion, but I've talked to a number of other female teachers about this, and they say the same thing. The girls are all going down for the last time, sending a collective SOS in menthol smoke, but none of them will accept help when it comes round. My first year, I had a specially fading one; her bones stood taller than she did. So smart; still, smart couldn't save her, and they took her away, tubed her up. She didn't come back, but her face reappears sometimes, a haunted hollow Chesire floating above the baseball caps.

I like the way Jane takes up space, inhabiting the bed, her round thighs pressed together to form something accountable, their weight teasing resistance from my hands as I try to come between. I like her heaviness, knowing I'm holding something, not fearing the slip-away of a thin woman's arms when I circle round. But Jane likes closeness more than leaping; I like the catch, but only after breadth, and crossing. Jane's understanding of hunger is part of what I respect about her. She co-owns a catering company, Movable Feasts, with a fluttery socialite named Paula Chesley, whose kids go to Wylie. Jane's as theatrical as I am, but she likes to be behind the scenes, to let food itself stake stardom.

I thought ahead to tonight's dinner: the two of us sitting down to something spice-gracious, no flowers or candles but a blue speckled pitcher of water, wine glasses with thin green stems, rolls (always wheat, with butter tucked inside) in a basket the color of polished pine. Maybe tonight I'd arrive at her place, hang my toothbrush in the rack to stay. Or maybe I'd sit through another dinner with my eyes on the balance, watching comfort and boredom fight for the feather that would finally tip the scales. Her face would funnel to a question mark; I'd reach out to change the channel, then remember we were live, and keep my hands wound tightly together in my aching lap.

When we finally took off, and I'd opened a tome to ward off unwanted neighborly chatter, I remembered the note I'd left myself, with its glib oath. What does it mean to promise yourself something? The person who did the promising had to be different from the one who did the carrying-out, or there would be no need for oaths; the thing would simply happen. As the plane hurried towards its landing, I could see the patchwork realm of Carlstown's rooftops; I could see the sudden, gleaming surface of the river. Whose mirror? The plane nosed, I watched its flaps spike and stutter, felt the wheels spinning mercilessly; beneath us, the runway eyed the bird's wings warily. I buttoned my yellow coat: the only protection I had against cold new air, which promised anything, or nothing.

CHAPTER 6

Copeland

I went for a drive. I wanted to leave the house long enough for the food to rot, for the bread to harden into bone, then crumble. I wanted the meat to stink the way the crevice of her sex stank now: dirt and ash, embraced by a coffin. I wanted her food to become inedible, as her flesh had become untouchable.

The coffin was closed, but her mother asked that she be buried in a flowered dress. Nothing she'd ever actually have worn. When I see sky, I think of Dell; grass reminds my throat of crying; when I see roses, I imagine false-flushed cheeks, need to look away.

I drove 'til I crossed the state line, then turned back again. I drive for a living, but never get enough of the easy motion, the way the tires speak to the yellow lines. If I could live in this cab, I would: breakfast, lunch, dinner with one hand on the wheel; newspapers, mail saved for stoplights. You could raise a family in a cab, if you wanted to.

Can a ghost be a mother?

When I got home the milk had soured the air, but everything else was still whole.

It takes time for things to decompose.

"She's not dead for you, is she?" Nora's kind of music. "You still live with her, you bastard!" I'd slammed the door on it, but her words still echoed.

It was four in the morning when I fell asleep; I woke at eight on Friday, called in sick to work. I spent the next three days mostly in bed, trying to discern what I really believed. I needed to know if Dell was coming back—if I believed she really could—and I needed to know if I should leave my bed or die in it. On Sunday morning, I felt I'd come to a decision. Flies groped at the food, and the whole place stank; as I walked the length of the trailer, I realized that I liked it: it felt right to let things go. If there'd been whiskey in the house, I'd have stuck my face in the bottle like a gas oven. But this

93

seemed easier, maybe even quicker: the trailer would be my coffin. I'd just stay put, not eating, not moving; when they came for me, I'd make their job simple. I'd already be buried. I closed my eyes, slept the day long.

Don't know when I would've gotten up if the phone hadn't found me. Must've been around five when it rang for the first time. After she died, I got rid of the answering machine; there were never any messages, and the red light reminded me too much of stop. No one calls me, really; sometimes I think I should junk the phone, save myself a few dollars a month. No family to speak of, one cousin in town and a sister who works fishing up in Alaska, a drunk like I used to be, no one I'd be likely to talk to. The boys at the office conduct their conversations in person. My bills were paid. And Dell sure wasn't doing any calling, at least not through phone wires. So I figured it was Nora; had to be. Who else? I didn't pick up.

But it rang again an hour later. Nine rings. Whoever was calling knew I didn't answer very often. I shut my eyes, tried to fall back asleep. The third time it rang twelve times.

When the phone rang for the fourth time, I gave in. Figured I'd tell her off. I needed sleep, I'd say; I was sick, and I couldn't have her here speaking ill of the dead. When a woman's voice answered, I wasn't surprised; I realized pretty quickly, though, that it wasn't Nora. I admit it: for a moment, my heart sped, and I thought, Dell, that you? She was so alive for me, so alive it would've seemed perfectly natural. But the voice on the other end identified herself.

"Copeland, it's Maureen, Maureen Cleary. I'm terribly sorry to bother you this way, on a Sunday evening, especially since we've been out of touch. But it's an emergency." She was brisk, businesslike, as if nothing had ever passed between us; she almost made me believe it. She's good, Maureen, and I mean it two ways—a good person, and good at pretending. You have to be both. You can't be just one. So it wasn't hard to hear from her; fact was, I'd felt bad, thought before about calling her. She's someone I shouldn't have let go of without first explaining the why of it. So it felt right just then to let Maureen tell her story. She explained that her seventy-one-year-old mother, Deirdre, was still living in the house Maureen had grown up in, all alone since Maureen's father died. But two days ago, she'd fallen on the stairs, broken her wrist. She'd made it to the phone and called a neighbor, who'd taken her to the hospital, but the accident had shaken her up: what if she'd hit her head, or twisted her leg full under her? How would she have found help? Maureen hadn't wanted to suggest that her mother leave the house until she was ready. But now, Deirdre herself wanted to move out, into an apartment in a retirement complex nearby.

It was sudden news; Maureen needed to be there, no question. She wanted to help her mother around the house while her wrist was still fragile, pack her things up, and see to it that Deirdre was comfortably moved into her new apartment. So she'd taken two weeks off from work, bought a last-minute ticket to Seattle, packed her bags.

She'd nearly forgotten about Joey. "He can't go." I could hear music in the background, or maybe a television. "He can't miss ten days of school, not at this time of year. Besides, he's in a play, and doesn't want to give that up. He's been practicing for months; I can't blame him, and I don't want to take that away. Then too," and her voice slowed, "even if he wanted to go, there's no way I could afford another ticket. I've charged mine on my credit card and hit my limit; I just don't have any more money."

I waited; it seemed she was asking for something without saying what. I wanted her to come right out and say it.

"Copeland."

There was a pause; her breathing came through, and I felt sorry suddenly. Hard for me to imagine having a mother troubled like that, and in a state so far away it was almost a foreign country. Deirdre. The name sloped, like a hill. I wanted to say it aloud more than once. Deirdre, falling. Being old, knowing you were alone, knowing you weren't ever going to have your first body back, and then falling: watching the wallpaper come closer, feeling your hand lose touch with the wooden banister. What would that be like, I wondered. How would the scars look? I took a glance around the trailer. Who'll come for me when I start tumbling? What will they save of mine? I could see my reflection in the mirror. I put one hand on my chest, over my heart.

"Copeland, I need to ask you a favor."

I turned my head away from the mouthpiece, cleared my throat. "Ask away." I won't say I wasn't scared—hadn't Nora asked for too much?—but I liked Maureen, needed to hear what it was she wanted, even if only for curiosity's sake.

"I've called almost everyone in town. The sitter who usually stays with him? Her brother's getting married, too busy. His best friend's parents? Grandmom's coming to visit next week, everything's hectic. I even asked one of his teachers, his favorite, but she said no, she didn't have the extra room. And even though he's mature for fourteen, even though I trust him, I don't feel right about leaving him by himself for close to two whole weeks. I need to ask you to watch Joey, Copeland. I need to ask you to let him stay with you while I'm away taking care of Mother."

It was such a favor, it felt tangible. I held it in my hands, turned it this way and that, stroked it, brought it to my cheek. What she was asking from me was to care for what mattered most to her. I understood about that—about what mattered most. I cleared my throat again, wiped my palms against my sweatpants. "Well, sure, Maureen, I think I can arrange for that. Joey can stay here; long time since I had company to pal around with."

What I liked best? She didn't go all gushy then, didn't cry, didn't perform some kind of song and dance routine. Not that she wasn't grateful, not that she didn't thank me. But it was one soft sigh, a "thank you" like she meant it, like one was enough. That told me something about Maureen right there. She wasn't someone to need to do something over and over and over again.

After I hung up, first thing I did was shower. Second thing was to collect the dead food pitting up the trailer into a bag, and take it out to the dumpster by the crossroads. It was eight-thirty by the time I started really cleaning; I stayed up 'til one, scrubbed the shower stall even, and that's what I hate most. Dell used to do that; she hated doing the toilet, so we traded off. That's the bum thing about living alone: no trade-offs.

Got to work early the next morning, took the first call out. I won't say I wasn't feeling shaky—I'd had whiskey dreams all night, with Dell's face on the bottle—but it felt good to drive again. I wouldn't want to give up driving, not for anything. When the wind's coming in through both front windows, when there's someone in back gabbing about the headlines, when I've got a cigarette between my lips and my elbow out the side, I'm in charge. My cab's my own. I bought it, paid it off with a loan that ended some time ago, so I don't even owe for it. I drive it on my off time, take it where I want to. It's yellow, little checkered pattern in a line along the side. Shiny and clean because I keep it that way.

First thing Joey wanted to do when I picked him up? Drive the cab himself. Initially I said no way, no siree, this here's my partner. You're not taking it anywhere. But his face scrunched up, and I could tell right away he was the kind of kid to take things hard. A lot softer than I ever was; probably smarter, though. So I struck up a deal with him. We unpacked first, put his stuff on the shelves I never use under the TV set. Spread out his sleeping bag beside the brown chair, so he could see the TV from where he was parked. Got the toothbrush in the bathroom, towel on the rack. I made him brush right then and there, too. "Why?" he said. "I brush before I go to bed, and it's not time yet."

"Too bad." I wanted him to know I was going to be a stickler on cleanliness-type things. "In this house, you brush a whole bunch of extra times. Just in case."

"In case what?" His mouth was full of toothpaste. I couldn't think what to say back, so I pretended I hadn't heard him, headed for the kitchen.

"I'll be in here, scrubbing the sink," I called. "That's something else we do a whole lot around here, is scrub. Everything. Real often."

I let him drive because I thought he might need it. I knew he was anxious about Maureen; it seemed right to give him something that would take his mind off planes, Deirdre, falling, the run-down trailer of a man he barely knew. You know what worried me? Not that he'd crash the cab—no, I was sitting beside him, and my hands are too quick for that. I was worried that he wouldn't get the same feeling from it that I did, that it wouldn't seem like flying to him, that he'd laugh, say "You do this all day?" I'd have felt old then. I'd have been sorry I'd ever let him take the wheel.

But he was like me, a natural driver. We drove down to the parking lot behind Wilson's; he started out with lines, then moved to turns, curves, slow circles. Pretty soon he wanted to get fancy. Tried an *S*, a figure eight, then asked me if he could spell his name.

I hesitated. "Sure, just go easy on the gas. Take it slow on the *E*."

He did, too. He spelled his name, my name, and his mother's.

Then he stopped, tired out, and I took over. "Just one more thing," I said, heading for the top of the lot. I spelled *DELL* on the diagonal, and I did it fast, spinning the wheels a little on the last *L*.

"What was that?" he asked, when it was all over.

"Love," I said, and then it was time to head for home.

It was odd at first, having someone else in the house. Joey was very mature for his age, so it wasn't like having a toddler around. But there was still someone else to think about; made me realize all the quirks I'd picked up living so long alone. Take singing, for example. I can't sing worth a darn, but I do it anyway, loudly, and not just in the shower, either. I sing country western mostly, but also a little pop, some old rock tunes I grew up with, even bits of classical music Dell introduced me to. Second day he was here, Joey walked in on me belting "Shameless" into a dish sponge. I turned one long *S* into a cough, "SSssHackhahuhhuh," but I don't think he bought it. It embarrassed him more than me, though, that was the thing. Because Joey was shy. Shy like I'd never seen in a kid before. Not that I'm around kids a lot, but I have a memory; I know what I was like at fourteen, and there was more noise and motion involved. What I couldn't figure out was whether it was just me he was shy around, or humanity in general.

The second day was hard on me, because I was worrying about Dell. We have our time together blocked off; I save dusk for the two of us. So there I was, settled into the brown chair, preparing to shut my eyes, preparing for the conjure point. Then I heard the door creak, and Joey entered, shaking his arms out of his jacket.

"Yo."

That's what kids say now, instead of "Hi."

I "Yo'd" back at him, but wasn't merry about it. I missed Dell. Maybe she was even waiting.

"Where've you been? After school sports or something?"

"Naw." He took his baseball cap off, put it on again backwards. "Play rehearsal. Art's dad dropped me off."

I hadn't realized he was friends with James' son. "I know Art. Nice kinda kid."

He nodded, looked down at his feet as if surprised at how big they'd grown. He pushed at a hole in the carpeting with his toe.

"What's the name of the play?"

"*Hamlet* by William Shakespeare."

"Sure. *Hamlet*. I've heard of *Hamlet*. I guess everybody has, just about."

He went quiet on me. Damn, I thought, making conversation with teenagers is a genuine drag.

"Yeah," I said, "I guess everybody's heard of *Hamlet*, and Shakespeare, all that jazz. But you know what?"

"What?"

I liked the way he always answered, even when I wasn't really asking a question. If I'd been in the same class with him when I was his age, I'd probably have slugged him a few, but now, I could see what was unique and pleasant about him.

"I haven't ever read *Hamlet*. I haven't read anything by William Shakespeare at all. Not ever."

He looked impressed. "How'd you manage that?"

"It probably took some doing. Let's see…I was supposed to read *Macbeth* one year, eighth grade or ninth, can't remember which. Maybe *Romeo and Juliet*—that's Shakespeare, right? But I couldn't afford the books, and didn't like the library, so that pretty much decided it for me."

"Books are expensive."

"Darn right."

We waited some more in silence. Then I thought of a question I wanted to ask, only I was worried that it was cheesy. I decided to go ahead and ask it anyway.

"So Joey. Tell me what kind of story *Hamlet* is all about."

That's when something happened. His face was a typical teenage boy's face—acne, some nose hairs, shaving nicks, a sort of befuddled expression covering everything like a screen. But when he began acting out all the main parts of *Hamlet*, his greasy face lit up, and the gawkiness slid from his shoulders like his knapsack. How there's this awful deception and murder by Claudius, and then Hamlet's father's ghost comes to tell his son about the whole done deal, and Gertrude meanwhile's just going along with it, and poor Ophelia dies this very elegant but horrifically sad death by just freaking and drowning herself in the river. How Hamlet has to play his cards right, and it's sad and then gets sadder and at the end, it's all about bodies flinging themselves this way and that. Joey got to be Guildenstern, and Art was Rosencrantz, and even though they weren't big parts (only seniors get big parts), it was still something, considering how many people auditioned, and it was something extra too because Rosencrantz and Guildenstern were friends in the play, and here Joey and Art were friends in real life. Turned out he'd memorized some of Hamlet's speeches; he wasn't an understudy or anything, just wanted to be prepared in case of emergency, and who could blame him? So he started in with "To be, or not to be," which was something I'd heard before.

I wanted to hear about the ghost.

He didn't have that one memorized yet, so he pulled out his book, which was a little damp from the Coke he'd spilled in his knapsack, and started reading to me.

Then he stopped.

"Hey. Why don't we trade off? You be the ghost, and I'll be Hamlet."

Now, I'm not much of a reader, but I said OK, kid, I'll try it. I wanted to get inside this dead father of Hamlet's. What would it be like to be dead and be a ghost? Later when I was in bed, I started wondering, for the first time I guess, whether Dell feels anything when I see her on the inside of my eyelids. Does it give her a little shiver, does she know it's me thinking of her, does it feel good, like brushing her hair, or driving, or sex? Only maybe driving doesn't feel good to her anymore, wherever she is now.

But right then, I wasn't thinking about Dell's ghost, I was thinking about Hamlet's dead father, "whose love was of that dignity"— I liked that bit. Love should be dignified. And it was good that the ghost knew his love had been true, even if he'd gotten bounced off by his very own brother.

The next night, I had a late call, came home three, four-ish. Slept in. When I woke up the next morning, afternoon really, I found a bowl, napkin, cup, and spoon laid out real neat on the table in the kitchen. There was a box of cereal beside the bowl, and a little note: "Be sure to eat a good breakfast. Back home by four. Rehearsal seven-thirty to nine. J.C." He'd signed his initials in big block letters; I wondered if anyone ever called him J.C. instead of Joey. Then I realized I hadn't ever asked him if he had another nickname, if he liked being called Joey, or if that was his mother's thing. Ask him,

Copeland, I told myself. Ask the boy what kind of name he wants to have.

I got home around six to find that Joey had cooked spaghetti and heated a can of Ragu. It was good, it was fine. I eat spaghetti a lot, and this was just spaghetti, but he put onions in the Ragu, which I like, and cheese in the spaghetti before he poured the sauce on. That was new to me, and I told him so. Told him it tasted all right by me.

"You got another late call tonight?"

"Nope. Finished for today. Tomorrow night I do a graveyard shift, but tonight is for sleeping. You've got rehearsal, huh?"

"Yup."

"What do you do at rehearsal? Read lines back and forth so you get them right?"

"Mostly. Ms. Cintos listens to us read, makes sure we're using the right kind of tone. But we also block scenes. We walk around and she tells us where we should be standing while different people are talking, that sort of thing."

"Is it fun?" Ms. Cintos. She was Dell's friend.

"They're good. Sometimes things get boring but mostly we have a blast. Ms. Cintos is the greatest. She's smart, and so she makes you understand things about the words that you didn't get from just reading on your own. And I like watching the thing..." He waved his arms around, almost knocking over the salt shaker, "come together. Yeah. Come together. Because the first rehearsal? It's just a bunch of us kids standing around. But then, after a couple more times, it starts to look like something somebody planned. Then by the end, it's moving on its own, like a machine, and it can get really wild, because it's organized." He rubbed a pimple on his chin. "Seems weird. Like, it gets wild and exciting and stuff, but only after it gets organized first. But that's how it is."

"That's a rehearsal."

"That's a rehearsal. Hey," he rummaged in the refrigerator, found two doughnuts, handed one to me, "wanna come sometime? You could talk to Art, and meet Ms. Cintos. She's the greatest."

"What time you leaving tonight?"

"Seven-fifteen. I gotta call Art, ask him to get his dad to give me a lift."

"Don't bother; I can take you. I'll go, bring a newspaper in case things run dull."

He turned on the water, began filling the sink, squirted soap in; I collected plates from the table. Nice to have someone help with the cooking and the after-things.

"You don't have to. I mean, it's no biggie for Art's dad to pick me up."

"No, Joey, I want to. I'd like to see one of these doodads." Then I remembered about his name. "Hey, gotta question for you."

"Shoot."

"You like being called Joey? Or is that a mother thing?"

"Joey's OK. But you know what? It's kind of a kid name. I've been thinking some lately? And I got an idea for a better name, sort of a nickname."

"What's that?"

"Horatio."

Horatio?

"Horatio?"

"Yeah, that's the name of Hamlet's best bud. He's practically the only person who doesn't die at the end. And right before Hamlet croaks? He asks Horatio this favor. Guess what he asks him?"

"Hmm." I couldn't think of what it might be. "To visit Ophelia's grave?"

Joey rubbed his pimple. "Naw. I mean, maybe he asks him that, too, only offstage or something. I mean, Ophelia is important and all. But it's something else. Guess what."

"I think I'm out of guesses."

"But that was only one!" Joey had suds all up his arms. He was so tall and soapy that he looked scary, like one of those mutating teenagers in a slasher movie.

"OK, one more. Hmm. Maybe he asks Horatio to give all his stuff to the poor people in the town where he lives? Something to show what a nice guy he was."

"That would've been good, too, but it's even better. Shakespeare was so excellent; if he'd lived today he would've been big. So Hamlet says to Horatio, look, if people don't know the whole story, they're gonna think I'm a total dickwad. Oops," Joey looked over at me; I just shrugged.

"I've heard worse, kid. Go on."

He grinned. "OK. So Hamlet says, look, you gotta tell everybody the whole story, so they know the truth, and don't think I was a jerk. If you're my friend, you'll do it." He took his knapsack from the chair, rummaged inside for his battered book. "Here you go: *O God, Horatio, what a wounded name, things standing thus unknown, I leave behind me! If thou didst ever hold me in thy heart, absent thee from felicity awhile, and in this harsh world draw thy breath in pain, to tell my story.*

Isn't that cool?"

Absent thee from felicity awhile. I liked it. "OK, Horatio. You ready for the rehearsal? Get your stuff and let's scoot."

"I'm history." He ran for the bathroom, knocking the plant off the TV stand. While I waited, I tried repotting it; it'd fallen out in two big clumps. But the roots were tangled, and the dirt dry, and when I picked up the first clump, the one with most of the plant in it, it crumbled. I searched under the sink for the Dustbuster. End of plant.

The auditorium was small, but expensive-looking. Joey walked me to a seat near the middle, then yelled, "Ms. Cintos! We've got an audience!" I wanted to say something to Ms. Cintos then, about Dell, how I was glad they'd been friends. Because Ms. Cintos had been Dell's only friend, really. Or at least, the only person Dell ever hung out with besides me. She'd liked Terry Cintos a lot, and it had made me happy to see her get out more, go places, do things. Because I was gone so much, so many late calls, and I had the boys: fishing, pool, ballgames. So I wanted to talk some to Joey's teacher, maybe thank her for what she'd been for Dell. But she just waved from the stage, smiled; she seemed preoccupied, and who could blame her? All those teenagers with swords running full tilt around the stage. Maybe after, I thought. Maybe after, I'll talk to her for a little while about Dell.

The rehearsal got boring, so I was glad I'd brought a newspaper. Some parts were fun to watch, though. Maura somebody was Ophelia, and she was good, really good, probably the best of the bunch. There was something about her that made you want to listen, something that made you think she really felt the stuff she was talking about. Hamlet was kind of lame; in the car on the way over, Joey had explained to me that he was a senior who'd been in drama club forever, that there weren't any other half-decent senior boys to play the part, and that Ms. Cintos had a rule that seniors got priority in casting. Everyone grumbled about it until they turned seniors, when it suddenly seemed fair. But it was odd to hear him reciting lines I'd heard Joey recite earlier. Joey was a lot better, I decided, and it wasn't that I was biased. He was just better. He could act, he could make you believe he was somebody else.

At ten after nine, Ms. Cintos called everyone onstage; they huddled around her in a wide half-circle. It reminded me of the pep talks my old basketball coach used to give us after a game. I couldn't hear what she was saying, but it was fun to watch her hands; she'd sweep her arms up and out to the sides. Then it was over, and Joey was running up the center aisle, dragging Ms. Cintos by the arm. She pulled back some; I figured she was maybe a little shy.

"Copeland! This is Ms. Cintos. She's my drama teacher. Ms. Cintos, this is Copeland, and I'm staying in his trailer while my mom visits her mom. Copeland and I have been practicing some. Mostly I do Hamlet, and he does the ghost, but we might do some stuff with Hamlet and Horatio, too."

When she smiled, her brown skin darkened into creases around her eyes, and she was pretty. I wondered what she and Dell had talked about. Had they ever talked about me? About drama? About Wylie, or driving?

"I guess we met before." I couldn't manage to say anything else.

"That's right. I knew your partner, Dell. We met at the funeral."

It didn't hurt as much to hear those words as I'd thought it might, maybe because it felt so good to be standing near someone who'd been a friend to Dell. Someone who knew her story. Standing close to Terry like that made me remember a time with Dell that was so ordinary I'd almost forgotten it. We'd gone shopping together out at the mall: me for sneakers, Dell for toothpaste and things. She'd written a list on the back of her hand so she'd remember what she needed. I found the kind of shoes I like right away: nothing fancy, no air pumps or racing stripes, just plain old black Chuck Taylors. Bought two pair, like I always do when something fits. Then I went to find Dell in the drugstore, even though I was twenty minutes ahead of schedule. I looked by the toothpaste and by the soap, but didn't see her, so I started wandering around, just ambling up and down the aisles. It felt good to be early somewhere. The drugstore was classy, everything was arranged nice and orderly on the shelves. I remember wondering how much money you had to have to start up that kind of business. Then I turned a corner and there she was, her back to me, one aisle ahead, in the stationery section.

At first I couldn't figure out what she was doing, messing around with pens and notebooks and staplers. Dell wasn't much of a writer; I think she wrote one letter the whole time I knew her, to her sister-in-law Francine when she had a miscarriage. Then I realized that Dell was having a conversation. Right there in the drugstore, like it was something normal for her to make small talk with folks on a regular basis. It was a woman she was talking to, a black woman in expensive-looking clothing. I couldn't see her face, but her hair was in braids; while I watched, the woman bent forward, pulled a pen from the rack, and tore the wrapping off. Usually there's not much saleslady action in drugstores, but it looked like Dell had gotten stuck. I moved away then, because I hate getting trapped by salesladies into buying things. Went to wait in front of the Choc-O-Latte, where we'd agreed to meet for ice cream after we were through.

When I met Terry at the funeral, I didn't peg her for the saleslady in the drugstore, but there in the theater, I remembered watching Dell talking to her, and figured it out. It must've been around then that they began to be friends. You know the way when you learn a new word, suddenly you hear it in every conversation, spot it in every newspaper you buy? It was like that with Terry's name around the trailer. She was just part of Dell's language, after that.

"Ms. Cintos." The air in the theater made my throat tickle. "I wanted to...before the rehearsal, I was thinking that I wanted to thank you. For being Dell's friend, because I was gone so much, and I worried she'd be lonely, and you were there for her to hang around with."

Terry's face had gone plain, like a folded napkin. "No." She touched my sleeve. "No, thank you. You were very good to her. She loved you a great deal."

I turned away, shuffled my newspaper. It took a while. Had to get the pages back into some sort of order. When I faced her again, she looked like Ophelia when Hamlet was telling her to go be a nun.

"She did love you. I know she did."

"Thanks." I tapped Joey on the arm. "Hey, Horatio. Time to get a move on. I need my sleep; late call tomorrow." I put my coat over my arm. "Ms. Cintos, it's been a pleasure meeting you. I mean, meeting you again."

"Do call me Terry."

"Sure. Terry. And like I said, thank you. I mean that." Joey ran ahead, out the wide double doors; I followed, a little slower, rummaging in my coat pocket for my keys.

"Copeland." She was still standing where we'd said good-bye. Her feet were parted like a dancer's, and her hands were dangling down by her sides. She looked like she was getting ready to move, but couldn't decide which direction to take. "I was wondering," she took a few steps towards me, "oh, hell. I was wondering if you'd ever want to get together sometime, have dinner or something. I feel as if Dell would've liked for us to get along."

It surprised me, the invitation. And you know what? For a minute, I felt scared. I thought about Kathy, Heather, Marsha, and especially Nora, and wondered if maybe Terry was trying to ask me out. The thought made me tired; I just didn't want anything from anyone right now. It wasn't that she wasn't nice, pretty, smart, good at her drama things; I just didn't want anything.

But as she approached me, something in her face told me that I was wrong. About the invitation, I mean. Because she didn't have that maybe-sexy look on her face. There wasn't anything there for me to evaluate. She was looking at me the way Dell used to look at me sometimes, very calm and steady and trusting. It was friendly, almost familiar.

So I told her yes, I'd like that. I'd like that very much. And we made plans, me and Terry. She took a notebook out of her purse, one of those appointment doodads. It was stuffed full, you could see names and times and things all over the pages. But then she said the night after next was almost blank, and asked me some things, and we settled on dinner. I wrote the date and time and place down on the back of my left hand.

When I got to the parking lot, Joey was sitting in the driver's seat, his legs stretched longways, feet propped up against the window.

"What took you so long can I drive?" He made two questions into one.

I didn't answer, but I let him. We drove home, and we were both smiling. In the little park three blocks before the trailer court, the trees were like hands reaching for him as he drove, but inside the car, it still felt safe.

"Hey." We were almost home, but I had just gotten a craving. "Turn back around in that driveway up ahead, and let's go to Wilson's, bring us back something with lots of sugar in it."

"You bet." The cab skidded and screeched, but made it round. We did a sugar tour of Wilson's, loaded up, and then Joey drove home, to the doorstep this time.

The inside of the trailer looked blue in the darkness. While Joey fumbled for the switch, I went back out to the car for the groceries. The bottom of the bag started to break as I hauled it out of the back-seat, but I made it to the door without losing anything.

"Want some hot chocolate?" I'd bought the little kid kind, with the tiny marshmallows that taste like rubbery sugar cubes.

"Sure. Throw me a Twinkie, will you?" He snapped the TV on, channel surfed for a few. "Nothing. Everything's shitty." He looked up at me, the way he always did when he cursed. I wasn't sure what he was waiting for. Disapproval? Laughter? Shock?

"I'm not a TV man myself." I spooned some ice cream into a plastic bowl with rabbits on it. It was Dell's when she was a kid. She was obsessed with Peter Rabbit, had the bowl, cup, plate, all that stuff. "I prefer the radio."

"Can I play something?"

"Sure. Whatever you want." I settled into the brown chair.

"Naw. Your house. What do you like?"

"Country. Try 103."

His gawky fingers found the station and we sat quietly, taking in the song's story, with the static of traffic interrupting now and then from the highway.

"So Copeland." Joey was cutting the Twinkie with a knife and fork. I stared until I realized I was staring. "What did you think of Ms. Cintos?"

"I like her. She's a friend of someone I used to know." The kettle whistled; I got up, took out two mugs for hot chocolate.

"Is that what you guys were talking about while I was waiting in the parking lot?"

"Sort of. Yeah. Not exactly, but sort of."

He speared a piece of Twinkie with his fork. "You know, Art's dad hates her."

"Why?" I wasn't very surprised by that: James can be a bigot. Says evil stuff about people for no reason. I mean, he's my buddy and all. But he's still a bigot. He probably hated Terry just because she's black.

"One time, I was over at Art's. And his dad got so angry! Because Art hadn't told his dad that Ms. Cintos is black. Only, you know what?" He got up, put his plate in the sink; I handed him a mug, settled back into the brown chair while he lay on the floor in front of the TV.

"Hand me that box, will you?" He passed me the microwave carton. "Go on. You were saying?"

"My mom says there should be more black teachers at Wylie. She thinks it's racist. The whole school, I mean. But she said something else, too, only I wasn't supposed to tell anyone, but I can tell you, I think, because my mom really likes you."

"Your mother's a good woman. Decent and smart."

"Yeah, she's pretty cool. My dad's an asshole, but Mom is good as moms go. But hey. So I'm gonna tell you something but you have to promise not to tell."

"Scout's honor." I wasn't ever a scout but it's just an expression.

"Mom told me one time? That Ms. Cintos is a lesbian. Like, you know when people say 'fag'? It's like that, only for girls. But you can't tell, because she looks like everybody else."

I tested the chocolate with my finger. It was still too hot. Had Dell known that Terry was a lesbian? What would she have thought? It wasn't the kind of thing Dell and I ever talked about, so I didn't have a clue. But I felt scared for Terry then. Had she tried to hide it from Dell? Would Dell still have been her friend if she'd known?

"So what do you think?" Joey had the same expression on his face that he got when he swore.

I put a spoonful of ice cream into my hot chocolate. I've been afraid of being called a faggot before, but what would it mean? Love is something hard to shake. Someone can't just push beauty from their hearts or legs that easily. What opens to you, opens. So I told Joey that I liked Terry, didn't think it rightly mattered much either way. I told him, Terry is a fine woman. Let her be your friend.

"She is." He took a sip from his mug. "That's what Mom says, too. Only thing is, with Art? It's hard. Because his dad is mean about Ms. Cintos, so Art has to pretend he doesn't care so much about her, or about drama." Even with the lamp on, the trailer was shadowed, but I could see enough of his face to sense that he was getting serious on me. "But Art does care; he cares about Ms. Cintos, and he cares about acting. He wants to go to college, study drama like Ms. Cintos did. And she's coaching him on the side, in secret so his dad doesn't find out. You know what?" He rubbed the skin under his ear. "Art's good. He's really, really good at acting. You think I'm good, but no way, not compared to Art."

"Is he better than Ophelia was today?"

Joey gestured with his sloppy hands. "Way better than Maura Michaels. Like, a hundred thousand times. He's the greatest. One time? We were at his place, when his dad was gone. And he dressed up in one of his dad's suits, and he did Hamlet, and I did Horatio. He looked really good, like a prince is supposed to look. It was at the end—when Hamlet's dying—and it was so awesome."

"You two are pretty good pals, huh?"

"He's my best. Why? I mean, why do you ask?" The tone of his voice then had changed.

"No reason. Just that it's a good thing to have a friend in this world." I took the empty mugs and bowl into the kitchen. "That's all."

The next night was another late call, but the night after was my dinner with Terry Cintos. She'd said she'd cook something for us, and told me where she lived, but the address had rubbed off the back of my hand. So I looked it up. It was funny, because her number was circled in red ink in the old phone book. There it was, another little thing Dell had left behind. And I'd never have found it unless Joey had stayed over and I'd gone to see him be Guildenstern and met his drama teacher who was Dell's only friend. I cut the page out, looked the circle over carefully. It was shaped almost like a mouth. I copied down Terry's number and address and threw the page in the trash. Most of the numbers were old anyhow; I needed to do something about getting a new phone book.

After I'd called her to find out what time I should be there, I changed into my beige slacks and a clean shirt. Then I drove by Wilson's, picked up a loaf of Italian bread. Figured she could save it if it didn't go with the stuff she was making. I started to get nervous then, the way I always do when I get invited places. Mostly I worry that people will have wine or beer and ask me if I want any and then I'll have to say no and they'll look at me funny. Or at least, I always feel as if they do. I hoped she wouldn't be drinking, or that at least she wouldn't be pushy about it.

Her apartment was in one of the nice complexes, out beyond the mall. I liked the place right away; it suited her. She had soft music on, classical. I handed her the bread, and she seemed so happy with it. I like it when people are pleased with the gifts I give them.

"How does eggplant parmigiana sound?" She led me into the kitchen, which smelled like basil. "If that's no good, we can call for take-out."

I laughed 'til I read her face and realized that she was serious. Then I moved to reassure her, but she stopped me.

"Don't. I know, I'm being silly." She turned back to a square of mozzarella she was slicing on a thick wooden cutting board. "I'm nervous, OK? You're the closest thing to Dell that's left on this earth, and you really, really make me nervous."

I stood with my hands by my sides, quiet. What do you say to that? The knife made little "thunk" sounds against the wood.

"Copeland." She handed me the knife. "You do it, OK? I'm going to fix this bread, make a garlic loaf. How did you know to bring Italian?" She opened the refrigerator, then started back up with her thoughts on Dell, nerves, and me, as if she hadn't interrupted herself. I felt as if I'd walked into a conversation that had been going on for hours; it had that sort of an intensity to it. That was when I realized why Dell had liked her, why she'd liked Dell. Because Terry was the only other person I'd ever met who could do what Dell did: dive right into the deepest level of talk, and push past where people usually go. Mostly, when you talk to someone, even someone you're close to, you start out on the surface, and move real slowly down to what matters. It's like digging, and it takes a while. But with Dell, and now Terry, there wasn't any surface, and there wasn't any second, third, or fourth layer, either. It was like starting somewhere near the bottom, or what you thought was the bottom, only it never turned out to be; that was the extra thing. Because she always took you somewhere further, past bottom, past rock.

I used to wonder how Dell stood living, because she always started from a different place than everyone else. She couldn't do surface even if she tried, and I know, because I've seen her try. She looked awkward, sounded fake; I remember going to some party with Dell, watching her try to make small talk, chat about the weather, sports, TV shows. She couldn't do it, just planted herself on a chair at the far end of the room 'til I came by and we went home. She was shaking when she got inside the car; I even had to drive. I sometimes wondered what it would be like to live near the bottom all the time, because living with Dell wasn't the same thing as being Dell. Sometimes she just looked so scary, like her nerves were all on the outside of her skin. I guess part of the problem was that she could see into people, almost see through them. But no one ever seemed able to see through her.

"That's why I asked you to dinner. It seems important, doesn't it?"

I'd missed what Terry was saying, dreaming of Dell. It seemed OK just to tell her that I'd spaced out, so I did. She walked over to me, put her hands on my shoulders. I could smell the wool of her sweater. Her fingers gripped so hard they almost hurt.

"I said she's not dead for me. I said I need to move on, to let go of her. I thought maybe you could help me."

Help her let go of Dell? "I think you asked the wrong person."

She took two plates from a cabinet, spooned eggplant parmigiana and salad onto both. Pointed towards the bread with her elbow; I picked it up, and we walked into the living room. As she set the plates down on the table, I watched the way her sleeves cupped her wrists. She walked away from me, towards the sofa, snapped on another lamp. I glanced out the window; all I could see was my own face, and the wall behind me.

"Do you still see her?" she asked.

The question hurt, like drinking coffee before it's all the way cooled. I liked Terry, but I liked my secret life with Dell much better, and I wasn't ready to share it with Dell's friend.

"Naw. Not anymore. Maybe the first year. Not anymore."

Then that was all about Dell. It was as if she changed before my eyes, Terry, into someone softer, more delicate. It felt like she was acting; it turned right away from something nervy into an ordinary dinner. Good food, laughter, talk about daily things: her job, my job, Joey, the play. We didn't linger. Everything seemed clocked out. At nineish, after a small slice of cheesecake, I moved to go, and she didn't stop me.

But as I walked over to the couch to pick up my coat, I looked at the art work on the walls for the first time. There was a sketch of a black woman in a blue robe holding a baby, a poster featuring two men in old-fashioned costumes standing in profile with their backs to each other, the words *Foster College Shakespeare Festival* printed across the bottom, and a small painting done in blues, deep greens, black, and a little grey—three women facing each other in a circle. She caught me staring.

"Which picture do you like best?"

"This one," I pointed to the women in the circle. She smiled.

"Yes. That was Dell's favorite, too."

I slipped my coat on; then suddenly she was beside me, reaching for the picture of the women.

"Here." She thrust it at me. "I want you to have this."

I pulled my hands towards my waist. No way. I couldn't take someone's things like that.

"No, really. Thank you, but I can't."

"Dell would've wanted you to have it."

"No, I really just can't."

"Take it." She held the painting out to me; suddenly I had a question for her, something I wished I'd asked earlier in the evening, before I lied to her, and told her I wasn't still seeing Dell. I realized looking at the painting that Terry had spent time alone with Dell, time I couldn't ever recreate for myself. I wanted to know what she knew about Dell that I didn't. What did it mean that Dell had liked this picture best, and never told me about it?

My hands were flat, turned up, lying on air as if on a table. The painting lay across them like a knife across a plate. I gripped the frame, lifted the scene to my face, inhaled, but couldn't smell paint or wood or canvas. Nothing. I smelled nothing. Up close, the paint was just little dabs and dashes, blurry, a meaningless jumble of color.

"It's not three women." I looked Terry in the eye. "It's just paint. There aren't any women here at all."

When I got home, Joey was lying stretched on the floor in front of the television, watching MTV without the sound.

"Copeland." He didn't look up. "Make yourself at home."

I walked over to him, tapped him on the back. "Take a look." I showed him the painting.

"What's it of? Looks like splotches to me." But he helped me find a nail, and watched while I positioned it on the wall above the table in the kitchen. After that, we sat together in the living room for a few, watching dancers and guitars swoop and crinkle on screen. A big tall man in a skin tight dress spiked his way across a highway. He looked so happy, there beside the trucks, in his platform heels and pink feather boa. The next song took place in a desert; someone set up a tow truck and hung a disco ball from the metal arm. Under the glittery flecks, about a million people danced while snakes and cactuses watched with eyes that gleamed and shot sparks. Then I went to sleep, and dreamed of knocking over the plant on the TV stand again and again, trying each time to untangle the roots. It was as if my brain was stuck on instant replay. When I woke up, Joey was already gone; he'd set out the cereal box for me as usual, only this time the note read, "I like the picture better in daylight."

Two days later was the dress rehearsal for *Hamlet*; the next night was the performance. As the dress rehearsal approached, Joey began wandering around the trailer reciting lines aloud, acting out almost every part in the play, men and women both. That's when I noticed something odd: he'd read me bits of Ophelia, Hamlet, Horatio, Gertrude, Claudius, Polonius, Laertes. But never Guildenstern, or Rosencrantz, for that matter. Finally, I got so curious I had to ask.

"You've got Hamlet and Horatio down pat. But why no Guildenstern? Don't you need to practice your own lines a little?"

He ran his fingers through the bangs that covered most of his face. "Art and I made a pact not to practice our real lines with anyone except each other and Ms. Cintos, because we want to be totally focused on what we're doing when we're Guildenstern and Rosencrantz. This other stuff? It's fun for me, and it's good practice, but it's not real, it's not about being Hamlet or Gertrude, it's about making my voice do what it's supposed to. When I practice Guildenstern with Art? I try to be him. And Art's Rosencrantz, and it's just the two of us, and we work off each other. Sometimes we get so into it? That we forget who we are, that we're Art and Joey. And it's like the play is us and we can't stop. It's so good then, that sometimes we try imagining what they'd do in other places, like, if they were alive now and went to McDonald's. One time? We went to the mall, only he was Rosencrantz and I was Guildenstern and we walked around being them for a while, bought some stuff and looked at things, but all just like they would in the play. Art calls it getting inside the characters."

"Art sounds very intense." It was hard to imagine any kid of James' being so thoughtful and bright. James ran Carlstown Yellow, and he was my fishing buddy, but he wasn't someone I'd call for smart, or imaginative.

"He is intense. It's like," Joey scratched his nose, "all his nerves are right up on top of his body. I mean, he feels things and gets all excited and everything. That's why he's so good at Hamlet. But sometimes, oh man. This is embarrassing; I can't believe I'm telling you all this." He scratched his nose again. Sitting on the couch, his long arms dangling between his V'd legs, his red bangs falling like fringe over his face, Joey looked like a Sesame Street creation, only with acne and an aura of hormones speckling the image.

"Hey, no sweat; you know I can keep a secret, man to man, all that stuff." But I got up, went into the kitchen, kept my back turned to him. Sometimes it helps to look away when someone wants to show their secrets.

"I know. I mean, I trust you, right? We're pals." He got up, played a little air guitar, sat back down. "Yeah, well, but Art? I think it's hard for Art sometimes, because not many people understand him. And his dad's a dickwad, really mean, and he treats Art's mom like shit, and she's just a doormat who won't do anything about it." He stood up again, put his hands in his pockets. "Art takes things so hard that he gets very down sometimes."

"Dell was that way."

"Dell who?"

I hadn't shown Dell to Joey. He was just a kid; why teach a kid about heartbreak? He'd learn on his own, and I wanted him to know me as someone who had his stuff together, someone in control. Her pictures were up in a couple of places, but he hadn't asked. Probably thought she was my sister.

"Dell was my girlfriend, couple years back." I turned on the water in the sink: end of conversation, I thought. But Joey surprised me; he's pretty clever for a teenager sometimes, and this was one of those times. Because he started pushing me, asking questions, trying to get me to open up. It reminded me of Maureen, the way he did it; with both of them, it was like they actually cared, not like when someone asks, "How are you?" and doesn't want to hear any real kind of an answer. Maureen asked good questions; I just wasn't ready to answer them. But Joey was even more persistent; maybe it was easier for him, because he didn't want anything from me. He just asked out of curiosity. And because I was an adult and he'd be one eventually, I answered him. Maybe he needed to prepare his heart for what would come.

So I brought the boxes into the living room, and we sat on the floor, looking at pictures. He listened while I told the story. It was hard when I got to the semi, but his face scrunched up like he actually cared, so I got through it.

"What was she like? What kinds of stuff did you guys talk about?"

It was hard to describe her, because my memory of Dell living had gotten knotted and tangled with the woman I saw when I closed my eyes. I tried, but I could see he wanted something more. We just sat still for a few minutes, and I got to thinking that maybe I could tell him. Maybe I could explain what happened for me when I closed my eyes in the brown chair.

But he beat me to it.

"Do you ever still see her? I mean, not like a ghost but inside your head, or in your imagination, or whatever." He put the lid back on one of the boxes. "Because when dad left? Mom kept seeing him after. We'd be having dinner, and she'd get this funny expression on her face, look over at the front door like she just knew it was going to open, and be him again. Only it never was."

"How old were you when it happened?"

"Eight. It wasn't even a divorce, not at first. He just took off one day, didn't leave a note or anything. Only way Mom knew he wasn't coming back was that he'd taken a whole bunch of stuff from the house. She drove into the garage, saw that the cardboard boxes from moving the year before were gone, and just freaked out. I was in the car and she started crying and I didn't know what the fuck was happening and she acted like I wasn't even there. Just turned the engine off, sat in the car, and cried. We didn't even eat that night. She forgot all about me, pretty much, and I was just a kid."

I touched his shoulder. "Go on. Tell me the rest of the story."

But that was enough, or too much. "Nothing else." He stood up, went into the kitchen, put on the kettle. "Want some hot chocolate?"

I collected the photographs, put them back in the boxes. "No, I think I'm gonna hit the sack."

"Yeah, me too, I'm pretty tired. But Copeland," he sloshed water around in the kettle, "you didn't answer about Dell. Do you still see her?"

I didn't speak, just listened to the sounds the trailer made, keeping itself going. I wasn't ready to give up what I had.

He didn't wait for an answer. "Don't think this is wu-wu or anything, but I have this friend, Gaby, who's really into séances. She had a party last month and me and Art went and we had a summoning for a lot of really interesting dead people. She had this Ouija board? And when we sat around with our hands under it, it spelled out Kurt Cobain's name. So we knew we were onto something. Hey, what if we tried summoning Dell? Just you and me; Art and Gaby wouldn't have to come. We could just try it and see what happens and maybe I'll get to meet her, too."

I laughed. "Joey, I'm a grown-up. Grown-ups don't have séances."

He did something I'd never seen a kid do then: his whole body curved inwards, and his face went slack. He looked like a funeral.

"Yeah, I know it, I'm just a stupid kid. Do you think I don't know it?" He picked up the kettle, and poured water too quickly into a mug. The steam spilled, and the water splashed his hand, and he cried out, and I dropped the boxes on the table, walked over to him, put my hands on his shoulders and just stood, not watching as he cried, dribbling tears onto the still-red rings of the stove burner. "I'm just a stupid kid," but the words came out choked and sloppy.

"Joey, you're not stupid, and you're not a kid. You're a guy, we're pals, and it's been great having another man around. When your mom comes, it's gonna be hard for me to go back to living by myself." I started out saying it because it felt like I should, but as soon as the words escaped my lips I realized that they were true. I'd miss him. He was a smart young man, a decent young man; he brightened up the place. I wished for a son, then, a son that Dell and I had made between us, but instead I had this small time with Joey, and it wasn't going to be enough. Not for either one of us.

"Look, let's have a séance. You're right, it'd be a good thing to do." I agreed. He wiped his nose on his sleeve, pulled away from my hands. "Sure, let's do it. A séance. Who knows what could happen, who could show up? I like it. When?"

He'd stopped crying, but was facing away from me. I waited for him to decide to forgive me.

"Not tomorrow night; it's the dress rehearsal. And the next night is the show."

"How about after that?"

"That's the night Mom comes back."

I'd forgotten. "That doesn't matter, does it? It'll just have to be an early evening séance, instead of the midnight special. Deal?"

"Deal." We shook on it.

The night of the play, I wanted to take Joey out to dinner beforehand, but he insisted on getting to the auditorium an hour early. We arrived at five-thirty; the doors were still locked, so we sat outside. While we waited, Joey ran through his lines, Art's, and some of Horatio's for good measure. When I saw Terry's car pull into the lot, I stood and clapped.

"Bravo," I yelled; I'm not sure why. There was a woman with Terry; as they approached us, talking and laughing, I saw the woman's hand graze Terry's back. It made me wonder if I would ever start to know her in a real way, or if, now that the connection Dell had been was broken, Terry and I would get stuck, not close enough to count for friends, but not distant enough to be acquaintances. I figured I wouldn't know for a while to come.

Terry introduced us to Jane while she unlocked the auditorium doors. I watched the easy way they moved together, the way they shared space. Jane was short and plump and so pretty. She had on a long green-and-black striped dress, a black hat shaped like a box, and a yellow scarf wound once around her neck; her skin was very dark, and her eyes were green. When she shook my hand, she looked me straight on for what seemed like minutes, and I had to look away. But it didn't make me uncomfortable, it was pleasurable, just too much for me to start off with. She suited Terry; you could tell right off because of her intensity. Terry seemed almost calm in comparison.

Several more cars pulled up in the lot as Terry opened the doors for us, and we filed into the auditorium. A minute or two later, we heard the strung-out vocal cords of teenaged actors emerging from the top of the stairs behind us; I settled into a seat as Joey ran to meet his buddies. The instant the voices started, the two women's posture and walk shifted ever so slightly. They moved just that much further apart, held their arms closer to their sides, tensed their bodies a fraction. I tried to imagine how my life would feel, lived that way, but couldn't; I have a hard time understanding secrets. Seeing Dell is pretty much the only secret I've ever had of my own, and it's not much of a secret, since it seems everyone can see me seeing her.

I drifted in and out of *Hamlet*, losing track of the plot, missing large parts of the dialogue, trying to isolate what it was I understood about Joey, Terry, Dell. When the curtain fell and the clapping began, I shook myself out of the place I go to do my thinking, and began to worry about what to say to Joey. How to praise him for a performance I hadn't watched? But he'd been excellent; I knew he had, could say that without lying, and I did, and he was so excited that he didn't notice. I took Joey and Art out for pizza; while they ate, they recited lines that had gone awry. At one point, Art's arm made a wide arc, mocking a salute; he'd forgotten that he was holding a slice of pepperoni pizza, and a gob of cheese sailed through the air, landing in Joey's coke. They blew straw wrappers at each other and crumpled handfuls of napkins. When their energy finally began to dim, I took Art home. Margaret was waiting up; I could see her profile through the kitchen window.

Joey was still wired when we got back, so I made a pot of decaf, and took advantage of his energy by suggesting we clean the trailer. We scrubbed, moved furniture, vacuumed, even dusted, 'til about three A.M. Sunday morning. I didn't have to drive; when I finally woke up, Joey was scrambling eggs and scraping off pieces of burned toast.

"Eat a lot," he said. "Today's the séance."

Between the excitement of the performance and his mother's return, I'd been hoping he'd forget about ghosts, Ouija boards, and Kurt Cobain. But after we ate, before I even had a chance to look at the newspaper, he pulled out a notebook, and began planning stuff. We'd start at six, because the number had some sort of significance,

I forget what. We'd sit on the floor, making the best circle two people could manage; in front of us we'd arrange things that reminded me of Dell, things she would recognize. Then we'd close our eyes, clasp hands, say her name six times out loud. We'd try to summon up the woman in the photograph, concentrating so hard that, if she was anywhere at all, she'd be sure to feel us.

I wanted to do Joey a favor, to play along so that he wouldn't feel I was making a distinction between boy and man. Too, I wanted to end his visit on a high note, let him feel he'd left me with something I could keep. Soon, Maureen would honk the horn, stop by for half an hour or so to chat and thank me, and then Joey would disappear. I didn't want to think about cooking for just one person, talking to the television, knowing things would be exactly where I'd left them when I got home late in the evening. But Joey and I hadn't talked about it, hadn't discussed whether we'd make plans to see each other again.

What was there to say?

That afternoon, when Joey went down to the gym to play basketball, I sat in the brown chair and closed my eyes, not to conjure Dell, but to prepare my mind for the emptiness to come. I tried to imagine what to say to Maureen when she arrived. She'd called Joey several times; her voice made me think that things with her mother were stressful. I wondered what her face would look like, how she'd move, who she'd be after the trip. I thought back to the dates we'd had, tried to remember why I hadn't stayed in touch with her. As I sat in the chair, I remembered the way telling Dell's story to Jody Phelps had brought the old grief back in long, choking waves, and how I'd simply holed up in the trailer, not talking to anyone.

Had I hurt Maureen? I remembered one night we'd gone out to eat at Sam's Deli. I'd been fairly sure up 'til then that I didn't feel passionate about her. She was pretty and all, very pretty in fact: reddish gold hair just going grey, long and curly past her shoulders, wide blue eyes and lots of freckles. She wore big flowing pants, usually black, with billowy shirts, very bright, soft-looking. But when I thought of passion, I thought of Dell's hands on my body that first night, of sitting on the stoop beside her watching the way she bit her lower lip when she looked up at the sky. "Gonna rain," she'd say, and I'd have to turn to hide my wanting face. With Maureen, I just liked looking; I never needed to touch. But that night? She was studying the menu, and brushed her hair across her shoulder with one hand. I got stuck staring at her neck, and the line of bone just before her shoulders; there was a moment when I felt dizzy inside, like falling, and almost reached out to touch her. Then I caught myself, my hand halfway across the table, and picked up the sugar shaker, and poured sugar into my coffee, a long stream, dumping in two creamers for good measure, just in case she'd thought my hands were thinking of doing anything else. The whole dinner was pretty much like that, but when I got home I sat right in the brown chair and summoned Dell's face. Asked for forgiveness. After that, I tried not to look too long or too hard at Maureen Cleary, because it always started to feel like falling, and falling felt like cutting Dell's face with a razor.

So I sat in the chair, thinking about things I might do to visit with Joey: fishing, driving practice, hiking or hunting if he had a mind to it. But my thoughts slid like smooth soles on ice, and I found myself thinking about Joey's mom, first worrying for her because of her stressful trip and all, then remembering that night at Sam's Deli, how we'd laughed and talked 'til the sweep-up crew asked us to leave and our legs shook from sitting for so long. Then something happened, and it confused me, because the brown chair is where I sit to be with Dell, to see her face and remember what she gave me. But as I sat thinking about Maureen, I saw the curves her throat made, and the red of her hair in the light, and the way her shirt made a V at the neck. Then I heard tires screeching, and shook my head alert as footsteps found their way to the door, and the door rattled, and Joey came in, his boat-sized sneakers shaking the floor slightly. He threw his sweatshirt over the couch, headed straight for the kitchen, drank three glasses of water, and opened the refrigerator door.

"Damn, Copeland, did we really finish off all that pie?"

I stood up, remembering who he was: Maureen's boy, this stranger who'd begun to feel familiar. I reached over his bulky boy-head for the empty pie box.

"Guess so. But I can grill up a burger, if you want."

I completely forgot about apologizing to Dell.

It was running on five; we ate, and then Joey pushed the couch and TV back against the wall while I searched through my bedroom for pictures and things. I found what I wanted quickly: my favorite snapshot, the one where her hair is all loose, barely out of her eyes, held back with those barrettes she liked, one on either side just above her ears. I wanted to use the Foster cap she wore nearly every day in the months before she died, but that's the one thing of Dell's I never could find in the messy pile of things she left behind. So instead I took a toothpick wrapped in plastic, the kind she used to scoop up by the handful from Sam's Deli, and the Clapton tape I'd found in her car the day we'd first driven to the office together. The tape had come unwound; the ribbon lay in a tangled double loop, like a figure eight. I carried everything into the living room; Joey had turned the lights off and opened the door an inch or two, not wide enough to see in, but enough to let in a breeze, "and anything that wants to visit."

"Sounds good to me," but I bit down on the inside of my lower lip to keep from laughing. He was a kid, Joey; just fourteen. I had to keep reminding myself of that, because sometimes he just plain acted old. But then his goofy arms would fly up and he'd knock something over, or he'd rub his pimples and look anxious, or he'd do something preposterous, like plan a séance, and I'd remember that he wasn't really a man yet. Just smart, kind, and creative for his age, and resourceful: things Maureen had given him.

It was hard to imagine any man leaving the two of them: a decent, pretty lady, smart and warm, and a goofy, good, bright kid the two of them had made together. It boggled my mind. It must've hurt beyond measure, like when Dell died, only more tangled, because Dell was gone from this world for sure. She wasn't coming back, séance or no séance. But Joey's father? He could reappear at any moment. Had she waited up for him, those first few weeks, thinking he'd be back? How long had it taken her to know that gone was gone? I thought about the puns she made when she was excited, and the way she explained things to me when I asked questions about stuff she knew: computers, Irish folk music, birds. How could anyone leave them behind? Joey's dad wouldn't know that his son's feet were like boats, that he had big ears and fiery hair, liked acting, liked Art, and wanted to be nicknamed Horatio. The clock would be frozen for him, stiff hands stuck on the minute and hour that he left the house, as if stopped on impact.

I put Dell's photograph face down on the carpet with the tooth-pick and the tape on either side. Joey and I sat facing each other; the room wasn't quite dark, but getting there. I heard the highway for a moment, and thought about the way sounds move in and out of con-sciousness, becoming white noise, then careening trucks, then white noise again. When Joey gave the signal, I closed my eyes, listening as he began to speak: not Dell's name, as I'd expected, but a poem, maybe a song. I didn't understand the words at first—he was mumbling low in his throat—but soon they took shape and became a child's rhyme: something about a fox, something about a forest. When Joey finished, I opened my eyes to find him looking at a photograph.

"This is him." He let it drop to the floor; I picked up a dog-eared snapshot of a tall, thin man in jeans and a camouflage jacket, stand-ing beside a car, one hand on the hood. He wasn't smiling, but his face was relaxed; he looked pleased with himself.

"Your father." It wasn't a question, but Joey nodded anyway. "It's him you want to summon, isn't it?"

He didn't say anything, just took the photo from my hands and put it beside Dell's picture. When he began mumbling again, I let myself see what was printed on the inside of my lids: a deep black, blacker than black, with faint light spots that shifted slightly. Then the noise of the highway flickered back, and the sounds of the kids next door playing with their dog on the narrow rectangle of grass between our trailers. I could feel sweat starting on my palms; the room was too warm, and my knees hurt from sitting on the floor. The dog barked three times, loud and short; tires screeched right out front. Joey's breath and my own. A car door opening. Footsteps. The rattle of the screen, and the door creaking. My eyes flickered open; as they adjusted, I saw that the doorway framed a body, its outline etched against the blue and black of nightfall in the trailer park. It wasn't Dell, because Dell was gone. It was someone else, maybe a mother, maybe a woman just looking, or looking for some-one she'd lost or left behind.

CHAPTER 7

Maureen

FOR almost two weeks I forgot all about being somebody's mother and became a daughter again, holding my body in the old way, using the cadences and slang of my girlhood. The house smelled the same as it always had, of the commingled scents of lemon furniture polish and yeasty bread. The plaster clowns on the shelves wore the same wan smiles, the porcelain ballerinas still held their legs stiffly in attitude and arabesque, and the gold enamelled plates were stacked neatly inside the glass display case, as if awaiting company that would never come.

No boxes.

That was the first thing I noticed when Ma and I got back from the hospital, and the first thing I set out to remedy. I fixed her up fine in bed, toast and tea within easy reach, telephone beside her on the pillow, magazines stacked on top of the covers.

"Ma, I'm going to buy some boxes."

Her nose was buried in a magazine; she didn't seem to have heard me. I put my hand on the doorknob.

"Maureen Cleary." Her very voice. What is it in a mother's tone that tells us who we were, yet keeps from us the knowledge of how to get back to that old self again?

"You needn't waste your hard-earned money buying piles of cardboard. Plenty of boxes to be had in the attic. Plenty to be had." She poked her nose back in the magazine; I put my hand on the doorknob again, twisted it to the right.

"Maureen." The voice stopped me; I was frozen, age thirteen again. "I need some tea, but how's a body to pour when one hand's swaddled like a newborn thing?" She sighed, and the sound was like curtains. "I need you to pour for me. For your poor mother." Pouting. I fixed a cup for her: sugar, and a dash of cream. I knew what to do for her, because she was my mother.

"Not so much!"

I didn't know what to do for her, because she was my mother.

Boxes in the attic, yes, but they weren't empty: yards of babies' lace, crumbling letters, newspaper clippings. Dusty, broken china; dresses hand-made for bodies now dead.

I drove to Packages Plus, a tiny stucco bungalow with a bright orange roof, and filled the back of my rented two-door with cardboard. I bought four rolls of masking tape, and wore them home, two on each arm, like bangles.

When I arrived, there were five cars in the driveway. Five? What sort of emergency would need five cars? I flew through the door, my voice spreading my mother's name like light from a beacon, clutching my purse, heading towards the stairs. Where was safe? Who was safe?

They stared at me, the grey ladies. Six heads looked me over from above china cups. Two blue dresses, one purple pantsuit, one skirt and sweater set, one pair of jeans and a red sweatshirt with PETA in black letters, and Ma, in her peach quilted robe, with matching fuzzy slippers.

"Maureen Cleary. Why ever must you hurry so? You might slip on the stairs and fall."

Laughter from the purple pantsuit, laughter from one of the blue dresses.

"Have a cup of tea. My gardening club's come to visit; they're fixing dinner for me. Would you like to join us? It'll be..." Ma paused, glanced at the PETA sweatshirt.

"Vegetable stir-fry with tofu, and wild rice."

I lied smoothly, like a teenager. "No, thanks. Claire Morgall invited me to dinner when I ran into her a few minutes ago."

I ate at McDonald's, because I couldn't bear to watch my mother eating with her friends. It seemed indecent.

Would their hands shake as they spooned food to their lips?

Did they eat tiny portions, and feel bloated afterwards?

I ate two burgers, a large serving of fries, and an apple pie. I wolfed my food, pretending eating was a gift that could never be taken away.

Did they dab their napkins at their lips, as if their flesh was too fragile for cloth?

That night I dreamed I was standing at the foot of the stairs, preparing to climb. I put my left hand on the banister, my right foot on the first step. Then something flew towards me from above; I shielded my eyes, but it hit the side of my face, wet and slick: a photograph, only partially developed and smelling of chemicals. When I lifted it to my eyes to try to discern the picture, my own face stared back: it had become a mirror.

Coffee, toast, and eggs were arranged on the table when I made my way down the next morning, wet from my shower. I felt I should have on my school skirt, a cross nestled precariously between my breasts. It was hard to imagine how she'd managed the meal with a single hand; then I heard voices from the living room, and realized she hadn't.

The grey ladies entered the kitchen in single file. Today, there were three dresses, all polyester blends, a zip-front jogging suit, cotton slacks and a terrycloth top, and Ma, in her blue quilted robe with matching fuzzy slippers.

Dad had given her the same robe three years running; when I asked her if she minded, she tilted her head. "Just so long as he doesn't do it on purpose." Hard to tell, though, since the colors were all different.

"Fine morning, isn't it, Maureen." Ma motioned towards the eggs and toast; I helped myself to a plate.

"Fine morning to you, Ma." I drizzled salt onto my palm, then onto my eggs. "And to the club." They hadn't heard me, though; they were busy munching, cleaning, chatting, and caring for Ma, who was seated at the head of the table. They knew what to do for her, because she was their friend. No one paid any attention to me; I felt I'd gone invisible.

They were thick friends, the grey ladies: all of them widowed or divorced; not one of them Catholic but Ma. The latter surprised me; when she first joined the club years back, I asked her if it bothered her to work with women she'd always called "non-believers." My mother startled me then, giving a long speech about tolerance and difference. It was the first of a series of seemingly sudden transformations and turnabouts. She didn't renounce her faith; said she preferred to think of herself as "expanding it." She continued to attend Sunday Mass, but in her daily life she followed different orders, arranging her life in patterns I could no longer predict. In her sixties, my mother had become a free spirit.

I shouldn't have been so surprised when, almost two years after my father died, after mourning herself thin and worn and nearly speechless, my mother called me one evening to say that she'd had an epiphany. My mother had often had epiphanies in the past, usually about new ways to fit the Virgin's teachings into her life, or how to spice a meatloaf properly, or how to re-do the furniture in the guest room so that the scuff marks on the dresser didn't show. But this epiphany was startling, the more so since she herself didn't seem to see anything extraordinary in it.

"Maureen, Mary Winston had a supper party last week, and introduced me to a very pleasant man, name of Joshua Borders."

I remember thinking how nice it would be if Ma began dating again, "taking the air," like her widowed or divorced lady friends, who were dutifully courted by grey-bearded, gentle old men whose hands stayed put, and who appreciated country-style dinners and evening Mass.

"Mr. Borders came to call this afternoon, and we decided to embark on an affair."

At first her words didn't strike me, so often did we use the same words to mean different things. I assumed that "affair" in my mother's parlance meant "somebody's sixtieth birthday party," or "visit to a restaurant that serves bland and spongy food." It didn't occur to me that the word "affair" might mean to Ma what it meant to me.

"That's nice."

"Yes, isn't it?" We talked a bit longer, about the weather, Joey, neighborhood gossip, then hung up.

Two weeks later, I called early in the morning and got Joshua Borders. When I asked to speak to Deirdre, he said, "Certainly." Ma's voice came on the line almost immediately.

"Hello, dear."

"Am I interrupting anything?" I didn't really expect an answer.

"Yes. Could you call back in about an hour?" In the background, I could hear Joshua cough. When I called back and asked how their breakfast had gone, she corrected me gently.

"Oh, we weren't having breakfast. We were making love."

I held the phone at arm's length while my mouth decided what sound to make; "um-hmm" was what eventually came out. Then she began talking about the weather, Joey, neighborhood gossip. That was when I had an epiphany of my own: my mother was a tease.

After that, I hesitated to call; it seemed every time I rang, Joshua answered, and Ma asked if I could call back later. When I suggested one day that she get an answering machine, she just laughed.

"It's much more fun this way."

Maybe for you, I thought, but I really don't want to hear about it. "Are you planning to marry?" It didn't seem out of the question; why should they wait? Gather ye rosebuds while ye may, and all that. But the question was met with silence, then a burst of hearty laughter.

"Oh, no, my dear, I've done that already. This isn't about marriage, it's about sex."

What could I say? I asked her if she took precautions, and she giggled. I asked her if she was worried about heartbreak, and she giggled. I asked her what the neighbors might think, and she giggled, wished me "God Bless," and hung up. When Joey arrived home some forty-five minutes later, I was still sitting at the kitchen table, doodling absently on a pad of scratch paper. When he asked how I was doing, I simply threw my hands up, and started dinner. How to explain that I was jealous of my own mother?

After Eric left us, there was no one for so long. At first it didn't matter; I felt sure he'd come back eventually. But I moved slowly from knowing to hoping to worrying; time came when my heart discovered that he wasn't ever coming back, and that if he did, I wouldn't have him. That was the biggest realization: that my husband could never come back, not really, because he'd be a different man for me now, someone whose potential beauty or justice or love would always be tainted. Someone I could never trust. At that point, I began to mourn, as if for the dead, which for all I know he really is. That took time, too, so it was a long while before I began to think about finding someone new. When James offered to fix me up with Cope, I resisted; I wasn't sure I was ready. I wasn't sure I wanted anyone, except maybe to help with Joey.

Cope changed things.

Written into the way he moved were letters, and those letters spelled *safe*. Safe was what I wanted. Oh, I'd had passion, and could find it again, if I wanted to. But passion wasn't what I was after, not in the first place, anyway. I wanted someone I could wake up to knowing his heart was in the same place I'd left it the night before.

I wanted someone scared by the sight of boxes. That was Cope: a driver whose cab went in circles, not straight lines. But Cope stopped making me and Joey his destination after only about two months, leaving me sick at heart, mourning for a man so caught up in his own grief that he couldn't see the wreckage he'd left behind. He simply stopped calling one day; I tried ringing him up but he never answered. Pretty soon I decided to stop pretending before I'd started.

I didn't need him.

I just wanted him.

It was the way he clung to Dell's memory. Loyalty's a beautiful thing, like a painting; Cope's was some Renaissance master's opus, all deep browns and burgundies, lush brushstrokes invisible beneath the satiny surface. I wanted that for myself, only in living colors; what I didn't realize at first was that Cope's loyalty to Dell was precisely the problem: it kept him from seeing me. I understood, though. For a long time after Eric left, I stayed loyal to the one thing I thought he might come back for: a dull brown cardboard box, the ordinary kind, with beige tape holding the pleated sides together, and *Kitchen—Appliances* scrawled on the top and sides.

Three days after Joey's seventh birthday, we moved from the cramped apartment we'd shared since our marriage into a rented house: a small brick two-bedroom on Chelsea Drive. The move was easy; it was unpacking that was hard. We couldn't agree on where to put anything: not one piece of furniture, not a single spoon. We began by bickering over which room should be ours, and which should be Joey's, and moved slowly through the entire house, arguing about the placement of every single one of our possessions. It took more than two months for us to unpack; I spent the mornings of those months shading beige foundation and powder over the black and blue residues of Eric's temper. Each time we'd finish a box, Eric would vacuum the insides with a Dustbuster, tape the top, and place it in the right corner of the garage. "For the next move," he'd say, and I'd nod without asking what he meant. We'd planned to live in the Chelsea house 'til Joey went off to college, to put at least a decade of our lives into that house, letting each room accumulate ten years' worth of stories, whispered gossip, lovemaking. We'd planned to watch Joey grow through awkwardness into the poised, dependable, ethical young man we were certain our son would be.

We'd planned a life the way you plan a road trip: dotting the map with certain stops, pencilling in possible detours.

Then one day I pulled the car into the garage, and all the boxes were gone. I knew without having to look what else was missing.

Those first few months were hell, because I wouldn't let myself know that he was gone for good. I made every sound into the music of his return, every letter his handwriting, every ring of the phone his voice waiting to reconnect with mine. I'd sit and stare, willing the doorknob to turn under the pressure of his callused palms. I ignored Joey, partly because it hurt too much to see that mixture of my features and Eric's etched into the skin of someone wholly new, and partly just because I neglected everything that had ever loved me back. What was hardest was not being able to communicate with Eric: at least to call, or send a postcard. But the past was flattened beneath the soles of his travelling shoes, and the future a great blank space where a map should've been. There was no way to reach him, no tracing a face that threatened rapidly to turn to memory.

About a month after he'd gone, I did a sloppy job of parking the car in the garage one evening, and had to climb over the passenger's seat to get out the other side. That was when I realized that he'd left one box, pushed almost out of sight behind the tool bench.

One box.

Would he come back for it?

I took it inside with me, carried it to my bedroom, and waited until I could hear Joey snoring through the adjoining wall. Then I undid the tape sealing the top. Inside, it was vacuumed clean like the rest: no shreds of paper, no plastic bubbles, no shards of china or metal shavings. Clean; I ran my hands along the sides and bottom, letting my fingers explore each crevice and corner. Then I took off my clothes, crawled into bed, and brought the box with me, letting the open end rest across my torso, so that it covered my chest and hips, stopping halfway to my knees.

I put one hand inside the box, felt the way the air hung stagnant, smelled the dampness the cardboard walls exhaled. Then I let my fingers rest lightly on the top of my thighs. Closing my eyes, I found Eric's face; because I did not want Joey to hear me if he woke, I clenched my mouth shut, even as I came, letting my legs and hips speak their fill to the mattress's coiled springs. It was the first time

I'd allowed myself to imagine Eric inside of me since he'd gone, and I pretended that the slight weight of the box and the faint pain of its edges digging into my clavicle and the round columns of my thighs were his weight and raspy nails. Beneath that box, I couldn't move from side to side, could only press my hips deeper and deeper into the mattress; I couldn't cry out, could only bite the insides of my lips to remind me to seal my mouth. When it was over, I wiped the wetness on my fingers along the sides and top of the box, then put on my robe and carried it back to the garage, leaving it exactly where I'd found it.

If he ever came back for it, he'd take me with him.

But he never did, and the box grew moldy around the edges as the seasons shifted, and finally I junked it, tearing off the tape all around, folding it flat, setting it out beside the garbage can for the trash collectors to inherit. Three years after driving into that unboxed garage, I got a call from my lawyer, who'd been contacted by a lawyer out in Reno, Nevada. Eric kept his own whereabouts secret, but had the dignity to sign divorce papers, and send them on. "Till death do us part" was erased via Federal Express; I went to an office one afternoon on my lunch break, signed on the dotted line, and returned to work more or less a single woman. I changed my name, and Joey's, almost immediately: Cleary, not my maiden name, but my mother's.

When Joshua Borders moved to Palm Springs, I expected a similar crisis. I thought she'd pine for him, the way I'd pined for Eric; I half-wished she'd follow him, for I thought that if she were attached to a husband, I'd worry less, feel less responsible if anything happened. But neither one of them seemed interested in continuing what had been, after all, only an affair. They wrote on occasion; if either she or Joshua had taken a new lover, my mother hadn't mentioned it to me. Instead, she'd found the grey ladies; they seemed close as lovers, those six, but without the jealousy. They watched over each other like raggedy angels, giving the impression that they were everything to each other, and that outsiders might be scorned, if not rejected outright.

Watching them caretake Ma, I sensed her deja vu: most of my mother's life had been spent within the circling arms of women. As a girl, she'd attended a convent school along with her twin sister

Eileen. The Cleary's had been firm with the twins: one of them would be a nun, the other would raise a family. Both vocations were about salvation; both were, their parents reminded them, equally necessary and worthy. The problem was, both Deirdre and Eileen wanted to join the sisterhood. Part of it was intimacy; close, like twins often are, the thought of separation burned their hearts like a brand. Moreover, they'd each fallen in love with the calm, predictable life of the convent. The clean, spare walls of the rooms, the scented air, the quietude—all contrasted sharply with the claustrophobic atmosphere of a large working-class family living in near-poverty. The tumult of six brothers, the dry smells of tobacco, rust, onions, and spoiled milk, all made the sterility of the convent seem novel, even elegant. The punishments and constant criticism, the exhaustion of kneeling for hours, the sharp sparks of hunger on fast days, could not deter them from wanting a life that seemed larger than the one they'd live as the wife of a chimney sweep, factory lineman, or milkman. They pleaded with their parents who refused to allow both daughters to vanish behind convent walls. "Choose between yourselves," they said. When the girls would not, could not, their parents approached Sister Joan to make the choice for them.

It was Eileen who got to stay, because it was Eileen whose eyes stayed open all through chapel, Eileen whose Hail Marys were spoken slowly and enunciated distinctly, Eileen who resisted the temptation of "particular friendships," and who'd once broached Sister Joan to ask whether, if she gave up her bread at dinner, she might leave it for the old man who slept on the steps in the summer evenings. Eileen was gentler, closer to godliness; it wasn't a surprise to see her chosen. Yet something happened to my mother when the news found her. She was sweeping the stone walkway that led to the dining room when Sister Joan approached her. As the nun took the broom from Deirdre's hand, and placed one palm on her shoulder, my mother claims she felt and heard something snap. It was as if she'd been holding one end of a rubber band, and the girl on the other side had let go of her stretched end. When she met Eileen filing from chapel into dinner, the two turned their heads away from each other at the same instant, without any sort of signal given. They did not speak at dinner; nor did they speak washing up in the bath before bed. The thread that bound them had broken; they no longer felt twinned. When they kissed good-bye the day of Deirdre's leave-taking, their lips tasted cold each to each, and their eyes were flat pools in a drought, no depth to the water beneath.

My mother had been out of the convent for only six months when she was married. Her parents had been making inquiries among their friends and acquaintances; they rapidly settled on the son of one of my grandfather's factory co-workers, Matthew Rourke. During the months of November, December, and January, Matthew was duly invited to Sunday dinner each week; Deirdre cooked, served, and sat without speaking. Matthew himself didn't speak unless spoken to; they were long dinners, slow, awkward, and formal. He was expected to propose mid-January; when he didn't, my grandfather had a talk with Father Rourke, and so one Wednesday evening, towards the end of an especially cold January, Matthew Rourke knocked on the Cleary's door with a bottle of wine in one hand, and a pound of flour in another. The wine was for my grandfather, the flour for my grandmother. He did not go down on his knees, for it was thought to be unnecessarily frivolous, but in his pocket was a tiny silver circlet that refused to fit over my mother's work-swollen knuckle. Her hand had to be greased with lard, and then scrubbed clean with the grainy soap that was usually saved for wash day.

It was neither a hellish nor a heavenly match. My father was not a drunkard, nor a gambler, nor an adulterer; he showed no violence to those within the walls of his home. Yet his ways sometimes seemed unfeeling; before he began working for Ivy Dairy, he'd had a factory line job, and indeed there was something of a machine about him. Watching him butter his bread, you could see that piecework had left a permanent imprint on his gestures; his knife always slid back and forth in the same groove. I suspect that Deirdre often had to remind herself that this man was a creature with appetites like other living beings. There was something cold about him, and distant; his piety nearly, but not quite, made up for his lack of spirit. Yet the first child came along quickly; Luke was born safely within a ten month duration. Five months later, my mother was pregnant again.

Luke's birth had been relatively easy; he was, by all accounts, a cheerful and lively infant. But my mother's second pregnancy was a nightmare; I sometimes dream about a faceless woman bent over a bed crying, and I know that the dream is the impossible memory of the miscarriage that preceded my birth. When she lost her second child, the doctor cautioned her not to become pregnant again, and indeed she and Matthew complied, focusing their energies on care-taking Luke.

As a child, I was once told by an uncle that Luke's death was the catalyst for my birth; there's little to suggest he was wrong. Though the family likes to forget it, Luke's teachers and friends remember him as a rebel; at fifteen, one Saturday night he joined a handful of high school senior boys on the back of a pick-up truck headed for Hideaway Lake. That afternoon and evening, instead of fishing as they'd ostensibly planned, they drank, drank some more, and more, until all the beer cans they'd brought were crushed flat by workboot heels. Then someone—Murph Mullins?—got it into his head to swim; the boys jostled each other into the water, making the motions and gestures drunken wild ones will. There were six of them when they met the water, but by some sorry arithmetic, only five boys' bodies emerged from the lake. They found Luke the next day; they had to drag the lake for the corpse. No one knew why his skinny bones were so far out from shore; the mystery of it lent itself to local legends, so that by the time I was old enough to join the neighborhood kids' games and storytelling, my dead brother's memory had become mythical, and I had to search hard for any history even remotely resembling fact.

Despite doctor's orders, Matthew and Deirdre took comfort in each other's arms after Luke's death; when my mother found her-self pregnant at thirty-nine, she spoke no words of complaint or fear. Yet both she and Matthew expected her to die in childbirth; cer-tainly her doctors feared for her. My mother grew belly-round again, preparing for my birth and her death at the same time. When the both of us lived, Matthew said it was a miracle; the force of his belief propelled Deirdre into something like sainthood in his eyes. And me? I was tended to with care, certainly, yet with something like remorse as well. After all, I came on the wake of Luke's death; too, my parents had spent most of my nine months' evolution resigning themselves to Deirdre's impending death, not to mention my own. I was a surprise, and a happy one, but mourning wreaths were all they'd prepared at home to signal my arrival. To remind them (as if they needed reminding), they gave me a single middle initial, not even a name: *L*, ostensibly for *Love*, but I read it differently: *L* for *Luke*, and also *Loss*.

I grew up an only child in a neighborhood where the next smallest family was five, and to be singular at anything was to feel oneself ostracized. Without siblings to ward off attackers, I was teased and shoved and beaten by my more ferocious classmates; looking back, I wonder what it was that kept me from becoming a fighter myself. I waited for protection; when it failed to come, I retreated into caring for our myriad pets, and reading voraciously. I escaped the only way I knew how. I met Eric at eighteen, at a formal dance given in honor of St. Mary's seniors. I wore a green dress with a matching pocketbook; he had on a red tie, and someone joked about Christmas when they pointed him out. I let my eyes meet his for half a second, then waited for him to walk the long width of the gymnasium floor to ask me to dance in front of my tittering girlfriends. Afterwards, he offered to drive me home; I turned up at his door three months later, pregnant, and, as they say a young man should, he married me.

I knew even less about him than my mother had known about Matthew.

To support a wife and child, Eric gave up on the idea of community college, and moved the three of us to Carlstown, the small city he'd been born in. A friend of his owned a gas station, and right away offered him a full-time job. By the time he left me, he'd become the day manager; he worked hard, Eric, there's no disputing it. After Joey was old enough to go to kindergarten, I found a job as a typist, and eventually, after Eric was gone, as a secretary in a small publishing firm. I got the job by accident, really; underqualified, I was almost turned away, but when the outgoing secretary saw my face, she opened the door again. She was a woman I knew from Joey's day-care center who was leaving the firm because her husband had been transferred to another city. She had a kid at home, too, and I think she could see in my eyes what she might become if her husband ever chose to steal away some night from the house they'd planned to rent in that strange city. Perhaps she read something else there, also; certainly in earlier days it was obvious enough to require make-up and stiff-necked blouses. Eric beat me and I believed in it;

it did not occur to me to protect myself. My world was full of martyrs; to be bruised by love seemed only natural. I wonder sometimes what might have happened if he'd stayed with me, if he hadn't lusted after cardboard boxes, motion, and the mystery he knew he'd leave behind him when he vanished. If he'd stayed, who would I be now? Would I ever have left him?

How deep would his violence have gone?

Hard to explain why I didn't fight back, or walk, Joey in one hand, a suitcase in the other. It had to do with money, with the girl I saw when I looked in the mirror, and with the God I'd been taught to love "like a husband": such blind faith, such dumb devotion. With Eric, bruises became flowers, shouts became sweet boyish whistles. He got me all mixed up; at first, the thing I missed most was the violent tension I'd breathed for eight solid years. In my dreams, I'd miss his arms around me, and then the flat of his palm against my cheek. I missed his cruelty as much as I missed his kindness, and indeed confused them, 'til they were indistinguishable. Not until much later did I begin to allow myself to feel them as separate.

One Saturday night, perhaps two years after Eric's disappearance, I was home alone while Joey spent the night at his friend Art's house. I'd turned on the television, the radio, the tape player; I was washing dishes and wanted to pretend, while I let the water run over my wrists, that the house was occupied again: parents and child all making different noises at once, enjoying the chaos of togetherness. I tried to take in all the noises simultaneously, fighting the urge to isolate one and try to make sense of it. For a moment, the noise enveloped me like a cloak; the water felt close enough to hands to comfort me. Then something harsh—the slap of a screen door, a dog's bark, a passing truck—broke into the enclosure, my right forefinger ached, and I remembered what family actually felt like.

Eric and I were dressing early one morning, maybe a Monday; I was handing him clothes from the chest of drawers on my side of the bed. He was standing beside me; when I reached into the second drawer, rummaged for a pair of socks, he moved like hail, slamming the drawer shut on my hand.

"Who's in charge?" Through the pain of a broken finger, I answered him. He listened, his face impassive. Then he lifted my hand to his lips, let his eyes meet mine.

I waited to see what he would do.

He kissed my finger, then finished dressing. When it came time for his jacket, he asked me to get it from the bathroom, where I'd hung it over the tub to dry.

Then he left for work, leaving me to dress myself, to fix Joey's breakfast, and to drive to my job, where I explained to my boss that I'd slammed my hand in the car door and could I please take an hour to visit the hospital?

Standing by the sink that Saturday in the empty house, feeling water run across my fingers, thinking about Eric's frantic urge to motion, thinking about the light rain of his kisses on my collapsed hand, I suddenly realized what it was that had bound me to him. Always before, I'd seen that Monday's event, and many others like it, as one brief uninterrupted sequence: a camera panning slowly across a single scene. But water, white noise, and some sharp sound triggered recognition. Not one event, but two: breaking my finger and kissing it weren't related. They only seemed so because he'd made their juxtaposition seem normal. It was the mixture that had drawn me to him; I'd become addicted to the reward that always followed his violence, and I could not think of one without the other. Kindness without cruelty to accompany it was not only unreal to me, it was unimaginable. I don't know how long I stood there, letting the recognition become body memory. The new knowledge felt nearly mystical; I housed it beneath the shriveled skin of the scars Eric had left behind.

To my knowledge, Eric never touched Joey; I promised myself a thousand times that if he ever hurt our son, I'd leave my husband. I like to think that's one promise I would've kept. Eric seemed proud of Joey; he joined a father-son program at the local YMCA, took him fishing and sledding, sat up with him when he was sick. It was Eric who insisted I take Joey to Wylie Academy to apply for a scholarship program he'd heard about from the night manager. I resisted at first: why set the kid up to expect wealth, when he'd only be working class? But Eric prodded and pushed, reminding me that Joey deserved the best education he could get. What I liked was his confidence that being around money wouldn't spoil Joey; the more I thought about it, the more it made sense. Why shouldn't he take advantage of Wylie, if they'd have him? What bothered me most was the feeling that the place was a cookie cutter: all the kids looked like Barbie or Ken. I didn't want Joey to grow up unaware that he was white; I didn't want him to hate his origins, to fall in love with money or its accoutrements, or to believe that the bland face of Wylie mirrored the world. But I also wanted to trust him; I even felt fatalistic about it. If Joey was going to be decent, he'd be decent no matter where and how he did his learning. If he was going to be a mess, it wouldn't matter which poison he chose. A few months before Eric took off, I drove Joey to Wylie for a day-long series of tests, interviews, evaluations. They gave out three scholarships; Joey got one of them. It was a two-year deal that would end in June, after which it would be renewed as long as he continued to make outstanding academic progress.

I wasn't sure what constituted "outstanding academic progress" for an eight-year-old; truth be told, I'm still not sure. But the scholarship's been renewed every year, no fuss or questions; Joey assures me it's a certain thing once you make it to the seventh grade. He says he'd have to fail all his classes, or get caught doing crack under the headmaster's desk; unlikely, since he's a straight-A nerdboy. Nerdboy: that's what he calls himself. I don't know what the other kids call him; he keeps his school life pretty private. I want to know, though; I want to know more than the grade he got on his History midterm, or what they're reading this week in his English class. I want to know about the rest of it: whether he's popular or an outsider, who he hangs out with, if he has friends to sit with at lunch. I worry sometimes that being a scholarship boy with a secretary for a mom has kept him out of the loop; I used to worry that not having a father would make him stand out, until one day he came home from Art's with a quizzical expression on his face.

"Art said he was jealous of me." He was unloading his backpack at the kitchen table.

"Did he say why?"

"He said he's the only person he knows whose parents aren't divorced, and he feels like a freak."

That made some things better, but it made some things worse, too. Because it got me thinking about how little I know of Joey's world. If things are so different for him—and they are—how can I help? How can I protect him if I don't know what constitutes a threat? When I visit Wylie, it's overwhelming, like a foreign country. Everything's about money; these kids are rich enough not to realize how rich they are. They've all got cars, bikes, their own telephone lines; everything's top notch, down to the littlest stuff. You'd think they could just buy Bics like the rest of the world, but they all have serious monogrammed fountain pens. And backpacks: Joey's is Kmart cheap, blue nylon, adjustable straps, one front pocket. But his classmates carry these tan leather bags, European looking, with nine million pockets inside for pencils and notebooks, watches and datebooks. Which they also carry. Imagine a fourteen-year-old with a datebook. It scares me. And then there's the way they dress. Everything is ironic. The girls wear little baby barrettes in their hair, only you can tell it's supposed to be a joke; the boys wear ripped jeans, and that's supposed to be a joke, too. Everything is extreme, either baggy or skintight. The girls let their nipples show through their blouses, and wear hiking boots, only they don't ever go hiking. The boys look like tractor salesmen, only their fathers are all lawyers fighting to buy out the farmland around Carlstown and build condos with man-made lakes and faux rock gardens. Joey just wears Levi's and t-shirts, sometimes some of the clothes Eric left behind.

For myself, I think Joey's a little odd. Not in a bad way; he's just different, hard to say how. I had a talk once with his drama teacher, Terry Cintos, because I was kind of worried about him, and knew she was his favorite teacher. I called her up and asked to talk with her; she was real nice, suggested we have lunch some weekend afternoon. We went out to Friendly's, ordered coffee and sandwiches, and talked about my son for almost two hours. The thing I need to remember is that Joey isn't just a combination of me and Eric. It's hard, because that's how he looks; he's like a perfect blend of the two of us. He got the best of both, lucky for him: not my slumped shoulders, not Eric's bad teeth, but my thick, reddish hair, and his father's build. So when I look at him, I expect to hear him speak like either me or Eric; instead, he's his own person, not a mix but something other. What's surprising, in fact, is how totally different from either one of us he really is; he's way smarter than me or Eric, for one. Likes acting, something neither one of us knows much of anything about. Likes poetry, for Christ's sake. And plays basketball. I fall if I walk too fast, and Eric, well, Eric wasn't ever much of a jock.

But that wasn't why I was worried. It was on account of Art. Because Joey and Art spend all their time together. I mean, all their time. When they were eight and nine and ten, it was great. Margaret and I would take turns watching them, give each other time alone. They played well together, too; rarely fighting, roughhousing some but never reaching violence. But now they're teenagers, and the other boys I know are all starting to take girls out to Pizza Hut and a movie. Joey doesn't hang out with girls a lot, and Art doesn't either. They like girls well enough—they both love Terry Cintos, and get along very well with Art's sister—but they're not interested in them, if you know what I mean.

It worried me.

So I picked Terry Cintos to tell, and wouldn't you know it, I picked the wrong person. Only really I picked the right person, it just took me a bit to figure that out. We sat in Friendly's, looked the menu over, decided on a BLT (me) and a grilled cheese (Terry). Then I fiddled with my coffee, adding sugar and cream, stirring it slowly, trying to think of how to say what I wanted to say. Terry did a nice thing then: reached across the table and put her hand on mine.

"You don't have anything to worry about. Joey's a great kid, smart and lively."

It helped to hear that. I mean, I know he's great, and he knows I know he's great, but how do I know what the rest of the world thinks? What she said made me feel brave. Brave enough to stammer out my story.

"You know Joey's friend Art?"

"They're best friends, that's pretty clear. Art's another great kid. Fantastic actor."

"Mmm." Would she understand me if I wasn't explicit? I hate saying things directly. I'd rehearsed the words into a mirror before I left the house, but a mirror is different from another person.

The waitress came with our food; that gave me a minute or two to think. When she'd set our plates down, I busied myself taking the little plastic toothpicks out of my sandwich, and spreading on extra mayo. While I was fussing with the lettuce, I told her. Said it right out loud.

"I'm worried that Joey is gay."

Terry could've done or said anything; maybe that was why I was so worried. Because I didn't know much about her, didn't know if she'd be scared, grossed out, or perfectly fine. No idea. But she was just calm, asked me why I thought so. Said kids Joey's age tend to have intense same-sex friendships. Asked why I thought things with Art were different from plain old best friends.

It was hard to say everything but I got most of it out. Told her what I'd seen and heard. When I was done I felt shaky, but I also felt better. I've carried too many secrets with me in this lifetime; it felt good to share one with someone, especially someone who listened.

She talked some then. Said what I was describing made it sound like Joey and Art had maybe been fooling around, but that didn't make them gay for sure. Said I should wait and be patient. Then she lectured me a little, something I hadn't expected. But it was OK, I didn't mind. She said if he was gay I should be open to letting him talk to me, that a lot of gay kids kill themselves, or try to, because they feel so alone. Basically, she sat there and said it was OK if he was, and OK if he wasn't. One wasn't better or worse; he'd need my support either way.

It wasn't what I'd expected to hear, but I liked it.

We'd ordered dessert; she was eating strawberry ice cream from a glass bowl. I remember how she poked her spoon around the edges, trying to keep the ice cream from melting down the sides. I was cutting a bit of crust off a slice of apple pie with my fork when Terry said, "I'm gay myself."

Well, you could've knocked me over with a breath. I got anxious for a second; would she think I'd been insulting her with all my worrying? She must've read my face because she smiled.

"Joey's going to be fine, no matter what he does with his life. He's got a good heart, and he'll find someone great to love. Just be easy with it."

I tried to pay for her lunch but she wouldn't let me.

There have been times since when I've wanted to call and talk to her again, but I don't want to burden her. She works too hard; I know that from Joey. But I'd like someone to talk to. It was something I wanted to do with Cope, only we never got around to it. I think Cope would understand because he's so easy-going, and because he really doesn't give a damn what other people think of him. He goes his own way. But we stopped seeing each other before I had a chance to tell him.

Funny how long it can take to get deep inside another person's head, enough to know what they think about big things. When I try to imagine what Eric would've said, I can't even. We never talked about real stuff, just daily things, what happened at work, what I'd made for dinner, TV shows, all that. He made fag jokes, sure, but that's not the same as talking serious about Joey. Sometimes I wish I knew how to make conversation go further than it does; I get tired of talking about the weather. Like with Margaret. We do things together once in a while: lunch, tea, school functions. Sometimes when the kids are hanging out, we'll hang out, too. But all we talk about is the price of apples, the way the boys' feet are growing, who was on last week's *Oprah*, those sorts of conversations. Mostly they're OK, but once in a while I start feeling, oh, I don't know, hemmed in, and I get this urge to ask her something serious: about life, sex, God, politics. Funny thing is, I know exactly what her face would do if I ever did. Her cheeks would blanch the way they do when we're watching TV and a tampax commercial comes on. She'd change the subject neatly, trimming the edges off anything serious the way she trims the edges of the pies she makes. That would be the end of me and Margaret, and I don't want that, if only for Joey's sake, so I still my lips and listen to the smallness of her world with patient eyes.

Listening to the grey ladies make small talk at my mother's table is sort of the same thing. Their conversation is like their clothing: it shields everything just so. They want their knees covered, and who can blame them? Yet there's a caring to their motions that I don't sense with Margaret. They're not cold, these ladies, just cautious; while I watch, they hand things round the table, their arms dancing a slow waltz, stirring the air just barely.

Who are they?

They move like sisters. Funny, isn't it, how women always bundle good girlfriends around them like blankets to shut out the cold. They kiss their husbands at night, but call Lori or Esther in the morning, first thing, to share what their hearts can't contain one minute longer. Ma always had a lady, or several, to take tea with, sort of a rotating cycle: Father out the door at eight, then in around noon would come Linda or Vicki, who'd stay 'til two, or three, or four. Around six, Dad would walk back in, but it never felt like his house, always someplace he'd stopped for the night. The women were blood to her;

days I was home from school, I could sit with them in the kitchen if I asked special. I saw it in her face; when they told stories, she drank those stories in, letting her lips rest nearly at their throats, pulling the red from their cheeks to keep her heart afloat another day-to-night-to-noon. They'd feed from her, too; when I saw that, I always felt queer, the way I still do when I watch someone eat pleasure. Because pleasure embarrasses me, makes me turn my face away. I remember when Eric would shake, and I'd know he was ready to come, and he'd say, "Watch," but I just couldn't, I couldn't look at the wild of his eyes then. It's easier for me to see sorrow on a face than joy; joy's uncontrollable, and I like things neat and easy.

When the grey ladies filed out the front door, the dishes were washed, and the leftovers neatly wrapped in yards and yards of plastic and foil. I listened to them go, then looked to Ma. Time.

"Which room shall we start with first?"

Only it wasn't "we"; with her bad hand, I did all the actual packing while she sat and directed me, bossing the way she used to do before I married Eric and she turned my welfare over to him. I did my father's study that day; sorting through papers took most of the afternoon and into the evening. It was odd to discover that his files were in such disarray, because I knew he'd been a keen businessman, moving up from milk delivery to manager to co-owner of Ivy Dairy. I suppose that, like everyone, he'd had his own private system, ideas about order and organization that had served him well, but died with him. Sorting through everything was like putting together a puzzle with my eyes closed; finally, surrounded by papers, Ma sitting on his swivel chair swathed in blankets and sipping her fifth cup of tea, I slammed shut in despair the drawer I'd been sorting.

"Does it matter, any of this stuff, now that we've sold the dairy?"

"Of course not." She looked at me as if I'd asked whether she'd like to go for a swim. "Maureen. Really now."

I didn't bother to ask her why she hadn't told me that before, just shrugged, then dragged the trashcan in from the kitchen and began dumping handfuls of paper down its white plastic throat.

There were two kinds of boxes: to go, and to stay. The boxes going to Ma's new apartment were my responsibility; I'd drive them over using the next-door's borrowed truck. The boxes that stayed would be hauled up the ramp of the Ryder van that was coming in several days, and deposited in storage. To distinguish, I'd bought two packages of stickers, red and green circles the size of my thumb: red for the boxes going to Ma's apartment, green for the boxes headed for storage. But after several days of packing, I woke in a panic at three in the morning. Wasn't red for stop? Wasn't green for go? I had it backwards; the boxes going to the new place should be green, and the ones staying for the Ryder, red. I untangled the quilt from among the sheets, wrapped it around my shoulders like a shawl, and stumbled downstairs into the kitchen, where the stickers stared up at me, florescent in darkness. I carefully placed red over green, green over red, 'til all the boxes were redone and I could sleep again.

Stop and go. No yellow here. I'd been worried that decision-making would be hard on Ma, but she wanted things packed more than I did. It wasn't what I'd expected; I'd heard horror stories from Margaret about her trip to pack up her father and mother's house when they'd decided to move into a small apartment near a shopping center some years back. The way she told it, they clung to the open lids of boxes, nearly scarring her arms when she tried to tape them shut. They wanted to take everything with them. When it actually came time to leave, to begin sleeping and eating and living in the new place, Margaret's father welded himself to the front door with an entire roll of masking tape. So I'd expected antics from Ma: melodrama, protest, tears—something. After all, I'd grown up here, and Father had died here (literally in the kitchen). I'd assumed it would hurt her to leave, that as each box lid shut, she'd hear echoes, and eventually the noise would sting too much, she'd fold, and I'd become her comforter.

Only that wasn't how it happened. By the second week of my stay, my mother's energy level was soaring. Her coarse curly hair looked windblown, and her cheeks were rosy with new energy.

"Can't you go any faster?" she snapped one afternoon, when I began re-folding the linens in the guest room. "I want to move in by Friday, remember."

"I remember, Ma." I smoothed a popcorn coverlet with the side of my hand. As I half-tossed it, then caught it by the fold, I remembered something else: how, nights when the temperature dropped too quickly, Ma would come into my room, drape the coverlet and a second quilt over my knobby knees.

"Be warm, Maureen," she'd say. Then she'd wait for me to turn off the flashlight I was hiding beneath the covers, and put my book on the floor beside my bed.

The year I turned sixteen, she stopped; I thought then that it was because those last two years at home, our winters were mild. But thinking back, maybe it was intuition: at sixteen, I climbed out the window for the first time to meet my friend Cindy's baby-faced brother Richard. I'd assumed that the mild winters were a neat coincidence, but as I folded the spread, I wanted suddenly to ask her if she'd known all along. Why hadn't it occurred to me then that she'd come in late one evening, seen the empty bed, and simply turned, turned back, letting the pieces of my life fall where they might? I tried to ask but what came out was a silly sort of question, something about tea, sugar or cream, a sweet biscuit on the saucer?

She tapped her foot impatiently. "No more tea; let's finish this room first."

I put the popcorn spread aside, marked it yellow in my mind's eye.

As we made our way through each room, leaving a trail of tightly sealed boxes, Ma's body swayed to private music while I grew greyfaced and sour. This trail wasn't what I wanted. As I sealed each lid, I heard the stiff sounds of paper unwrapped beneath a gleaming pine on Christmas morning; I heard the crinkle of newsprint as my father turned pages with one hand, sipped black coffee with another; I heard the crumpling of notebook paper as I scratched another effort at an essay or math problem I was struggling with at the kitchen table on late-homework afternoons. The sounds I was making now—the fffpt! of tearing tape, the twhup! of tense cardboard opening into a box—weren't sounds I associated with anything like happiness. But Ma sat in each room beaming while my hands flew through their packing-dances, as if her life had led up to these folded, noisy moments. She wanted to move in by Friday. She wanted to move.

I wanted her to stay.

I wanted her to outlive me.

To occupy the spaces I'd once occupied, to keep the floors warm, the air breathable. Come holidays, where would I go to visit her? Some stuffy generic apartment with two real rooms, a bathroom, and a crevice for a kitchen. We'd have Christmas there, me and Joey and Ma, but I'd mostly feel like a manger animal.

"Maureen, make your fingers hurry. I want to move in by Friday, remember?"

"I remember, Ma."

I remembered too much. Wednesday night, after Ma was in bed, as I paced the wooden floor of the kitchen, unable to sleep or settle, I forced myself towards "why?" After all, living at home hadn't been easy; there were good times, but ugly scenes, too. I'd wanted out; getting pregnant was the easy way, and I took it. Why should nostalgia hit me now? It seemed false, like crying at a sappy movie simply because the music moves you. When Ma came downstairs, sixish Thursday morning, I was snoring away, my face buried in the kitchen tablecloth. She didn't tease me, for which I was grateful; just put cereal on the table, asked me to open the refrigerator door.

"Help me make coffee," and I did. We'd saved her room for last; it was mostly green from here on out.

I'd saved stacks of linens and towels to wrap fragile things; now I folded a blue sheet around the clock her grandparents had given her as a wedding gift. Each photograph was nestled in its own hand-towel; the perfume bottles and silver brush were tucked inside a battered child's quilt. While I moved around the room, trying to decide in what order to arrange things, I heard a soft, steady tapping: my mother's slippers beating time against the wooden bed-posts. I'd carry the boxes myself to the downstairs entry; tomorrow morning, I'd begin loading and unloading, a series of short trips, culminating in moving Ma herself.

Friday morning I woke at five, before Ma, before my alarm. I didn't bother to brew coffee, but spooned too much instant into a mug and microwaved it, watching the numbers flicker from two minutes to zero, and vanish. I spooned sugar and splashed an ice cube into the coffee, drank it like water as I made my way into the entry. I wanted the loading and unloading over with; I wanted to come back ready to take Ma to her new apartment.

The trips to and from the retirement complex seemed to take forever; it was raining, and I knew I was driving too fast. On all four trips, I'd unlocked the door as if the apartment were mine. After the second load, I'd rested a few minutes on the sofa, stretching full-length the way I do on the sofa at home. But when I finally came back for Ma, around eight, I handed her the keys at the door, and she stepped forward to open it in spite of her bandaged wrist. She didn't ask for help, and I didn't offer. When she turned the knob and stepped inside, I waited on the mat.

"Come in," she said, and I followed her across the threshold.

I hadn't realized 'til then how tired I was, and hungry. As I made my way into the living room, I yawned; Ma touched my shoulder.

"Can I make you some tea? Some toast?"

"Sure, but good luck finding it."

She turned and walked towards the kitchen. "I had the manager send someone by yesterday to turn on the refrigerator and stock it with groceries. And I brought over some cookware in that blue shopping bag. What kind of bread would you like? Eggs on the side?"

I sat on the sofa, leaned my head back, closed my eyes. I think I even drifted off; when I woke up, I realized with a start that my mother was in a new kitchen alone, fixing toast and eggs with a broken wrist.

"Ma!" I had that panicky feeling that comes from falling asleep for a few minutes and waking abruptly in unfamiliar territory. "Ma, hang on. Don't do anything. I'll be right in; let me make breakfast."

"Maureen Cleary." She stood in the entry to the living room, her good hand on her hip. "I believe you fell asleep on me. Breakfast is served."

And it was: eggs with cheddar cheese mixed in, toast with blueberry jam ("I asked for strawberry, the fool"), and strong dark tea. While we ate, Ma explained to me where she planned to hang her pictures.

"What'll you do the rest of today?"

"I'll unpack some of my things, and then at four o'clock, the club is coming by to see the apartment. Mary Louise lives six doors down, Maureen, did I tell you?"

"That's great, Ma."

"Yes, and Hester lives on the other side of Building F. It makes things fine and convenient." She took a small bite of scrambled eggs. "Would you like to take tea with the club when they come?"

"Ma, I'd love to. But my plane leaves at a quarter to four, remember?"

"That's right. I'd forgotten." She set her fork down on her napkin. "Well, why don't you help me start putting things up in the bedroom?"

We began with the cardboard wardrobe that held much of her clothing. I slit open the tape, made a square window in the top half, and began pulling her dresses through.

"Careful, Maureen. Don't let the fabric catch." Ma held out hangers for me; I placed each dress in the closet, smoothing the pleated skirts, straightening the sleeves. We worked slowly, methodically, no hurry in the air; she had time, and more time. It felt odd to remember the frenzied driving I'd done that morning.

We finished the wardrobe and two boxes by twelve, when I began to think about leaving for the airport. I needed time to park, check my luggage, and try to secure an aisle seat. As I glanced surreptitiously at my watch, Ma caught me.

"Maureen, perhaps you'd best go soon." It wasn't a question, but I nodded anyway. Now, I thought, now for the farewells.

But nothing much happened: she kissed me on the cheek, hugged me as best she could with one arm. I read sadness in her eyes, but not loss. No tears; her lips didn't tremble.

"I'll miss you," she said, "but you'll be back soon."

She'd miss me.

But.

Couldn't she miss me without qualifications? I hugged her back; she seemed distracted.

"Do I look alright? The club is coming at four."

"You look fine, Ma. Beautiful." I felt the old disappointment wrap me round like a winding sheet.

What did I want from her?

She was strong; did I want her to cling to me? She was happy; did I want to see her grieving?

Hadn't giving up her house meant anything?

But the loss was mine, not hers. This apartment was her new life, a warm one. She'd moved to create a future for herself, something the old house couldn't give her. Could I blame her that in the process my past had gotten lost?

"Good-bye, dear." She took my elbow and began to walk with me towards the bedroom door.

"Wait." I remembered something I'd forgotten to give her. "I need to run out to the car. Be right back." She nodded; the light coming in through the bedroom window whitened the grey of her hair. The sun had emerged, though it was still raining lightly; I hugged my arms close to my chest as I hurried to and from the car. Back in the entryway, I stopped to unwrap the package; the popcorn coverlet looked faded in the clean, bright light of Ma's apartment, but the stitches were strong, and the design remained clear. I held the nubby fabric to my cheek, breathed in the scent of the old house. The new apartment had a different smell; making my way to the bedroom, I tried to place it: sweet, a little spacey, like paint, only not as familiar. The door to the bedroom was closed but not shut; as I pushed it open with my shoulder, I realized the name of that peculiar scent. It was the smell of freedom. I felt the old urge to jealousy rise in my throat.

But she was sleeping. I spread the coverlet carefully across the bed, then held my hand up to her lips to reassure myself that she was breathing—she looked so still. She was, she was breathing, she was sleeping the keen sleep that comes on a woman unexpectedly when she finds herself confronting the beginning and end of something all at once.

Should I wake her? Our good-byes felt incomplete. Her eyelids fluttered, her chest rose, and in my mother's room, I let go for one minute while I watched the clock, allowing my head to rest on the coverlet as I knelt by the bed. I wanted to give her what I'd promised when I'd arrived here, in this very town, all blue-faced and witty with screams and smells and curiosity about her very breasts.

Bliss knows itself, and its location.

I let my head rest and counted the seconds. But when I got to twenty-five, I stopped. I risked everything, sleep without end, by closing my eyes and ignoring the clock's morris code.

On the inside of my lids, I saw her face. It was the only face I'd ever fully trusted.

I let my son slip from my parted thighs. I let my father's photograph slip from my mind, my ex-husband's hasty hands slide forever from my strapless shoulders. There was only my birth and this, its aftermath.

When I opened my eyes, the clock was moving faster; it breathed, it had a face, it had become her suitor. Her eyes were still closed, her breathing steady and slow and audible.

I left her with him. I turned the knob. I did not look back.

The flight home took off at three forty-one, too late to plan on being served any kind of lunch. So when I arrived at the airport an hour early, I made my way through a maze of corridors and frenzied suitcase-wielding wingtips to the International Food Court, a half-circle of desperate, greasy vendors selling hamburgers, pizza, and spaghetti under the garishly painted flags of such nationalities as Czechoslovakia, Wales, and Lybia. I decided to patronize Mexico, but when my tacos arrived, the meat looked suspiciously white; I pointed this out to the ponytailed attendant whose sex I could not discern.

"That's chicken," he/she said, sticking two fingers in and presenting me with a rubbery pellet. I explained patiently that I hadn't ordered chicken.

"We only serve chicken tacos. Guatemala does beef."

I took one taste and trashed the yellow paper box, then travelled to Switzerland for strawberry-chocolate chip nonfat frozen yogurt with Nutrasweet. I wanted the regular kind, with lots of fat and sugar, but the manager explained that they didn't sell regular anymore.

"No one will eat it."

I threw up before the plane took off, into one of those paper bags they stuff in the seat pockets along with information on what to do with your children if the plane crashes. First you cover your mouth with a little plastic cup, then you do your kid's, the idea being, I suppose, that orphanages are really terrible places, while childless adults often lead productive, interesting lives. After I threw up, the stewardess avoided my row, making eye contact with every seat but mine while demonstrating safety features. My seat belt was broken, and I'd landed a talker, a young nurse wanna-be who made chitchat about vomiting, why it happened, how to stop or induce it, etc. When he began on catheters, I gave a loud yawn, tilted my head back, and fell instantly asleep. I actually did fall asleep about five minutes later. When I woke, the plane was diving, diving, and Josi and Kristi, our flight attendants for today, were polishing their nails in the kitchen. I wanted to tell them that I could see them, could read the color printed on the bottle, but my tongue felt stiff in my mouth, and my head hurt too much to shout, even something short like "Gotcha!" The landing was mercifully brief; the airline had lost my luggage, for which I was mildly thankful, since it was a twenty minute walk to the parking lot.

All the long drive home, I unpacked boxes in my mind's eye. I put the china flower girls back on the mahogany shelves of the cupboard, unwound the sheets and put them back in the linen closet, shutting the door reluctantly on piles of pale, cool fabric. I hung my wedding dress back up, smoothing the layers of netting beneath the skirt so it fell evenly; I took the photographs and arranged them neatly in the living room beneath the television stand. After returning each item to its proper location in our house, I drove to the retirement complex, came home with Ma in the front seat.

"This is where you belong," I'd say, opening the front door for her, and she'd smile, satisfied because she was needed. The house needed her, I needed her to be a part of the house.

But she needed something different.

I drew maps of the retirement complex and its honeycombed lots in my mind's eye. What if Ma got lost on the way to bingo, or walked into the wrong apartment some dimly-lit evening? What if her neighbors were reliving their college days, and played swing music terribly loudly, guzzled rum, and left panties hanging from the bushes along her portion of the sidewalk? Would she complain? What if (my stomach dived) someone in the complex died, and she saw the ambulance carting off the body? Who would she talk to? What would she say? Why was she there? Who was she?

"Maureen Cleary." The very voice.

Now I wouldn't ever know. Had I once thought I might? I'd postponed trying for so long; now it felt too late. The gardening ladies had swooped in, taken over. She'd left me behind, or I'd left her, and since I couldn't tell which, it was over, over.

Dad had bought her the same robe three years running.

Who was she?

Among the moments I remembered best from my childhood were those spent preparing for Sunday Mass. Ma and I would sit in the kitchen, a bowl of water, a towel, and a hairbrush spread out before us on the table. She'd dunk the brush in water, then blot it on the towel before running it through my long, thick, unruly hair. No comb: for tangles she'd use her fingers. When my hair fell sleek and smooth down past my shoulder blades, reaching for my legs as if for the race of it, she'd thumb two lines into my scalp, scratching my skin just enough that it stung 'til after we'd settled into our pews. She'd braid a dense plait I'd fold myself in a coil at my nape. A hat on top, a ruffled dress, and we were off, to worship Mary in her blue folds, her son strung on the bloody cross that hung, larger than life-size, behind the altar.

Even then, belief seemed elusive, something to be desired but never attained, like the popular boys who drove convertibles and brought their girls roses on the first date. I made a good show of it—easy enough to act, kneeling and folding my hands in a pious crescent. Yet the lushness of the faith my mother experienced, a sensual, almost ecstatic communion with the imagined spirits of the dead, was never mine to be had. I found faith elsewhere, in bursts of smoke from stolen cigarettes, in Saturday night drives to nowhere with boys whose cheeks were barely stubbled, in hours spent practicing the flute, and in the twists and tangles of Victorian novels. At St. Mary's, we mocked the nuns whose lives our mothers envied; we climbed out our windows at midnight to meet young men from St. Joe's in the woods behind the chapel. Yet guilt never haunted me, because each experience seemed a religion unto itself. I remember putting my lips to the flute in front of the school for a Christ's Day performance, and feeling a shiver run from my belly through my legs, thrilled by my own music. The world seemed technicolor-brilliant; I couldn't understand my mother's urge to dream up another in order to pursue pleasure.

The window across from her bed was striped with thick off-white blinds; I'd left them slit open, just enough to let the sun in when the rain ended its sentence. She'd wake to find her bedcovers dappled; if she reached a hand to her face, that hand would be slashed with yellow light. I could see that, and could envision, too, the face she'd wear on waking, could see her climb carefully out of bed, walk first thing to her tiny bathroom and scrub her teeth with the orange toothbrush I'd bought her the day before. Then she'd dress, maybe the yellow skirt and sweater, maybe the blue slacks with the matching flowered blouse and zip-front jacket. She'd make her way to the kitchen, begin fussing with tea for the gardening ladies, who'd arrive promptly at four, not more than five minutes early, or ten minutes late. I could see all that, and know it was the

actual way of things. But I couldn't predict what she might be thinking or, more importantly, how she might feel. What if the light
frightened her?

I'd promised to call tomorrow evening, just to check up, see how
things were going. But as I sped past the familiar post-airport
scenery, my hands steady on the wheel, I anticipated the way my
palms would itch when I picked up the phone to make the call. It
would hurt, hearing her voice, knowing where she was was
nowhere special; mostly it would hurt to know she'd never leave.
What would it be like to move knowing the move was final? Would
she even unpack all the boxes? I tried to hold the thought in my
head but couldn't, the way I couldn't imagine death even when I
tried wrapping all my mind's strength around the idea of it.

She'd die in that room, and I'd be the one to pack the boxes again,
to fly or drive them back to Carlstown, where they'd sit in the garage
waiting for me to stop mourning long enough to unpack them.

How could I have left her?

I almost made a U-turn there in the middle of the highway. It
felt instinctual: my mother was dying. I needed to be there, to wait
the coming years out in the chair beside the bed until she no longer
needed me. I felt my hands give on the wheel and saw the blank
spaces of the lanes to my left and thought yes, yes, back you go Maureen, Maureen Cleary, who else *is* there?

It wasn't the thought of Joey that pulled me back, but a semi
that passed me on the left; then after that another, and then a car
toting a van, and by then the naturalness of the gesture had vanished, replaced by guilt, and a hole in my gut the size of the sprawl-
ing city I'd just left.

I drove on through the beginning of the evening, without stopping until I saw the lights of Carlstown's main drag. Usually neon
hurts my eyes, but that night I welcomed the garish streaks of color.
At the first stop, I squinted so that the startling reds and blues and
yellows bled and mingled, making me feel like a painter, 'til the
impatient mister behind me honked and I snapped my eyes open to
let in green. Fifteen minutes more, and I arrived at Casey Lane; one
right turn, two left, and I pulled into the gravel drive of Cope's trailer
park. It hit me then that the name on the weather-worn metal sign
marking the entrance—Green Acres—was the name of my mother's

retirement home. Green Acres. Acres of green. Acres and acres and ages of green, gone brown, gone weathered. Why is it we lie when we name things?

When I found his trailer, I pulled the car off the road, shut down the engine. But I was too tired to be a mother just yet; closing my eyes, I let my head rest against the wheel. The image of Ma's face floated up, drawn and grasping, a white lace collar closed like a hand around her throat. Her face was imprinted on the inside of my lids; she'd never leave me. I didn't know yet if this was a good thing, or bad.

I realized then why Cope had always seemed so familiar, why I'd trusted him with Joey. He wore the same mixture of grief and bewilderment as my mother invoked in me: a look that said he'd lost something, but was staving off the knowledge that the loss was irretrievable. Why is it we lie when we lose things? I opened my eyes again; I'd have to make peace with this picture.

Joey. It was as if a thread had snapped en route to Seattle; now I searched for it again, running my fingers across a spool whose surface had gone slick, the end of the thread clipped so neatly that it had become invisible. Joey. Who was he, what did he want from me, what had he given? I remembered the chorus of a song he liked to sing, about being the king of pain; I remembered his favorite colors, brown and gold, and I remembered the book about the turtle, the one I'd read to him over and over again the year he turned seven.

I pulled myself back to him slowly, hand over hand, remembering a son, until I was almost a mother again.

CHAPTER 8

Terry

I'VE got a habit of making lists. I paste them on the bathroom door, look them over while I'm foaming and flossing. Sometimes they hang for months, sometimes they come down before day's end. But I've had one up for I don't know how long. The edges are curling, like a white girl's hair when it's too short for long and too long for a bob; the ink is green, and the title's bold along the top. Calligraphy makes the words look official: *Things I Never Told Her.*

Number one is the Maidenform ad.

Number two is the crush I had on Marie Osmond in fourth grade.

Number three is Robert.

But it's number eight that matters. Number eight, two circles joined at the hip: I never confessed that our first meeting wasn't an accident. I hadn't called Parker's, hadn't ordered shuttle service at all. I'd intended to catch a bus home, but as I walked away from the airline terminal, into the desperate weather, I saw a woman striding towards me, shaking off snow with each step, and thought, why not take a risk? What have I got to lose? Seeing Dell take those overambitious steps in snow, I felt that here was a woman who wouldn't lie to me. Her walk was honest, and the snow appreciated her boldness. She seemed untouched by the weather; it merely echoed around her. I left some poor soul stranded, waiting for a cabbie who never came, but all I could think was how much it bothered me that I couldn't see her face behind the sign she held, shielding her eyes from the icy flyers. I took the liberty of slipping in beside her; she grumbled, but once I'd seen her up close and learned her name (Dell—she was Dell, no doubt about it), I wasn't going anywhere. My suitcase could take up space in back; I wanted to know what only proximity could teach me. We buckled up. We sped off. We talked, and began the slow, delicate process of unpeeling.

When she dropped me off at my destination without a word towards tomorrow, disappointment stung my chest like ice striking glass. Had I read her wrong? I didn't think so; after running into her a few times around Carlstown, I came to understand that the signal she was sending was curiosity, not desire. Then I assumed it was only a matter of time; if you feed it, curiosity easily becomes desire. Not until we met in passing on Fourth Street did I realize that things were complicated. Naomi and I were on our way to dinner when out of the snow, I spotted her: that unmistakable long stride. At first, I thought she was with another gay girl, and I pointed them out to Naomi.

"Butch-on-butch," she laughed. "Never a good idea." But as they approached, Dell shook off her companion's arm and stuffed her hands in her sleeves; as her companion turned towards her, I saw that she was with a man. I watched his lips sound out a question ("Cold?"), watched as he offered her his jacket and she refused. As she recognized me and stopped walking, her lips pronounced my name without giving any of the usual greetings.

After that, I thought often about calling. Once I even dialed, got the poor fellow she was preparing herself to betray. I liked his voice, which made it harder; after all, I was preparing myself to betray him, too. But I didn't leave a message. What was there to say? She needed to make up her mind, show me what her decision looked like. Once she did, she practically knocked me down with her enthusiasm. I was standing in the stationery aisle of some florescent drugstore, my eyes preoccupied with inks of different colors, when I heard a skittering; without looking up, I knew it was Dell. Her time had come, and how convenient: she'd gone to the drugstore for tampons and dental floss, and discovered Truth along the way.

"What do you think, Dell? Should I try grading in red ink? I've never been able to stomach the connotations, but perhaps the time has come."

"Red's good," in that calm way she had, not giving an inch, not flirting back even a bit. "You should show a little authority now and then, keep them on their toes. You're probably too nice."

No one had ever called me "too nice" before; it made me laugh stupidly, snorting a little. I wanted to know what she meant by "Red's good." Red for passion. Red for dead stop. Why is it that one color means both?

"How about green?" Watching her eyes for clues. "Green for go. That way, they won't take *F* to mean *stop*."

We chatted some then about Wylie Academy, but also about the fierce high school she'd gone to, little more than a prison. I was aware that I was talking too much, running on, waving my hands about in the clumsy way I do when I'm around a girl whose body makes me thirsty. The conversation pulled me towards her, like our talk in the car that first day. But I felt the pressure of my watch band against my wrist; sooner or later, she'd skitter back around the corner to her man's cold arms and her own lonely confusion. Speak, Dell, I thought, just speak. Say what your body is thinking.

"Terry, I have to ask you something."

Was she going to ask which brand of dish detergent I used and then stride backwards in slow motion, vanishing, the way some do?

She wanted to go out for a beer. "It wouldn't have to take long. And if you don't drink? We could have a cup of coffee. Or maybe you don't like caffeine. Well, then we could try tea. I don't like tea much myself, seems kind of nasty, like flavored water, but I could certainly try it. And if you don't like...."

That was the go-ahead. "Dell, why don't you ask me for my phone number?" I didn't have a pen, so I pulled one off the rack, tore away the plastic, and scrawled her number on a page she pinched from a miniature memo book.

I spent the next few days trying not to call.

When I gave in, the boyfriend's voice was friendly and benign. To his credit, Cope did a lot for Dell, more than I realized at first. I could see it in the photographs she kept, a sort of before and after picture show. She was an introvert, Dell; seriously, almost fatally shy. Never did like people very much. In high school, she ran track, set a high jump record for her school that was still unbeaten when she died. But outside of track, there was almost nothing: a few dates, two or three acquaintances, no close friends, parties, proms, clubs. In her high school pictures, she's too thin, near scary-looking, her long, straight hair straggling across almond-colored eyes. Her skin's pale enough that she could pass for a ghost, if it weren't for her lips: stark, bright red. The day we met, I remember thinking it was odd that a tomboy dyke like Dell was wearing lipstick. Found out later it was natural, a permanent red flush. In those pictures, you can see the loneliness through her translucent skin. The ones Cope took later show a different girl: closer to graceful, at ease in her own body.

"He gave me inside," she once told me, when I asked her why she'd started something with him, and why she was staying in something that looked so much like sleep. "He was the first person to give me enough space, to leave me alone enough of the time that I could be with him the rest. I was always outside, wanted to be. Cope made outside inside sometimes. I could rest with Cope."

Whatever else he couldn't give her, he made human contact nearer to bearable; he made her feel safe for the first time. Safe enough that, when I came along over a year and a half later, she was ready to want risk, the way once, back before meeting Cope, she'd wanted safety.

We do this for each other: tug on the skins our friends and lovers need to discard. It's a beautiful thing, but horrible too, because once it's done, you're so often left with the skin and not the body-in-motion. That's what happened to Cope, though she died before he had to face finding out. I don't know which pain would've been worse for him: finding her dead, or finding her gone. I shouldn't think on it, but of course I do. And me? Would she eventually have discarded me, too? Moving in *S* swirls along the ground, stirring up dust to blind me from the sight of the papery shards? Dead skin's something elegant, all criss-crossed with lines and shadows. If she'd left me, years from now, or even sooner, what would it have been for? Not safety, not risk. Does death always come after?

But before after came before. It was as if we'd escaped the present, not for the past or future, but for another outside. That first night, I looked and looked and it was like hunger for me, something that hurt inside, looking at her body. She was violet and yellow and garland and dusk at once; her arms made a circle that smelled of sweat and sudden motion. The edgy red of her lips flew at my eyes, I put one finger there, as if I could feel her pulse, as if her heart was hidden there. Dell's lips were the first I'd ever kissed that made no distinction between answering, asking, and giving pleasure. We played at flaws, showing each other our worst selves, daring the other to look, exploring the limits of empathy.

Show me the sagging or withered flesh, the puckered scars, the frizzled hair on the insides of your thighs. Let me put my hand beneath, not your clothing, but your very skin. Let me feel the blood making its way, and touch the ugly, lumpish heart that forces you on past what you think you deserve.

Now that beautiful girl is dead. I can't think it; I've seen the coffin, but that wooden memory isn't real. I can still hear the knowing that was in her voice when she made "we" something dark and particular; when I close my eyes, my face is burrowing between her legs, my tongue finding spaces that taste of summer. I keep thinking such body-memories can't lie, must eventually transform themselves into flesh in the real, that one night my own hand clenched to the point of pain between my legs will go translucent, become Dell's, and she'll watch, her eyes going liquid, as I tease my fingers across her upper thigh. That's what stays, that's why I can't believe in a semi, spinning, taking the top off. No stupid truck's as strong as memory; no memory's as strong for me as Dell's. She was the first one to bring my life to a screeching halt, red for passion and dead stop both.

Yet no one at the funeral knew my face or name, much less who I'd been to Dell: her best beloved, the one who'd peeled back her skin, the one she'd been planning to live with after she'd settled into the idea of "forever." I wanted to grieve with every part of my body, to make an opera of mourning; after I'd crept past her sleek, sealed casket, I wanted to take scissors to my hair and eyes 'til there was no beauty left of mine to remind me of hers. But who was I to weep so loudly? Instead I let lie body and voice, walked past the coffin quickly, the way acquaintances do, showing respect but not the paralyzing grief I actually felt. I spoke in the calm, distant accent of a visitor, not the frenzied tones of an inhabitant; no one knew that my hands had climbed up and inside her, that my tongue had spared no reaches its root-flavors. I spoke and moved with gentile coolness, arid in my grey wool dress. I look terrible in grey; that seemed apropos. At least my deliberate ugliness echoed her accident. Why cultivate beauty when beauty was gone?

I met Cope at the funeral for the first time, not counting the day we passed on Fourth Street. Made a point of walking up to him, shaking his hand. We'd talked on the telephone so many times that I recognized his voice from across the room, even though all I'd ever said was, "May I speak to Dell?" and all he'd ever said was, "Who's calling, please?" He looked the way she'd described him, only hollow, worn-through with grief and sadness.

"I'm Terry Cintos, Dell's friend. She spoke very highly of you."

"She told me you were a good pal to her."

I wanted him to say more, wanted for us to talk, to grieve together, but when I tried to ask him a question, he didn't answer, and I let him be. It made me sad, even angry, how little comfort I could give him; I tried not to think about how little comfort I'd been given, the few close friends who'd known about me and Dell. None of them knew her well enough to go to the services. I was on my own; it didn't help that it was nearly an all-white crowd: a sea of blond lashes and pastel faces, row after row of people I didn't know, people who didn't see me, or didn't want to, people who claimed kinship to Dell and would've denied mine, had they known.

About a year and a half after Dell's death, I put on a production of *Oedipus* at Wylie. Not an easy task, but I thought it might distract me from my silent mourning. *Oedipus* is the kind of challenge I enjoy. I'd rather watch my students struggle with the classics than goof their way through a musical, or some *Saturday Night Live*-style spoof. The performance had gone well; not stellar, but better than I'd expected, given the seniors I had to work with. I make it a rule to let seniors take the lead roles in each year's big drama; mostly I feel proud of that, but once in a while I'm sorry, find myself wishing I could break my own rule, or at least bend it.

This was one of those years. Ed Chesley, Jr. was the senior boy with the most Drama credit hours, the perfect attendance record, and the highest quiz grades. I had no choice but to let Ed play the lead, but what a grand piece of miscasting: imagine Oedipus qua veejay, and you've got the idea. To make matters worse (as every teacher at Wylie knows), working with Ed Jr. meant working very closely with his mother, Paula Chesley.

It was Paula's idea to have a real cast party after the show. That was her word: *real*. What *real* actually means, in Wylie-speak, is *expensive*: she wanted it catered. Now, who ever heard of catering a cast party for a bunch of hyperactive, hormone-tickled teenagers? But Paula insisted; since she wanted to pay for it, I couldn't very well say no. Didn't have the heart to tell her that the kids really wanted pizza and Little Debbie's snack cakes. She orchestrated the whole thing with her catering company, Movable Feasts. Which should've worried me, since Jane is her business partner, but at the time, I just assumed that Jane would have the dignity not to cause a fuss on my professional turf.

It wasn't that I did Jane any cruelty when we split; I let go the way a child lets go of a balloon. One night Dell kissed me in my car outside Cope's trailer, a smack-deep flying kiss she fled from. Even though nothing had been spoken between us, even though I knew she'd open the trailer door and head for her boyfriend's O-shaped arms, I realized that I had to break things off with Jane. I didn't force Dell's hand so that I could be sure of her before giving Jane up; I didn't play the two of them against each other, or go behind Jane's back. No, I left that kind of confusion up to Dell, and instead drove home and phoned Jane. By the time her car pulled up in my lot, I was already gone; when I answered the door, it was for a friend, not a lover. I made no move to kiss her, and she brushed past me, ready for anger, not thinking flight, but plunge, and cold water.

Yet after Dell's death, in the midst of my deepest mourning, I thought often about calling Jane. What stopped me was that I knew how ungracious the gesture would appear; what I wasn't sure of was whether my motivations were indeed ungracious. Did I simply want her back to fill the void now that Dell was gone? Or did I miss Jane for who she was, and want contact—of whatever sort—because seeing Jane reassured and even cheered me? I didn't want to call unless I understood my own reasons for calling; clarity failed me, and I never dialed.

When I arrived at the cast party, I remembered two things I'd forgotten: that Jane stays angry until she has a reason to forgive, and that she usually fights silently, lets food do the talking. So it was Oedipus' mother's idea, but when I saw the spread, I knew I was in the middle of a Jacobean revenge plot.

Banana everything.

Banana bread. Banana-walnut pie. Ambrosia. Lime jello with banana bits. Cole slaw with banana slivers. Shish kabob with chicken, onions, and bananas. While the kids were gnashing (they devoured everything except the slaw), I slipped into the auditorium's kitchen, in search of the chef herself.

I'm allergic to bananas.

"Wasn't Ed Jr.'s performance stunning?" Paula Chesley was smiling her preppy smile. "Terry, do you know Jane, my partner?"

"We've met before."

Jane stretched out a hand. "When Paula told me she'd suggested our services for your cast party, I told her, just leave the planning to me. I'll design the menu myself."

I did something coy. Took the hand she offered, grasped it tightly, then let my fingers seek out the coiled silver ring she always wears on her thumb, and turned it, easing it halfway off her finger. The last time I'd taken off that ring, she'd left it on my dresser the next morning by accident.

Or maybe on purpose.

Paula didn't notice me making trouble; her vision isn't keen enough. She knows I'm gay; I've been out at Wylie since my job interview, though Paula insists on treating my sexuality as a secret to be ferreted out, hoarded, whispered about. Her eyes smirk when she looks me over; the way she looks at Jane is more complicated. Jane isn't out to Paula, and I'm sure Paula hasn't guessed. Jane's high femme, passes easily. She says the partnership would end if Paula found out.

Seeing Jane in the kitchen startled me, because I'd forgotten so many distinct things about her. Like the depth and black-violet of her skin's brown; like her hats, this day's a deep blue that matched her skirt, which met her ankles just at the point where the t-straps of her brown shoes made their crosses. Fine and fancy, that was Jane; there was a confidence about her that clashed with Paula's arrogance. Yet Moveable Feasts is a success story: preparing food is an art and a passion for both of them. How many people can say they earn a living pursuing their passions? What I don't understand is how they manage to work together.

Because they hate each other.

Don't even make a secret of it. Their ubiquitous disagreements raise room temperature; the air in the kitchen is steamy no matter what they're cooking. Naomi once suggested that their antagonism is the secret ingredient, the spice that makes their food specially tasty, and maybe she's right. Their bickering has a snappy, almost musical rhythm to it, and their put-downs are always witty and pungent. What they won't do, can't do, is express affection or appreciation for each other; instead, their love goes through the wringer and comes out twisted: cruel entertainment.

Why does passion take such circuitous channels?

Like this habit of mine. I test the temperature with my exes when we meet. I like knowing whether there's still a spark, but it's a cruel habit, because not everyone wants to be reminded of what they've lost, or let go of. So I let go of Jane's ring, and dropped her hand, and gave her something for her trouble: "I can tell you worked hard on the menu, and I don't blame you. I don't blame you at all."

Why waste good breath on blame? She had a right. It was just hard for me to get back to the hurt Jane was still feeling over the demise of our relationship when, in the time that had passed, Dell had come and gone. Hard, too, to measure what I'd ever felt for Jane; Dell had become my point of reference. Nothing that preceded her made sense any more.

I watched Jane buzz about with Paula; they reached around and across each other's bodies easily, like lovers. Jane caught me staring, and raised her eyebrows. "Have you tried the jello, Terry?"

"Special. But I've got to get back to the kids before they tear the place apart."

Another exit without good-bye. I'm bad at closure.

Half-hoped Jane would do it for me; I checked my answering machine that night and the next, thinking our meeting might trigger some reconciliatory impulse. But the machine tape played only the usual voices; on the third night, when I came home to a wrong number and a message from my mother wanting to know if my shoe size had changed, I gave in, and prepared to dial Jane's number. The digits looked strange to my eyes, but the feel of the pattern my fingertips traced was familiar.

She wasn't surprised to hear from me. But angry.

"I owe you an apology."

"You do."

"I'm sorry."

"Apologies mediated by electronic circuitry don't count."

"Do you want to hear it in person?"

"I do."

"Should I come over?"

She refused; smart, because an impromptu reunion might've pushed us towards some cruel or passionate response that we'd have regretted later.

"Should we meet, say, Friday or Saturday night? At Maxwell's?"

"Not not not romantic locale, Terry. What are you thinking?"

What was I thinking?
Was I trying to get her into bed?
I was.
I felt like slime.
"Jane, I'm sorry."
"Apologies mediated..."
"Look, I know. Why don't you choose where to meet? Someplace public. Make it as unromantic as possible, OK?"

After she hung up, I sat on the floor, address book spilling my life's shifting emotional geography onto apartment-complex carpeting; I sat, and tried to think through what I'd just done. Why was it I insisted on flirting with Jane when I knew how much it hurt her? Was it a sign that I wanted her back, or a sign that I didn't take her seriously?

I dreamed that tears came in little kits: purple vials of water, and tiny cellophane packages of salt. You mixed the two, then drank the potion; the taste induced sadness, and the tears that fell were recyclable.

What did I want from her?

Saturday night. Pizza Hut was jam-packed with the family values crowd: be-ringed het two's with kids in tow, guys and dolls on dates. There was even a table full of prom-goers, Sweet Christines in taffeta and dizzying spangles, Buff Matthews in multi-colored tuxes with cummerbunds to match.

Pastels to die for.

"Brings me back," Jane murmured. No nostalgia for me, though; I never did much of that stuff. But Jane was married, briefly, to an Air Force pilot. Sometimes wishes she'd had children then, while it was cheap and easy, though the words "custody suit" snap her out of it. She'd have lost them, and she knows it. We don't go down that fantasy often.

We found a booth in the back, with a window behind us. Our waitress brought a pitcher of soda, and we took turns pouring for each other, then clinked for a toast. I was fine with making small talk to start us off, but Jane moved in for the kill.

"I've never understood what happened." When she said it, I felt sadness rise in my throat. Wanted to plead confusion, say I hadn't understood it either. But more than wanting to escape, I wanted to tell the story.

I began with the wheel.

How her hands slid along that circle, keeping the cab steady on even the frozen roads. How I couldn't stop thinking of the steering wheel spokes as the hands of a clock, and of time as something precious, held in hands like hers. How I couldn't stop thinking of hands like hers, of her, how she'd kissed me and fled, leaving me to fly home, where I'd called "you because it felt like the beginning of something. Honest, Jane, I'm sorry. I should've told you about Dell. But it wasn't 'til her kiss that I knew where she was taking me."

Jane stayed quiet.

I kept on, over ice. About loving my driver, and wanting her to leave Cope. About how she wouldn't give him up, and how she died, bloody and shapeless beneath gored metal. How, after the funeral, I couldn't see: faces blurred to the same dull pale, featureless. Everybody smelled and gestured and spoke as if weighed down with salt.

Jane played with a napkin, folding it until it looked like one of those little toys you play with as a kid, predictions folded underneath each flap: who you'll marry, how many children, whether you'll be business-rich, or sew socks for a living. She had questions. I could tell by her hands' busyness. The waitress came by and we both looked out the window. Jane took another napkin. Wadded the first into her empty glass.

"You really loved her."

"Yes."

"Did you ever really love me?"

"Yes."

I don't know if I lied; I can't decide. But then, it's not possible to tell the truth about the past, only about the future. Without a signal, the subject shifted, and we talked of other things. That was enough for a first night out.

Because we'd gotten too close. Too close to "why else," and "what now," and "why not." I didn't want to think more about how much of leaving Jane was actually about Jane; best to leave it at Dell, and turn off that highway. Before the storm started, or the easy driving.

What we didn't finish, we took home. The waitress gave us two boxes; we both moaned about the wasted tree pulp, but took them anyway. Cold pizza's a familiar breakfast. As we stood to leave, the neon *L* in the *SALAD BAR* sign flickered and died, leaving us all

with a sad bar, and an extra *A*. We hugged good-bye in the parking lot, then drove our separate ways home.

I can't say what she played to drive by, but my tape deck sang
blue songs that night.

We hang out a lot nowadays, Jane and I. At first we circled round
the important stuff; finally one night she spilled and there were
harsh words I had to hear and hated to and salty water and sullen
looks and then a door and a week and a day to think, and now something's climbing. Since we're both single, folks often mistake us for
a couple; I admit it's something I've given thought to. Naomi says I
should ask her what she's feeling. Says since I'm the one created the
leavetaking, I'd have to be the one to start things up again. Sometimes I feel my mouth moving in that direction, but then my skin
goes cold and prickly, and I stop myself.

Because I'm just not sure it's what I want.

If Jane and I had never been together? If she was someone I'd
just met, someone new? I'd risk it, no question. Because if it didn't
feel right for either one of us, there'd be no huge heartbreak. We'd
retreat, nurse our wounds, count it a diversion, not a set-back. But
given our history? If anything happened with me and Jane, it'd be
dead serious from the start. I'd need to be sure before starting things
up again; right now I'm not certain about anything to do with loving.
So I keep my hands to myself, and she holds her passion in, though
I know she's got the thought tucked underneath her hat.

But for now, we just hang out, and then there's Kyla, and Naomi
and Katelyn too, and their sons Harvey and Edward. Times, I catch
myself thinking about who else there might have been if Dell hadn't
vanished, about Kelvin and Annalee, the children we imagined.
Then I stop myself. Because Dell's dead, and the dead don't come
back, whatever the *National Enquirer* might say about Elvis. Gone
is gone: you can't retrieve, only create. I don't want all my creations
to be about a dead girl; I want to save some passion for whoever else
comes along next, out of the snow or sun, shielded or starring her
name, her mouth open, bright or muted, someone who'll know me
as a best self, and feel the same certainty I do, make me know she
knows it in her goodly bones.

Because the thing about Dell was certainty.

I just knew.

And certainty is what usually confuses me. Oh, there've been lots of girls who've loved me. Sometimes deep, like Kyla and Jane; sometimes shallow, like the others who've come and gone too quickly to leave a curve in the lines of my left palm. There've been lots of girls, but I haven't ever felt that I knew what I wanted, that it was right and natural to be with this one instead of that one, to make a choice and stick with it, to follow one lifeline instead of another.

With Dell I felt certain.

What I can never be sure of was whether she felt certain about me.

She told me often enough that she loved me. But there were so many differences between us that I couldn't help but worry that our very similarities must, of themselves, be differences in disguise. How could Dell use the same words, how could she say "I love you," being Dell, and have it mean the same thing "I love you" meant to me?

There's that fear, but there's also another, deeper and colder. One that makes trees look like pleasant places to park; one that gives knives and razors sexy voices.

Cope didn't know her.

Who am I to think I did? Was I so naïve as to think I could find my way inside that girl: that beautiful, guarded girl, whose face was always an austere door?

Would she eventually have discarded me, too?

I can't shake the feeling that if I could just talk to Cope—really talk—I'd find the missing pieces, enough to know if Dell was the girl I took her for, enough to know if she'd have stayed with me, or left me behind, the way she left Cope, even before she died in the steaming metal snow. At the funeral, I wanted so badly to talk to him. To put Dell's story together between the two of us. But he was blown away, and my tongue was so heavy with the taste of her. I knew if I spoke at all, I'd say too much.

A few months ago, I ran into Cope at Wylie, during a rehearsal for *Hamlet*. It was the last place on earth I expected to see him; the only explanation I could think of was that he'd found out about me and Dell, and driven to the rehearsal in a lover's rage. Copeland's not the violent sort, but who knows what someone will do when you wrench their history away from them? He gave this weird half-shrug from the back of the auditorium, but just sat down and whipped out a newspaper, so I kept on with the rehearsal. Ran the

166

kids through their paces as if I was sleepwalking, then let Joey Cleary drag me out to meet him.

Turned out Cope had no clue. He was there on account of Joey; he and Maureen Cleary are friends, so he was looking after Joey while she visited her mother. I was so relieved once I realized why he was there that I couldn't stop grinning, even after Cope went serious on me, and introduced himself. Then he started thanking me for being friends with Dell, and I stopped smiling.

"I was gone so much, and I worried she'd be lonely, and you were there for her to hang around with."

I couldn't trust my tongue. I still couldn't trust it, after all this time. I reached for his sleeve, took the fabric between my fingers. Held tight. "No, thank you. You were very good to her." What was missing? "She loved you a great deal."

He pretended to shuffle his newspaper around. Was it on account of me or Joey that he hid his face? As I watched him play with the newsprint, I remembered the first time I ever drove Dell home. After we'd exchanged numbers in the drugstore, I'd called her and we'd gone out for a beer. Nothing got said, nothing honest anyway; when I dropped her off at the trailer, I asked if it was hers, or if she lived with someone.

"I have a roomie," she said. "A pal of mine I used to drive with, when I was with Carlstown Yellow." She unlocked the car door. "He's...it's cheaper this way. It's just cheaper, that's all."

I looked at her eyes. That odd almond color. Then I shut off the ignition. "Dell."

She leaned towards me, kissed me, full hard long on the lips, and then fled the car, fumbled with the door to the trailer in darkness. I didn't see the inside of that trailer until almost a month later, one night while Cope was out on an overnight shift. The first time Dell and I slept together.

"She loved you." My words, but they came out of nowhere. "I know she did."

"Thanks." That was all. Joey ran off, and Cope turned to go, but I stopped him.

"Copeland. I was wondering...oh, hell. I was wondering if you'd ever want to get together sometime, have dinner or something. I feel as if Dell would've liked for us to get along."

Concern creased his face; he looked at me as if I'd insulted him. Then it passed, and he went all polite, even eager, in that puppy-dog way he had. I took out my datebook, and he wrote the date and time and place down on the back of his left hand.

The night he was supposed to come over, he called first, asked what time dinner was. Said he'd washed it off the back of his hand. I couldn't laugh. The detail reminded me too much of Dell. When he arrived at my door, he handed me a loaf of supermarket Italian, and I laughed then instead. The whole evening was like that: my emotions all misplaced, laughter and anger always emerging at the wrong moment.

"I'm nervous, OK?" I said. "You're the closest thing to Dell that's left on this earth, and you really, really make me nervous."

I explained to him why, then, as best I could without telling too much. About trying to remember and forget, both at once. About how he had scars on his wrists, for the world to notice, while I'd tucked mine inside, under the skin, where no one could see them unless I chose to peel that skin back. Maybe I was hoping something would spark, spread through us both like whiskey. That we'd feel Dell's presence, and then let go of her at last.

"That's why I asked you to dinner. It seems important, doesn't it?"

His face was blank. He hadn't heard a thing I'd said.

"Say again? I'm sorry; I spaced out there for a second."

She was gone again, and he'd followed her.

I walked over to him. Put my hands on his shoulders. I bit my lip to ward off memory, but it came crashing, like someone breaking furniture in the apartment above. A few nights after she kissed me in my car, I invited her to my apartment. Figured we had things we needed to talk about, Dell and I. As I shut the door behind her, I let my hand rest on her waist, and we walked that way into the kitchen until she leaned against the counter and I moved my hand away. Rummaging through the cabinet for glasses, I said, "What do you want?"

"Water, or wine, if you have it."

I shut the cabinet door. "That's not what I meant, Dell." I didn't turn to look at her face, but I can see it now: the expression she wore when she was serious, her pale skin flushed slightly at the temples. Instead, I stared at the wall: white, rough, and knobby. Why texture a wall, I wondered. Why not leave it smooth, why waste roughness on something people rarely touch? My legs stiffened beneath me; that's good, Terry, I thought. Now you can't move. She'll have to pick you up and cart you out of your own apartment, straight for the dumpster: stiff girl, body like a board.

I'd like to say that the stiffness vanished when she came up behind me, put one hand on my back: very gently, nothing heavy-duty. It was a friendly touch, but my legs shook so hard that they sent a jump through my body. I've forgiven her since, but at the time I was red-angry, because you know what Dell did? She laughed. Sweet, but still a laugh. I whirled on her then, fierce the way I get when somebody finds me funny.

"Don't you dare laugh when you touch me."

"Terry." Her voice wasn't a song anymore, but a yellow light. "Terry, I'm sorry. I'm nervous, too, you know." I have so many pictures of Dell in my head, but I've lost that one: the way she looked when she first told me she was nervous. I put my hands up to my face, across my cheeks, because I wanted not to think, not to be in that place. Too much feeling hurts me in the marrow of my bones; I should've lived someplace even colder. But Dell took my hands away from my cheeks, made me see her. I wish my mind still had that picture of her face.

My hands were gripping Cope's shoulders, fingers digging into bone. "I said she's not dead for me. I said I need to move on, let go of her. I thought maybe you could help me."

"I think you asked the wrong person."

I busied myself serving. I filled two plates with food, and carried them into the living room. But after I set the plates down on the table, I walked over to the sofa, snapped on another light. I had to know if I was still sharing her.

"Do you still see her?" I asked.

He was watching his reflection in the window. He cleared his throat, adjusted his left shirt cuff, then his collar.

"Naw." He pulled out my chair, gestured for me to sit. "Not anymore. Maybe the first year. Not anymore."

I dream sometimes that I've told Cope by mistake, let it slip while we're talking about the weather. I see clouds, point, and say "lover"; I hear thunder, cover my ears, and say "betrayal." When he told me he didn't see her anymore? That it was over for him, that her face had vanished from the inside of his lids? I thought I heard rain begin beyond the window: a faint drumming, like a heart when your ear is to her breast. I thought I heard rain, but through the window I could see blurred, dense light, and realized it was only a driver pulling into the parking lot out front.

He was lying.

For a minute I could see right through him. Past the face he saw mornings when he combed his speckled hair. Past the face he showed to customers when he dropped them off and pretended not to be waiting for a tip. I could see past the face he showed Joey when Joey practiced Horatio, and the face he showed me when he handed me the bread, his eyes shying away from the empty wine bottle in the recycling bin.

He was lying.

"Have you heard any news about Maureen Cleary's mother?" I asked him that question, then something about driving: how much a mile costs, how much a minute. We exchanged anecdotes about Joey, he asked questions about teaching, and I told stories about acting. All the while I was watching his face, and what I saw chilled me, because it was what Dell had seen all along.

He moved to leave. But as he reached for his coat on the sofa, he stopped to look at the pictures on my wall. He stopped, and looked, and one of the pictures he really seemed to see. It was Dell's favorite, the one Jane painted for my birthday years ago: three women, facing each other in a circle. He looked it over, and as I watched, something crossed his face like a shadow.

"No, I really just can't."

"Take it."

He stood, his face covered with questions, his body curling away from the painting I held, the edge of the wooden frame pointing towards his belly. Neither one of us moved. Then his arms rose, almost of themselves, until his hands stretched flat, palms to ceiling, and I set the painting to rest.

CAROL GUESS was born in 1968 and moved eight times before the age of fourteen. She studied ballet for nine years, quitting in 1989 to focus on writing. The following year, she received a BA in English from Columbia University. She is currently teaching English and Women's Studies at Indiana University, where she received a MA in English in 1993 and a MFA in Creative Writing (Poetry) in 1994. Her second novel is forthcoming from Cleis Press.

Books from Cleis Press

Sexual Politics

Forbidden Passages: Writings Banned in Canada introductions by Pat Califia and Janine Fuller.
ISBN: 1-57344-020-5 24.95 cloth;
ISBN: 1-57344-019-1 14.95 paper.

Good Sex: Real Stories from Real People, second edition, by Julia Hutton.
ISBN: 1-57344-001-9 29.95 cloth;
ISBN: 1-57344-000-0 14.95 paper.

The Good Vibrations Guide to Sex: How to Have Safe, Fun Sex in the '90s by Cathy Winks and Anne Semans.
ISBN: 0-939416-83-2 29.95 cloth;
ISBN: 0-939416-84-0 16.95 paper.

I Am My Own Woman: The Outlaw Life of Charlotte von Mahlsdorf translated by Jean Hollander.
ISBN. 1-57344-011-6 24.95 cloth;
ISBN: 1-57344-010-8 12.95 paper.

Madonnarama: Essays on Sex and Popular Culture edited by Lisa Frank and Paul Smith.
ISBN: 0-939416-72-7 24.95 cloth;
ISBN: 0-939416-71-9 9.95 paper.

Public Sex: The Culture of Radical Sex by Pat Califia.
ISBN: 0-939416-88-3 29.95 cloth;
ISBN: 0-939416-89-1 12.95 paper.

Sex Work: Writings by Women in the Sex Industry edited by Frédérique Delacoste and Priscilla Alexander.
ISBN: 0-939416-10-7 24.95 cloth;
ISBN: 0-939416-11-5 16.95 paper.

Susie Bright's Sexual Reality: A Virtual Sex World Reader by Susie Bright.
ISBN: 0-939416-58-1 24.95 cloth;
ISBN: 0-939416-59-X 9.95 paper.

Susie Bright's Sexwise by Susie Bright.
ISDN: 1-57344-003-5 24.95 cloth;
ISBN: 1-57344-002-7 10.95 paper.

Susie Sexpert's Lesbian Sex World by Susie Bright.
ISBN: 0-939416-34-4 24.95 cloth;
ISBN: 0-939416-35-2 9.95 paper.

Lesbian and Gay Studies

Best Gay Erotica 1996 selected by Scott Heim, edited by Michael Ford.
ISBN: 1-57344-053-1 24.95 cloth;
ISBN: 1-57344-052-3 12.95 paper.

Best Lesbian Erotica 1996 selected by Heather Lewis, edited by Tristan Taormino.
ISBN: 1-57344-055-8 24.95 cloth;
ISBN: 1-57344-054-X 12.95 paper.

Boomer: Railroad Memoirs by Linda Niemann.
ISBN: 0-939416-55-7 12.95 paper.

The Case of the Good-For-Nothing Girlfriend by Mabel Maney.
ISBN: 0-939416-90-5 24.95 cloth;
ISBN: 0-939416-91-3 10.95 paper.

The Case of the Not-So-Nice Nurse by Mabel Maney.
ISBN: 0-939416-75-1 24.95 cloth;
ISBN: 0-939416-76-X 9.95 paper.

Dagger: On Butch Women edited by Roxxie, Lily Burana, Linnea Due.
ISBN: 0-939416-81-6 29.95 cloth;
ISBN: 0-939416-82-4 14.95 paper.

Dark Angels: Lesbian Vampire Stories edited by Pam Keesey.
ISBN: 1-57344-015-9 24.95 cloth;
ISBN 1-7344-014-0 10.95 paper.

Daughters of Darkness: Lesbian Vampire Stories edited by Pam Keesey.
ISBN: 0-939416-77-8 24.95 cloth;
ISBN: 0-939416-78-6 9.95 paper.

Different Daughters: A Book by Mothers of Lesbians, second edition, edited by Louise Rafkin.
ISBN: 1-57344-051-5 24.95 cloth;
ISBN: 1-57344-050-7 12.95 paper.

Different Mothers: Sons & Daughters of Lesbians Talk About Their Lives edited by Louise Rafkin.
ISBN: 0-939416-40-9 24.95 cloth;
ISBN: 0-939416-41-7 9.95 paper.

Dyke Strippers: Lesbian Cartoonists A to Z edited by Roz Warren.
ISBN: 1-57344-009-4 29.95 cloth;
ISBN: 1-57344-008-6 16.95 paper.

Girlfriend Number One: Lesbian Life in the '90s edited by Robin Stevens.
ISBN: 0-939416-79-4 29.95 cloth;
ISBN: 0-939416-8 12.95 paper.

Hothead Paisan: Homicidal Lesbian Terrorist by Diane DiMassa.
ISBN: 0-939416-73-5 14.95 paper.

A Lesbian Love Advisor by Celeste West.
ISBN: 0-939416-27-1 24.95 cloth;
ISBN: 0-939416-26-3 9.95 paper.

More Serious Pleasure: Lesbian Erotic Stories and Poetry edited by the Sheba Collective.
ISBN: 0-939416-48-4 24.95 cloth;
ISBN: 0-939416-47-6 9.95 paper.

Nancy Clue and the Hardly Boys in A Ghost in the Closet by Mabel Maney.
ISBN: 1-57344-013-2 24.95 cloth;
ISBN: 1-57344-012-4 10.95 paper.

The Night Audrey's Vibrator Spoke: A Stonewall Riots Collection by Andrea Natalie.
ISBN: 0-939416-64-6 8.95 paper.

Queer and Pleasant Danger: Writing Out My Life by Louise Rafkin.
ISBN: 0-939416-60-3 24.95 cloth;
ISBN: 0-939416-61-1 9.95 paper.

Revenge of Hothead Paisan: Homicidal Lesbian Terrorist by Diane DiMassa.
ISBN: 1-57344-016-7 16.95 paper.

Rubyfruit Mountain: A Stonewall Riots Collection by Andrea Natalie.
ISBN: 0-939416-74-3 9.95 paper.

Serious Pleasure: Lesbian Erotic Stories and Poetry edited by the Sheba Collective.
ISBN: 0-939416-46-8 24.95 cloth;
ISBN: 0-939416-45-X 9.95 paper.

Switch Hitters: Lesbians Write Gay Male Erotica and Gay Men Write Lesbian Erotica edited by Carol Queen and Lawrence Schimel.
ISBN: 1-57344-022-1 24.95 cloth;
ISBN: 1-57344-021-3 12.95 paper.

Politics of Health

The Absence of the Dead Is Their Way of Appearing by Mary Winfrey Trautmann.
ISBN: 0-939416-04-2 8.95 paper.

Don't: A Woman's Word by Elly Danica.
ISBN: 0-939416-23-9 21.95 cloth;
ISBN: 0-939416-22-0 8.95 paper

1 in 3: Women with Cancer Confront an Epidemic edited by Judith Brady.
ISBN: 0-939416-50-6 24.95 cloth;
ISBN: 0-939416-49-2 10.95 paper.

Voices in the Night: Women Speaking About Incest edited by Toni A.H. McNaron and Yarrow Morgan.
ISBN: 0-939416-02-6 9.95 paper.

With the Power of Each Breath: A Disabled Women's Anthology edited by Susan Browne, Debra Connors and Nanci Stern.
ISBN: 0-939416-09-3 24.95 cloth;
ISBN: 0-939416-06-9 10.95 paper.

Woman-Centered Pregnancy and Birth by the Federation of Feminist Women's Health Centers.
ISBN: 0-939416-03-4 11.95 paper.

Reference

Putting Out: The Essential Publishing Resource Guide For Gay and Lesbian Writers, third edition, by Edisol W. Dotson.
ISBN: 0-939416-86-7 29.95 cloth;
ISBN: 0-939416-87-5 12.95 paper.

Fiction

Cosmopolis: Urban Stories by Women edited by Ines Rieder.
ISBN: 0-939416-36-0 24.95 cloth;
ISBN: 0-939416-37-9 9.95 paper.

Dirty Weekend: A Novel of Revenge by Helen Zahavi.
ISBN: 0-939416-85-9 10.95 paper.

A Forbidden Passion by Cristina Peri Rossi.
ISBN: 0-939416-64-0 24.95 cloth;
ISBN: 0-939416-68-9 9.95 paper.

Half a Revolution: Contemporary Fiction by Russian Women edited by Masha Gessen.
ISBN 1-57344-007-8 $29.95 cloth;
ISBN 1-57344-006-X $12.95 paper.

In the Garden of Dead Cars by Sybil Claiborne.
ISBN: 0-939416-65-4 24.95 cloth;
ISBN: 0-939416-66-2 9.95 paper.

Night Train To Mother by Ronit Lentin.
ISBN: 0-939416-29-8 24.95 cloth;
ISBN: 0-939416-28-X 9.95 paper.

The One You Call Sister: New Women's Fiction edited by Paula Martinac.
ISBN: 0-939416-30-1 24.95 cloth;
ISBN: 0-939416031-X 9.95 paper.

Only Lawyers Dancing by Jan McKemmish.
ISBN: 0-939416-70-0 24.95 cloth;
ISBN: 0-939416-69-7 9.95 paper.

Seeing Dell by Carol Guess
ISBN: 1-57344-024-8 24.95 cloth;
ISBN: 1-57344-023-X 12.95 paper.

Unholy Alliances: New Women's Fiction edited by Louise Rafkin.
ISBN: 0-939416-14-X 21.95 cloth;
ISBN: 0-939416-15-8 9.95 paper.

The Wall by Marlen Haushofer.
ISBN: 0-939416-53-0 24.95 cloth;
ISBN: 0-939416-54-9 paper.

We Came All The Way from Cuba So You Could Dress Like This?: Stories by Achy Obejas.
ISBN: 0-939416-92-1 24.95 cloth;
ISBN: 0-939416-93-X 10.95 paper.

Latin America

Beyond the Border: A New Age in Latin American Women's Fiction edited by Nora Erro-Peralta and Caridad Silva-Núñez.
ISBN: 0-939416-42-5 24.95 cloth;
ISBN: 0-939416-43-3 12.95 paper.

The Little School: Tales of Disappearance and Survival in Argentina by Alicia Partnoy.
ISBN: 0-939416-08-5 21.95 cloth;
ISBN: 0-939416-07-7 9.95 paper.

Revenge of the Apple by Alicia Partnoy.
ISBN: 0-939416-62-X 24.95 cloth;
ISBN: 0-939416-63-8 8.95 paper.

Autobiography, Biography, Letters

Peggy Deery: An Irish Family at War by Nell McCafferty.
ISBN: 0-939416-38-7 24.95 cloth;
ISBN: 0-939416-39-5 9.95 paper.

The Shape of Red: Insider/Outsider Reflections by Ruth Hubbard and Margaret Randall.
ISBN: 0-939416-19-0 24.95 cloth;
ISBN: 0-939416-18-2 9.95 paper.

Women & Honor: Some Notes on Lying by Adrienne Rich.
ISBN: 0-939416-44-1 3.95 paper.

Animal Rights

And a Deer's Ear, Eagle's Song and Bear's Grace: Relationships Between Animals and Women edited by Theresa Corrigan and Stephanie T. Hoppe.
ISBN: 0-939416-38-7 24.95 cloth;
ISBN: 0-939416-39-5 9.95 paper.

With a Fly's Eye, Whale's Wit and Woman's Heart: Relationships Between Animals and Women edited by Theresa Corrigan and Stephanie T. Hoppe.
ISBN: 0-939416-24-7 24.95 cloth;
ISBN: 0-939416-25-5 9.95 paper.

Ordering information

Since 1980, Cleis Press has published progressive books by women. We welcome your order and will ship your books as quickly as possible. Individual orders must be prepaid (U.S. dollars only). Please add 15% shipping. PA residents add 6% sales tax. Mail orders: Cleis Press, PO Box 8933, Pittsburgh PA 15221. MasterCard and Visa orders: include account number, exp. date, and signature. FAX your credit card order: (412) 937-1567. Or, phone us Mon–Fri, 9 am–5 pm EST: (412) 937-1555.